The Devil
Walks on Water

The Devil Walks on Water

a novel by

JOHN F. MURRAY

LITTLE, BROWN AND COMPANY · BOSTON · TORONTO

LIBRARY OF CONGRESS CATALOG CARD NO. 69-15072

FIRST EDITION

The history of Southampton that appears on pages 85–87 of this
novel was adapted from Eunice Telfer Juckett's "Social Life in
Southampton Reshaped," as published in *The New York Times*,
July 14, 1957.

Published simultaneously in Canada
by Little, Brown & Company (Canada) Limited

PRINTED IN THE UNITED STATES OF AMERICA

To my brother Tom

Acknowledgments

To Wilson F. Reynolds, former Mayor of Westhampton Beach; Stanley J. Teller, former Police Chief of Westhampton Beach; W. K. Dunwell, Historian of the Town of Southampton, for chats and material.

To the nice lady librarians at the Rogers Memorial Library in Southampton, who gave me access to their newspaper files.

And to Theron Raines, period.

J. F. M.
Greenwich Village, N.Y., 1969

A touch of love, and the devil walks on water.
                                        —*Anonymous*

The Devil
Walks on Water

1

BRINEY MITCHEL SPAT AT HIS OWN REFLECTION.
It was one ball of spittle on the Kelly green hood of
the Ford Phaeton, and it straightaway began to sizzle
and split into small balls of frothy white wet, like
mercury. But unlike mercury, they were not inclined to
return to the original ball.

No, the balls of spit split and sizzled, trying to
evaporate in the awful heat of the still-hot motor cooking them. But before they could, he leaned over, not
touching the hood, and huffed on the gleaming steel,
then ran a chamois from the glove compartment over
the spit, wiping it away with a couple of sweeps. He
looked at his face in the mirror of steel, and it was
green, and when he showed his teeth to the steel, they
too were green.

His nose came off big in the steel green mirror,
though it was not a big nose. And his ears retreated to
nothing at the back of his head, though they were, in
reality, big by most standards. He smiled at the carica-
ture, as he had once when he was a child looking at
himself in a distorted mirror at Coney Island's Steeple-
chase Park. But this smile was pure irony; his reflection

came off as the face of his father, Lucian Mitchel, who was behind all this anger.

Briney Mitchel polished away the memory of it on the hood, the last vestige of spittle, and replaced the chamois in the glove compartment. Then he went away like an Indian hunter for quarry.

He did not walk like ordinary men; he padded in soft, oiled moccasins, his whole body hulking, rocking from side to side. He wore a faded polo shirt and white ducks — frayed at the pocket and cuffs, and here and there rust-marked from the laundry. His arms were not too long for his body but they seemed to be. Like an ape, he did not swing them much; and when he was angry, as he was this afternoon, he clenched and un-clenched his big fists. His black Irish head hung for-ward of his body, as if he were preparing for physical combat, and as he approached the steps of the big Meadow Club porch, the chauffeurs clustered around the admission gate began to make an uneasy path for him.

Briney knew them all: Joel and Frank and Marchie and Herbert and the rest in their black habits and stiff peaked hats, and some of them in tight dove and fawn and clay tunics caught at the neck, and puttees en-casing their varicose-veined legs from standing around waiting for their employers too long, and some of them in black shiny high-button shoes. And all of them seem-ing like generals, or even Hitler corporals on leave, gos-siped and smoked in the shelter of the porch on this terribly humid day, wishing they could unbutton their tunics and get a swill of beer, for God's sake.

And the young man knew they were hot and thirsty,

but he had no sympathy for them, because he had absolutely no compassion for a man who got paid for the privilege of driving a beautiful automobile. Poor as they were, he held no brief for the chauffeurs of Southampton — not even his father's chauffeur — for doing what he loved to do so well. And when he brushed past them after mounting the porch, none of them except Herbert said anything to him, and some of them turned their backs to him. "Hello, Mr. Mitchel," said Herbert, the thin one with the mustache. He got no answer.

The clerk at the admissions desk, the man in the Meadow Club green blazer, also greeted him, but Briney Mitchel did not answer him, either. And some of the prep school kids hanging around the entrance said something to him, but he did not answer them. He stopped at the edge of the porch, posturing just enough to give a stranger the impression that he owned the place, and surveyed the tennis courts. When he found Millicent Crocker, he bounded onto the grass and walked quickly through the players and their games on the other courts to where she was playing. Then he slipped down on his haunches against the backstop, the rub of the wire like the firm fingers of a woman on his hot, perspiring back. Or was it more like being back at Princeton wrestling with some bastard from Muhlenberg or Swarthmore or Penn? No; there was the old familiar heat in his pants, too. It came, it always came from being close to Midge Crocker. He could have stayed in the comparative coolness of the long porch, but he preferred it where he was; he was closer to Midge, and the closer he could get to Midge, the better it was for him and everyone around him.

His mind began to grapple with Millicent Crocker, who was smashing away at Carley Harris. He loved to wrestle with this girl, trying always to get her top off, and he always ended up with his shirt off instead, as when he wrestled at Princeton, and he quite unconsciously began to peel off his faded polo shirt. Carley Harris, about to serve in the far court, stopped with the ball in midair and said, "Put your shirt on. This is the Meadow Club, not Ebbets Field!" And Briney said nothing; he simply finished peeling off the shirt. Carley Harris let the ball dribble at her feet, and Jonathan T. C. Carpenter, playing with Denny Washington in the next court against the Borland twins, stopped dead in his tracks, and glared at Briney Mitchel, who was now scratching the hair on his chest and muttering dark things aloud.

"I'll get the club steward to make you put it on," said Carley Harris.

"Get Mayor LaGuardia," said Briney Mitchel.

"And wash his mouth out, too," said Jonathan T. C. Carpenter. And then Jonathan T. C. Carpenter dropped his racquet and began to march over to where Briney Mitchel was squatting, still bare-chested.

"Get President Roosevelt."

The prep school kids on the big porch began to laugh, and some of the old ladies who rocked away their lives during the summer at the Meadow Club, clucked with their tongues. Meanwhile, Denny Washington intercepted Jonathan T. C. Carpenter and said, "I know this fellow pretty well, Mr. Carpenter. Let me take care of it, sir." The older man grunted and went back to get his racquet and Denny came over to Briney. "Put it back on, you idiot."

"It's too hot." He did not look up at his friend; his eyes were glued to Midge.

"T. C. is on the Board." Denny squatted down beside Briney, grimacing. "And Jesus, watch your language. What a place to mention *Roosevelt*."

Briney, a smile flickering across his face, started to put his shirt back on, and Denny stood up and went back to his game.

There seemed to come a collective sigh of relief from everybody, even from the kids on the porch. While Briney adjusted his shirt, Carley Harris, still waiting to serve in the far court, said, "And now you can get us some ice water," and Briney Mitchel laughed loudly at her, and the kids on the porch laughed loudly with him, and Carley Harris slammed her racquet against the backstop and stomped off toward the clubhouse, her legs two tanned chopping pipestems flying out of her one-piece gored tennis outfit, her black stringy hair bouncing in the ominously blistering humid afternoon. The Meadow Club, whose grass courts now dappled with players in white ran almost all the way down to Cooper's Neck Pond, followed the curve of Meadow Lane and the Dune Road, which ran along the ocean all the way to Quogue, Westhampton Beach and the Moriches. But there was no breath or even gasp of wind from the sea whatever. Up until today, it had been windy and overcast for weeks it seemed, and people were complaining about losing their tans. Today, the wind had dropped, and it was dead hot.

"You're in a swell-elegant mood today," said Millicent Crocker, flopping down beside Briney to await the return of Carley.

"That girl can be a nut buster," said Briney Mitchel, lighting a cigar. "I hope you whip her skinny ass."

"Well, it doesn't look as though I will."

"Maybe she'll drink too much water and have a bellyache." He took the cigar out of his mouth and glanced at Midge Crocker. She drove him crazy when she played tennis; she was perspiring through her white polo shirt; whenever she perspired, you could see the nipples through her bra, and Briney said, "I wish you'd take *your* shirt off, Midget. My what a lovely pair you have. But —"

"Mitch!"

"— but that stick of a Carley Harris, she'd poke holes in your flesh with her bones in bed."

"Don't talk like that."

"I'll talk any way I please. And don't you drink too much ice water when that stick brings it back. Just wash your mouth out with it. Or suck an orange. Do you have an orange?"

"Of course I don't have an orange."

"I'll get you one from the bar." He started to get up but Midge said, "No, that's not fair: to get me an orange and not get Carley ice water."

He said nothing, but he thought: I will never get that stick Carley Harris anything in my life. Then he went away to the clubhouse, crossing at net where Denny Washington and Jonathan T. C. Carpenter and the Borland twins were between points. He passed Carley coming back with the ice water and he blew cigar smoke in her face; the porch laughed again. Carley turned and whispered a curse at him that no one could hear except Briney.

When he came back from the bar with an orange for Midge and a frosty South Side for himself, he took the cup of water Carley had handed to Midge and gave it back to Carley roughly; then he gave Midge the orange. "Suck it," he said. "And then beat her skinny ass." Carley flung the cup aside and picked up a ball. Then he went back to his place against the backstop, Midge following him, peeling the orange, a California navel.

"Anytime you're ready," said Carley, practicing serves against the far backstop, even though such behavior was a breach of good tennis etiquette.

"In a minute," said Midge, sitting down beside Briney.

"Christ," said Briney. "Playing tennis on an afternoon like this."

"Why do you sit there watching and complaining then?" Midge said between sucks. "No one," suck, "says you have to sit here," suck, "there's no law," suck. "And Mitch, I wish you wouldn't smoke those awful cigars. God," suck, "they smell."

"They don't smell, they stink, and godammit, Midget, you stink, too, when you play this game in this heat."

"Sor*ree.*" She moved a little away from him.

"No, come back here, I like your stink, but I hate everybody else's stink, and that's why I smoke cigars: to kill the stink of people playing tennis."

"What in the name of God's got into you this afternoon, Mitch? Is it the weather? Really, I don't think the sun will ever shine again. And you need a shave, did you know that?"

"My old man and Uncle Aidan Carew's got into me this afternoon."

"Are you going to shave for me tonight?"

He rubbed his chin. "Of course not. Uncle Aidan's had my old man's ear about Princeton. He says to the old man: 'It's canon law that Briney should get a Catholic education. Encyclical number 6,978.' *Canon law!*" Briney took a long pull on the cigar. "As if I didn't get enough of the priests at the Priory. Anyway, he wants me to transfer to Georgetown next fall."

"That's nothing new, is it?"

"But this time I think the old bastard means it. I think he means to get the old man to cut off my tuition at Princeton if I don't transfer to the Potomac."

"What are you going to do?"

Briney flipped the cigar stub toward Carley Harris, still furiously slamming serves against the far backstop. "I'm going to spread rumors about Uncle Aidan that will get him kicked out of the Knights of Malta and the Knights of St. Gregory. In fact, I'll make it so bad that he won't even be able to get into the Knights of Columbus. I'll fix his wagon."

Carley Harris yelled, "Come on, Midge!"

"Soon's I finish," Midge called, still sucking and not being able to catch some of the juice that dripped down the front of her shirt.

Briney put his hand between his legs and rubbed a

little, and Midge said, "I wish you wouldn't always put your hand there all the time, Mitch, when you're sitting with me. Honestly."

"Put my hand where? Oh, there. Why, I've never been aware of it." He left his hand where it was.

"Well, I'm aware of it. You only do it when you're sitting down with me, you know. But other people notice."

"You should be flattered."

"I'm embarrassed."

He watched her for a moment, still sucking. He said softly, bending to her: "I'd like to lick the juice off your nipples right in front of God and all these people."

"Oh, Mitch." She began to blush hotly and perspire more. "I'm not *fast*, you know that," she said.

"What I'd give to have your sweet, sweaty little body under me right now!"

"Mitch, don't."

"You love it."

"No." She said it weakly. "Talk like that to your fast girl friends. Not me."

He bent closer. "You love every word of it, and why do you wear that lovely tight polo shirt? And if we had no other place to do it, you'd love to do it with me right in Macy's window." She had to get up, unsteadily, and having finally finished the orange pulp she held it out and Briney took the skin from her and said: "Now whip her skinny ass. For me."

His eyes following her, eating her, she went and picked up her Slazenger with the diagonally strung catgut, and prepared for Carley's serve. "Okay," she said to Carley, but she said it as though she meant it for Briney, too.

Midge Crocker was irresistible to Briney Mitchel. She had a sand-and-sun blondeness about her: her skin was copper and her hair almost white from the sun, and she had a cool saltwater look about her; she was sweet and fresh; she epitomized the tennis-playing, sun-soaked Southampton teenager in every sense of the word. People who wondered how she could be attracted to Briney Mitchel overlooked the fact that Briney and Midge were just the proper poles apart emotionally to be most strongly attracted to each other.

And so Briney, the hell-for-leather Irishman, lusted after Harriet Crocker's beautiful blonde daughter, and she, in her own innocent way, lusted after Briney — only partially realizing it and not fully understanding it.

No matter what people thought about the arrangement, however, they had to admit that — by the very nature of their physical contrasts — Briney Mitchel and Midge Crocker made a very handsome couple.

"And tonight . . ." Briney started to say, so that she could just barely hear it. He watched her small body with its lovely female movements, and he suddenly realized that his hand was still between his legs, so he removed it and started to rub the soft wet skins of the orange together. Absently, he began to suck the remaining pulp where her teeth and her lips and her tongue had been, and he put his hand on the grass, still warm, where she had been sitting.

2

THE OLD LADIES ROCKED AGAIN, THE KIDS ON THE porch gossiped and drank Cokes, and the matches continued on the courts. But the Meadow Club was simply not itself, and not just because Briney Mitchel was abroad upon its acres. No, it was the oppressive heat and the gray of the day that disturbed it; the Meadow Club had fully to be enjoyed when it was washed in sunlight, and there had been no sunlight for well over a week. And so the big club, like Briney Mitchel, continued its business as usual, but brooded.

Briney Mitchel gently laid aside the orange pulp, the sweet wet orange pulp, and picked up his South Side, holding it at eye level and appraising it before he began to sip it. It was lovely and cold and ever-so-pale greenish; a delight to his eye. He knew this South Side would taste good; as good as they tasted at Jack and Charlie's "21" Club in New York, where the glorious drink had been invented. Sammy, the Meadow Club bartender, had very carefully measured out one and a half ounces of Gordon's gin and a half ounce of lemon juice, added a few leaves of fresh mint from the Meadow Club garden, and just the right amount of sugar and cracked ice. Then he had shaken it all together in a silver cocktail shaker, poured it into a prefrosted four-ounce stemless glass, and sprinkled more shredded mint on top.

Briney Mitchel sipped, rolling it over his tongue, savoring it, then swallowing. In a moment there was a deep, cool pleasure within him, and he sat back against the hard wire fence, softer now, to watch these two very good girl tennis players smash at each other some more on this unbearably breathless afternoon at the famous Meadow Club; on the very courts that Frankie Parker and Frank Shields and George Lott and Sidney Wood and Don McNeil and Bobby Riggs and Bitsy Grant and Gene Mako and even Mischa Oschnik and a lot of other talented players had been invited to play in the annual Invitational Tournament during Tennis Week. Most of them wore hot, cream-colored flannel trousers, and a few of them even wore black spiked track shoes to get a better grip on the grass, and tear it up as well.

Oschnik. Briney Mitchel, then a small boy, had once asked this Russian, who had just been eliminated from the tournament, for his autograph, and Oschnik, angry and dripping beads of sweat from his great nose full of blackheads, had told Briney: "Get the hell out of here, you little bastard," and Briney had laughed in his face. But Oschnik, not a very good tennis player, but a good guy after all, later offered to give Briney the autograph he had refused before, and Briney politely refused it, telling Oschnik what he could do with the big Waterman fountain pen he was proffering.

Yes, one had to be a very good player to use these clubhouse courts at the Meadow Club in Southampton on a Saturday afternoon. In fact, if a person were just a kid spending the summer in Southampton with his parents, he could never get a court at the Meadow Club on weekends at all. He could start to play all right, but they would kick him off, the older people, and if he complained, the wife would say, "Mr. So-and-So only gets the weekends to play. He works in the hot city all week, you know. Now you run along. You have all the week to play." And some of the kids, off their prep school saltpeter diets and feeling their oats, said to themselves: "We don't blame your old man for staying in the city all week. With a face like you have, lady!" Then the St. Paul'ses and the St. Mark'ses and the Grotons and the others would gather up their balls, the new ones that had hardly begun to show any grass stain, and go back to the clubhouse and sign for a Coke that would cost Father twenty-one cents, and take it and sit and kibitz on the edge of the big porch overlooking the clubhouse courts, wagging their crew-cut heads and swinging their white-ducked legs and watching that old son of a bitch Jonathan T. C. Carpenter and his doubles partner, A. Dennis Washington, who had only one and a half arms, play their Saturday match against the Borland twins. Or watch that cute Midge Crocker, on whom a lot of them had a "crush," and the stringbean Carley Harris, who seemed to have a match that ran all summer, smashing at each other. And they kept an eye on Briney Mitchel, wondering what he would do next.

Hardly anyone knew what Briney Mitchel would do next, least of all Briney Mitchel. He lived with his parents and never had to worry about getting a court on weekends at the Meadow Club, for he never lifted a tennis racquet. He swam every day in the ocean and once in a while he borrowed somebody's Cape Cod Knockabout at the Southampton Yacht Club for a slow sail in Shinnecock Bay. But he really spent most of his time driving his Ford Phaeton, and when summer ended he took his Phaeton to Princeton, where he hid it "behind the Nass," in the Negro section of town. He was captain of the freshmen wrestling team, and he wrestled, some said, to keep in shape for his girls, for he almost always had one in the front seat beside him. She was most often a Southampton native girl. The summer girls, all except Millicent Crocker, weren't usually allowed to go out with Briney, not so much because he drove too fast or tried to seduce them. No, it was because he made enemies of their fathers in another way: he ripped up their lawns with the wheels of his car. Briney was simply incapable of sticking to a trim bluestone driveway if it had a nice green lawn running away from it.

The only lawn he never tore up was Harriet Carpenter Crocker's nice green lawn. When he called on Midge, he somehow found himself able to keep to the bluestone. Whether it was because he was fond of Midge or because he had too much respect for her mother, a woman whose husband had been a special agent for the FBI and who had once played professional football for the Frankford Yellow Jackets, nobody really knew. The other parents in Southampton only knew that Briney Mitchel had no fear of them at all.

"I never want Doris (or Nancy or Betty or Maria) out with that devil again!" said the fathers, surveying the damage from the breakfast room the next morning.

And then the house would be silent until later when Briney would send flowers to the mothers with a note.

"Who sent the flowers?"

"Briney Mitchel. With the sweetest note of apology."

"Is that so? Well, I've a good mind to return them with a bill for the lawn."

"It isn't so bad. The marks will go away in no time."

"He drives too fast. What's the matter with that boy?"

"That's just it. He's just a boy. Anyway, he never drives too fast with Doris (or Nancy or Betty or Maria). She's told me he's very careful with her."

The fathers cleared their throats or snapped their *Barron's* or took a sip of their second cup of Postum. "That's not the way I hear it. I hear he's not very careful with the native girls."

"Well, Nancy's not a native girl. And anyway, Briney is Denny Washington's best friend, so he couldn't be all bad."

Which was perfectly true. Briney Mitchel, swimmer and itinerant sailor, never swung a tennis racquet or a golf club, but he was Denny Washington's inseparable summertime companion. Denny, who did both of these things very well, was a good four years older than Briney, drove very carefully and stuck to the driveways when he dated Carley Harris, which wasn't very often, especially during the winter when he was studying for his law degree at Harvard and she was at Bryn Mawr. People said it was his one and a half arms, his premature baldness and his rimless eyeglasses that made him shy and look much older than his years.

They also said that Denny had been born with his handicap, at least the older people did. The younger people, overhearing their elders talking about the Great War, preferred to believe the other story: that Denny had lost the lower part of his left forearm in the Argonne, not realizing that Denny had only just been born when the war was fought. Denny shot golf at Shinnecock in the high seventies with one arm, and was the second-best tennis player at the Meadow Club. No one could quite understand why he always teamed up on weekends with Jonathan T. C. Carpenter — certainly he would have had no trouble keeping a court playing with someone else his own age, even though he lived with his mother. Besides Jonathan T. C. Carpenter, the only other thing that could have handicapped his tennis game was his service, but Danny overcame his inability to hold two balls in his left hand by pinching them one at a time in the crook of his left elbow, and depositing each ball in turn on the end of his racquet face to be tossed into the air and swiped at in one motion. Denny Washington served hard and well and almost never double-faulted.

His tennis was like his conduct: he did both with supreme self-containment and discipline, and for this reason alone people never ceased to wonder why Denny Washington was such a good friend of Briney Mitchel's, whose life seemed to consist of an unending train of major and minor crises. The most common explanation for the relationship was the simplest: opposites do attract.

3

BRINEY MITCHEL, WHOSE NAME, OF COURSE, WAS Brian, never tired of watching Midge Crocker play tennis. But he had finished his South Side and he wanted another one. Leaving his glass next to the orange peel, he got up and walked, this time along the backstop, to the long porch of the clubhouse. The prep school kids quickly made a path for him, and the old ladies stopped rocking when he went by. He went into the bar, which was empty of people except the bartender, who had the radio tuned to a baseball game between the Cincinnati Reds and the Boston Bees. Briney Mitchel asked the bartender if he had heard a weather report, and the bartender said, "Rain and high winds is all," and Briney said, "Good, maybe this humidity will break." It was dark and cool in the bar and Briney signed for another South Side and felt better until the bartender said: "Where's your glass?"

"What do you mean, where's my glass?" said Briney Mitchel.

"Just what I said, Mr. Mitchel. We ain't got no clean-up corps around here — things bein' what they are. You kids got to clean up for yourselves."

"Are you kidding?" Briney felt his body getting

warm again. "Why, do you know that the Meadow Club once had a lady's maid for each female member?"

"Yeah? Well, times have changed, ain't they," the bartender said with delight. "But I'll tell you what I'll do: I'll make an exception this time."

The bartender started to reach for another glass, frosting in the wooden icebox, but Briney said, "No, you won't."

"I won't?"

"No. You march your lazy ass right out on that tennis court and get my glass, that's what you do."

The bartender started to laugh, but Briney reached across the bar and grabbed him roughly by the shoulder of his starched white jacket. "I'm not kidding, Sammy. You sit here all afternoon not doing a goddam thing except bring Cokes to the kids on the porch and pick your nose, and you complain about no clean-up corps. Okay, this afternoon, you're *my* clean-up corps. *Get!*" He swept Sammy out from behind the bar with one motion and shoved him toward the door. "And pick up that orange peel while you're at it, too."

The kids on the porch made another path for the bartender. They laughed when they saw Sammy come back with Briney's empty glass and Midge's orange peel. When Sammy, red-faced and furious, got back behind the bar, he said, "Mr. Mitchel, I got to report you to the club steward."

"Go ahead," said Briney Mitchel. "But before you do, make me another South Side, and don't use the glass you just fetched. Use a new glass, Sammy, nice and cold and frosty."

The bartender got a fresh glass out of the icebox and

made another South Side just as meticulously as he had made the first. He placed it in front of Briney, cracking the glass smartly on the bar.

Briney took a sip of it. He was cool again. He said, "You know what, Sammy?"

"What's that?"

"You make the best South Side in Southampton."

Calmed down, he looked at Briney Mitchel. "Well, thanks."

"Better than that guy at the Beach Club. Better than anybody in Southampton. And as for that Bobby Motley at the Twelve Trees in Water Mill, I don't think he ever heard of a South Side before he came out here."

"I wouldn't know about that, Mr. Mitchel."

"Sammy," said Briney, hunching forward over the bar, "this is where everybody ought to be on an afternoon like this. Inside a dark, cool gin mill boozing a little with a girl. And then after a little boozing, a little loving in some air-conditioned place like upstairs in a movie house, since movie houses seem to be the only joints that are air-conditioned so far."

"Yes, sir."

"Did you ever knock one off in the balcony of a movie house, Sammy?"

"Beg pardon, sir?"

"I said did you ever make love to a girl in the balcony of a movie house?"

"Oh, why no, sir."

"Well, I have, Sammy. Of course, the whole place was empty except for me and this older girl who went to Bennington. That's a famous battle site, but it's also a college up in Vermont, Sammy. It was a famous battle for me, too, Sammy. It's terribly hard in those seats, but we made it. Yes, we made it."

"Good for you, sir. Would you mind signing for the drink?"

"Of course not," said Briney, taking up a pencil. "But I already have."

"Oh! Of course. I beg your pardon, sir."

"I'll sign again, if you want."

"No, of course not, sir."

"As long as the old man's got the jack. Your old man didn't have much jack, did he, Sammy?"

"No, sir, he didn't."

"Well, mine does. He's loaded. You see, his old man was a big publisher. And you know what, Sammy?"

"What's that, Mr. Mitchel?"

"I'm getting a little loaded myself. It must be this stinking weather."

"Yes, sir."

"That's a damn good South Side, Sammy."

"Thank you, sir."

"And thank *you* for getting my glass off the court."

"You're entirely welcome, sir."

"It's been a crazy summer, Sammy."

"Has it, sir?"

"Corrigan flies the wrong way across the ocean to Dublin. Only an Irishman would be dumb enough to do that."

"If you say so, sir."

"Three people get killed by lightning swimming off Riis Park."

"Oh?"

"That's where all the Brooklyn Irish swim, Riis Park."

"Really, sir?"

"The BICs — that's short for Brooklyn Irish Catholics — who haven't moved to Garden City yet. I don't know where they swim in Garden City, but it must be in holy water someplace." The bartender smiled. "A man aboard the *Normandie* strangled his wife and then jumped overboard."

"I remember reading about that, sir."

"Jimmy Foxx hit two home runs in one game for the ninth time this season, thereby breaking a record set by Babe Ruth and Hack Wilson. Are you a *Sawx* fan, Sammy?"

"Boston Bees fan, Mr. Mitchel."

"Good. Everybody at Portsmouth Priory where I went to school in Rhode Island is a *Sawx* fan. They all root for Jimmy *Fawxx* on the *Sawx*. I must be drunk."

"I wouldn't say so, sir."

"And the Dodgers used a yellow baseball as an experiment in a game with the Cardinals this summer. You know what happened when the ball hit the grass?"

"What happened, sir?"

"The ball turned blue. Experiment over." He slammed his glass down on the bar. "It must be the weather."

4

JONATHAN T. C. CARPENTER, PURPLE IN THE face and perspiring through his flannels, came into the bar and said to Briney Mitchel: "What do you mean by taking off your shirt out there in front of everybody? And crossing my court at net?" He shook the face of his racquet at Briney. "I've a good mind to have you suspended."

"You mean you'd drum me out of the regiment?"

"Don't be insolent with me, young man!"

"I took off my shirt because it was hot, Mr. Carpenter."

"The Meadow Club is not a WPA project."

"You can thank God for that."

"Why —!"

Denny Washington came into the bar and Briney took advantage of this to say: "Well, I thought you played great, Mr. Carpenter, but that one-arm partner of yours was lousy as usual."

Jonathan T. C. Carpenter, not quite sure what he had heard, managed a faint smile. "Well, we won, and that's the important thing, isn't it, Dennis?"

"Yes, sir," said Denny Washington, who was also perspiring through his flannels, and whose eyeglasses were steaming in the coolness of the bar. He and Jonathan Carpenter contrived to beat the Borland twins regularly, which was surprising, since both Borlands were ranking players at the Meadow Club.

Jonathan T. C. Carpenter ordered a Perrier water, downed it in several gulps, and gave Briney a mean look before leaving to go to the locker room in back of the pro shop. When Briney was alone with Denny in the bar, he said, "It's a chore with that old bastard, isn't it?"

"You're in a lovely mood today. What's the trouble, the weather?"

"Georgetown again."

"Because you've been on probation at Princeton for having women stay too late?"

"No, they don't know about that. It's the religious thing."

Denny sighed. "Ah, yes."

"This time I think they mean it."

"You should take it out on the tennis court or someplace," Denny said.

"What, and work as hard as you do with old T. C.?" Briney laughed shortly. "I have better ways of taking it out. But you, you like to work hard, don't you?"

"Today I didn't like it so much," said Denny.

"No?"

"My stump hurts. There's a storm coming."

"You've been saying that for days. Rain and high winds is all the radio says."

"Well, it's a good thing in a way."

"Yes," said Briney. "And then maybe after the

storm the sun will come out and people will stop complaining about losing their tans."

"Nature abhors a vacuum," Denny said.

"Galileo said that."

"And we're literally sitting in a very low pressure area."

"Galileo said that and the Pope put Galileo under house arrest for nine years until he died." Briney raised his empty glass. "Here's to Galileo and up the Pope's."

"We're sitting in a low pressure alley with two high pressure walls on each side. The alley runs all the way from Florida to Labrador."

"How do you know?"

"I read the *Times*. But there's not one mention in the paper or on the radio of a hurricane coming through here."

"Hurricane?"

"Hurricane. The one that's been out in the Atlantic all week."

"Well, nobody knows it but you. And I think I'll have another drink," said Briney. He ordered another South Side and Denny, who seldom drank liquor after tennis, ordered a cuba libre from Sammy, and the two of them settled back in a couple of wicker chairs.

Denny said, "Usually, though, I don't mind playing with T. C. I have to poach a little and all that. But it keeps me on my toes. He plays very well for an older man. He knows where to be at the right time, and he's, well, cunning."

"Like an old washed-up infielder."

"Yes, I suppose you could say that. But T. C. is far from washed up, you know that."

"He's washed up and he's not a very good tennis player anymore, either. Why do you play with him?"

"Well," said Denny, squeezing the lime in his glass, "it may seem odd to you, Brine, but I play with him simply because he asks me. I'm really quite flattered. I was always taught to respect the wishes of older —"

"Oh, don't be pompous! You mean you'd rather play with T. C. than with Bobby Borland?"

"No, of course not. But I actually don't mind playing with T. C."

Briney grinned. "You didn't mention that he's senior partner in a law firm you'd very much like to become associated with after the Law School, did you?"

"You think that's the main reason I play with him, don't you?"

"Well, it should be."

"Maybe it is," said Denny, leaning forward in his chair. "But don't forget that T. C. was an intimate friend of my father's. He's always been very kind to me — growing up, I mean. And the least I can do is play a little tennis with him." He turned to Briney. "He's rather fond of you, you know."

"He may have been, but he's not now."

"Why? Because you took your shirt off on the tennis court?"

"No. Because he knows I want to get Midge into bed."

"How can you tell?"

"Never mind how I can tell. But I can tell."

Denny said: "He told me once that he admired your independence. Something like that."

"The only thing T. C. admires about me is the fact

that I don't rip up his dear daughter Harriet's lawn. And the fact that as far as he knows right now, I haven't taken Midge to bed yet."

"You haven't, have you?"

"Well, I haven't tried very hard."

"It's funny you should like Midge," Denny said. "She's not your type at all."

"Yes, she is. She's vaginal."

"Vaginal?"

"I'm sure she's capable of having a vaginal orgasm."

Denny Washington almost choked on a piece of ice. "Vaginal orgasm. What the hell is *that?*"

Briney sat back more comfortably in his chair. "Some women, a very few women — at least that I've found — are capable of coming with the friction of the penis against the walls of the vagina."

"I never heard of such a thing."

"Of course you never heard of such a thing. Most men haven't. Not to mention women."

"Do you know what you're talking about, mister?"

"Do you want me to draw you a picture?"

"No, of course not," Denny said.

"Other women, most women, say a woman like Carley, they can only come with friction on the clitoris. You know, massaging the baby penis."

"The baby penis," Denny said vaguely.

Briney flexed the middle finger of his right hand. "This, Dennis, has got to be the strongest male appendage in all of the world. My, but it has to work hard in bed!"

Denny said nothing. He was frowning, thoughtfully.

Still flexing the finger, Briney said, "It's one hell of a tough thing for two people to come simultaneously when the man has to be massaging the lady's clitoris with his finger, this finger, and pumping in and out of her with his whole body at the same time."

"You should know," Denny said weakly.

"No wonder so many marriages are lousy."

"Why do you have to be so goddam *clinical?*" Danny suddenly said. "Especially about Carley." But then he was thoughtful again, and in a moment he said very quietly: "You ought to see how hard it is when you've only got one hand, when you've got to prop yourself up on a stump . . ."

"It must be terrible," Briney said.

"Vaginal orgasm, eh? Well, I've never come across one, but then I haven't had your experience."

Briney smiled. "Anyway, I have a hunch that Midge is capable of the big V.O. as well as the big C.O."

"The big V.O. Why are you so sure?"

"I'm not. It's just that I've discovered that tough, brittle women — women who try to compete with men — aggressive women — and, by the way, women who wear a lot of goddam jewelry and care more about girdles and bras and hairdos more than anything else — usually these broads have to come with the finger, so I avoid them. On the other hand, soft, sweet, tender women, like Midge for example — women who will surrender to a man's penis rather than having their own little bush league penis massaged — these women will usually be capable of the big V.O."

"The big V.O.," said Denny. "Sounds like a whiskey."

"Same thing," said Briney. "V.O. in whiskey means nothing more than 'Very Old.' Well, hell, vaginal orgasm is older than God."

"You exhaust me," Denny said, "just hearing about your experiences."

"Well, you play tennis. And I —"

"But you've never done it with Midge, have you, so you really don't know."

"No. And that's the truth. How about you and Carley?"

Denny shook his head. "I don't know either."

"Well, if I were you, I'd find out. And the sooner the better."

"I've given marriage very little thought."

"Who said anything about marriage? But since you've brought it up, you ought to damn well find out before you propose to anybody whether you've got a V.O. girl on your hands or a clitoral — a C.O. girl. Because, believe you me, A. Dennis Washington, it can make one hell of a big difference in bed."

Denny leaned back and sighed. "I think you place entirely too much emphasis on the whole thing. Certainly, there are other things in marriage besides *bed.*"

"Sure. There is the couch and the rug and the upper berth in a Pullman, and if you like to do it outside under the moon, there is the grass, and like I was telling Sammy a few minutes ago, the balcony of a movie house, and —"

"*Enough!*" Denny was holding up his hand, grinning.

"Okay. But the good bed life simply makes the other

things in marriage that much better. And minimizes the worse things."

"Amen."

"Sure," Briney said. "I like Midge's body, too, just the way, I suppose, you like Carley's body. Now I suppose you think Carley Harris is *your* type. She and her caustic tongue, sometimes like a longshoreman."

"She's amusing," Denny said. "And I don't take her out that much, anyway."

Briney was thoughtful for a moment. "Carley would poke holes in you in bed."

"Why do you think that?"

"Tall, bony, skinny girls poke holes in you in bed."

"Nonsense," said Denny. "Their bones have nothing to do with it and you know it."

Briney burst out laughing. "Of course not."

"All right. Why else do you like Midge? Never mind her sexual capabilities or her body."

"I honestly don't know."

"Maybe it's because she doesn't take any of your crap."

"You know something?" Briney said.

"What?"

"I don't have any to give her. No, I don't have to give Millicent Crocker any crap, so she doesn't have to take any of it. But Carley."

"Never mind Carley," Denny said.

Briney got up from his chair and stretched. "All this talk has horned me up. Suddenly, Dennis, I feel like some strange — some strange out there waiting for me to give 'em the big V.O."

"Oh, for God's sake, sit down," Denny said, looking around the bar to see if anyone but the bartender was listening. But there was still no one else in the bar, and Sammy only understood a little of what he could overhear.

"Yes, just talking about it makes me want some strange very badly." He pretended to head for the door. "Come on."

"No. We've got East Hampton tonight and I'm pooped."

Briney started to pace in front of the bar. "Sure, you're pooped, and from what? From running your ass ragged all over a damn lawn chasing a tennis ball in this wretchedly damp, sodden heat. What a way to get pooped! Wasting all that time and energy when you could be getting pooped in bed with some strange. People will think of anything as an excuse not to screw."

"You're demented."

"There are over two billion people in this world, and over half of them, over a billion, are strange — imagine that."

"You forget that some of them are married."

"All the better."

Sammy the bartender, who had been grinning transfixed at Briney pacing and talking in front of him, said, "Go get 'em, Mr. Mitchel!"

But Denny said: "Sit down, you idiot!"

"All right." Briney sat down. "I won't go looking for strange right now. I'll make an exception, since we're going to East Hampton tonight. As long as it's Devon and not the Maidstone. Christ, if it was Maidstone, I'd call up Paula Kalinski right now. Now there's a girl who really enjoys the big V.O."

"You would, wouldn't you?"

"You bet I would."

"Not even thinking of Midge or anybody else," Denny said.

"Little Paula knocks the pictures off the wall when she comes. Anyway, what's Midge got to do with it?"

"Don't be dense," said Denny.

Someone else was finally coming into the bar. It was Jonathan T. C. Carpenter, looking for another glass of Perrier water. He was dressed in a navy blue linen jacket, yellow shirt, Charvet tie, coral Daks and Panama hat. His face was slightly crimson, and he was still perspiring from the match with the Borlands. He was trying to light a cigarette, but it was too damp, and he was grumbling.

While Briney remained seated, Denny stood up and said, "Thanks for the game, sir."

"My pleasure, Dennis." He downed the Perrier water in several long gulps. "See you tomorrow."

"Yes, sir."

"Early?"

"Well, sir, not too early. You see we've got this thing at Devon tonight — we're taking Midge, as a matter of fact — and we'll probably be quite late."

Jonathan T. C. Carpenter glanced at Briney, slumped in the wicker chair. "Who's taking Midge?"

"I am," said Briney.

"No, you're not, young man. Not my granddaughter you're driving to East Hampton."

"Denny can drive then."

"No. Denny can drive whomever he wants to East Hampton, but not you with Midge." The old man went and put his empty glass on the bar. "No, I don't want you out with my granddaughter tonight." Briney stood up. "Yes, I thought I could get you on your feet," T. C. said. "Why don't you stand up like Dennis when older people come into the room?"

"This is a club bar," Briney said. "I'll stand up for you or any older person in a private room, but this is a club bar."

"I have a premonition about these things," the old man said, beginning to raise his voice in a tremble. "And, no, I don't want you out with Midge tonight."

Briney wanted to attack the old bastard, but he remained calm. "Have you talked to Midge about this?"

"No, but I will."

"You might break her heart."

"What colossal conceit!"

"No, I mean that sincerely. She's been looking forward to this thing, she has a lot of friends in East Hampton she wants me to meet."

The boy and the man stared at each other for a long moment and then the man said quietly, "By thunder, she can go alone with Denny, then, and whomever he's taking."

"Carley Harris," Denny said.

"Yes, Carley Harris, of course," T. C. said.

Briney began to seethe. "Godammit to hell, Mr. Carpenter!"

"Sit down, boy! And don't dare use language like that to me!"

Denny waved Briney down with a hand motion, then began to walk the old man to the door. Briney sat, his eyes riveted on the two. They spoke in whispers for a few moments, and then T. C. said, "Why can't he be like other young fellows? Like you for instance?" Then turning to Briney, he said, "Why the hell don't you play this damned game instead of sitting around all day and chasing girls all night?"

"It's too much effort for the reward, Mr. Carpenter."

The old man came back to where Briney was sitting. "Let's see your hands, boy."

"What for? They're clean."

"There, you see!" the old man said, spinning on Denny. "A civil request —"

"Show him your hands, for God's sake!" Denny said, in a rare fit of pique.

Briney extended them, palms up.

T. C. held one of them for a moment. Then he said, "Yes, just like my daughter's husband. Ex-husband. Good, big hands. Strong." He dropped the hand and looked at Briney. "My son-in-law, ex-son-in-law, played fullback for the Frankford Yellow Jackets, played against Red Grange when he came through Philadelphia with the Chicago Bears, did you know that, Brian Mitchel?"

"Yes, I knew that."

"He was a devil, that boy, like you, but he was also a special agent for the FBI, you know that, too, I suppose."

"I know that, too."

"Is that why you never tear up my daughter's lawn

with the wheels of your car? Because she was married to an FBI man?" T. C. began to smile. "Is that the reason?"

Briney, suppressing his own smile, said, "No, sir," and he never used "sir," not since he had left Portsmouth Priory. "It just never occurs to me."

Jonathan T. C. Carpenter leaned over and tapped Briney on the chest. "You're damned right it doesn't occur to you, because there aren't enough flowers in Southampton or the whole of Long Island to appease Harriet Carpenter Crocker's old man, if you tore up her lawn, and you just remember that."

"I'll remember that, Mr. Carpenter. I'll remember something else, too."

The older man, starting to go, turned and said, "What's that?"

"I'll remember this harangue, the God damndest spout of shit I have ever heard from a man of your intelligence. You remind me of my father."

Jonathan T. C. Carpenter stood rooted for a full minute staring at Briney Mitchel while Denny tried to get his friend out of the bar. But Briney Mitchel stood there, too, watching the purple come back in the old man's face, and the hand tremble, the tennis hand, and then, not wanting the old man to fall dead on the floor, took himself out of the bar and went into the lounge and sat down and picked up a copy of the *Social Spectator*, in Briney's view, a terrible resort magazine, which he started to thumb through and look for a monthly column called "Things & Stuff" which told about the social and physical exertions of the young people in and around Southampton. There was a picture of Midge in it someplace. He couldn't find the picture. He flung the magazine on the coffee table. No old son of a bitch like Jonathan T. C. Carpenter was going to keep him from taking Millicent Crocker to East Hampton tonight — nobody in the world. It would be tough, by God, but he would do it.

5

IN A FEW MINUTES DENNY JOINED HIM AND SAID,
"T. C. has gone to talk to Midge and find his chauffeur."

"Good."

"Well, congratulations. You did it."

"Sure I did it. But I cannot stand that kind of talk from anybody. From T. C. or anybody else." Briney, who had picked up the *Spectator* again and found the photograph of Midge, took a last lingering look at the golden girl in shorts going into the Beach Club. He almost wanted to rip it out and keep it, but he threw the magazine back down on the table.

"You didn't think of Midge, though, did you, you selfish bastard?"

"I thought of Midge. But I will not take that shit."

Denny looked down at his friend for a moment, fingering the towel he had thrown around his neck. "Let's go back in the bar."

They went back and sat down in the wicker chairs again and Briney said, "He's a killer. And I don't mean a killer-diller, either."

"Yes, and you are, too."

"I'm debating whether to have another South Side or

not. I mean he's a self-killer. He's going to buy it out there on court one, one of these fine hot Saturdays."

"I'll have another cuba maybe. No, he's in good shape," said Denny, wiping his glasses which had, oddly, steamed up again during the contest between Briney and T. C.

"He's too fat. He's too old and too fat and he's going to drop dead right on court one."

"He's been playing every weekend all his life. I hope I'm in as good shape as he is when I'm sixty-six, or whatever he is."

"You know why I left the bar?" Briney said.

"No, why?"

"I left the bar because I didn't want the son of a bitch to have apoplexy and drop dead right on the floor here."

"I hardly think that's likely to happen."

"All right then, not in the bar. He's trying to make a mess on court one. Ruin everybody's afternoon. Doctors, ambulances."

"T. C. plays tennis because he enjoys it," Denny said. "And to keep fit."

"Godammit, Dennis, what old Jonathan T. C. ought to be doing instead of playing tennis and trying to run his granddaughter's life, what he ought to be doing is sitting in the Southampton Club playing cribbage or bridge or whist or drop-the-soap or whatever the hell those tired old bastards do in that club on a Saturday afternoon."

"They play bottle pool, some of them. You didn't mention that."

"Instead of trying to do it to himself on court one and ruin everybody's day. He's a killer, all right, a self-killer."

"That's a gross exaggeration," Denny said, "and you know it."

"Well," said Briney, "each have our own way of doing it to ourselves, don't we?"

"Sure," said Denny. "I lost my arm under a street-car on Madison Avenue when I was a kid."

"What makes you bring that up?"

"You were talking about self-destruction."

"That was an accident."

"Are you sure?" Denny said.

"You mean you threw yourself under the streetcar on *purpose?*"

"Not exactly on purpose. I —"

"Oh, for Christ's sake!" said Briney. They ordered the drinks and glared at each other, and when Sammy brought the drinks, Denny said, "And you drive too fast. I may have had mine, but you drive too fast, and you be careful, mister. Yes, you drive much too fast and you rip up other people's lawns and you date married women, don't you, and you sleep with the native girls, don't you?"

Briney took an indelicate swig of his drink and slammed the glass down on the table in front of them. "Sure. We're about even. You throw yourself under a streetcar and I rip up lawns and screw married women." He looked out the window, away from Denny, and he couldn't find Midge or Carley on their court. They must have quit playing. "Married strange,"

Briney said, almost to himself. "And not just in South-ampton, either."

"And poor Stanley Kalinski's wife. Paula Kalinski, married to a motorcycle cop."

Briney looked sharply at Denny. "How can you compare that with old man Carpenter trying to knock himself off on court one?"

"If, as you say, Jonathan is trying to kill himself on the tennis court, you may very well be trying to do the same thing in bed with Paula Kalinski, mightn't you?"

"I can't think of a better way to go," said Briney.

"Suppose Stanley were to walk in on you sometime and catch you flagrante delicto? He carries a service revolver, the last time I looked, and he'd like nothing better than to find the very rich, very social Mr. Brian Mitchel rutting with his wife so he could put a bullet in his foolish brain. Stanley's a mean bugger, you know, for all his charm with women."

"Paula and I go to Aunt Margaret's. For God's sake, do you think we would do it in her house?"

"Quite frankly, yes — knowing you. Anyway, Stan-ley can stalk you to Aunt Margaret's, too."

"Well, Paula Kalinski's been passing it around Southampton for years."

"Yes, but not to the likes of you. Stanley might be tolerant of the native boys. His own kind, so to speak. But the phantom of Southampton? Never."

"Who's been passing it around Southampton for years?" a female voice said from behind them.

"I have," said Briney Mitchel without turning. "And furthermore, this is a men's bar. Or was."

"I only see one man," said Carley Harris. "And a boy."

Briney reached for his drink. He tasted it, swallowed it, but it was not comforting like the first two had been. "You be careful, Carlotta, or I won't run you over to Devon tonight."

"You're not running anyone over to Devon tonight, phantom. I just got the word from Midge, who, by the way, is in tears, and you might be decent enough to go into the lounge and say something nice to her." Briney turned around and looked at Carley, tall and triumphant, behind the chairs. The bitch, he thought. "Although why she's crying because she can't go with you is something I'll never fathom. Buy me a drink, Denny," she said, laying a thin muscled arm on his shoulder. "Cuba's fine. Yes, Denny can run us over, but not you, wrestler. We can take Denny's nice little Studebaker with that top that slides open, and Midge can sit in the rumble and keep an eye on me and Denny up front."

"Keep an eye on you for what?" Briney said.

"You'd be surprised for what."

"Who won?" said Denny, waving Sammy over.

Briney got up and went back in to find Midge. The lounge was sunken, a sunken glade of fresh-cut flowers from the Meadow Club gardens, and comfortable couches and easy chairs on oriental scatter rugs that seemed to grow out of the gleaming polished oakwood floor itself. The lounge said, "Sit down and relax" — but only the very old ladies who made the Meadow Club their home ever seemed to heed it. The younger genera-

tions were much too busy bustling about on the tennis
courts or drinking in the bar.

He found Midge seated at the big Steinway, almost
lost behind it, lightly fingering "The Moon Got in My
Eyes," a current Hal Kemp favorite. He sat down on
the bench beside her and took one of her hands, but she
pulled it away, so, with characteristic boldness, he began to stroke one of her breasts, very moist from the
tennis and very prominent, and she jumped and
slapped him hard on the arm, and he dropped his hand.
She smelled of that stale sweat that Briney remembered
so well back in his grammar school days when the girls
got through with gym. It did not matter; she was still
sweet and delicious.

"You had to ruin it, didn't you?" she said. "You had
to back-talk Grandpa."

"I didn't back-talk Grandpa. I just didn't think I
should take any of his crap. Besides, he's not your
father. What's he trying to do, run your life?" He tried
to take her hand but she wouldn't let him. "Are you
going to East Hampton with me tonight?"

"You know I can't."

"Be ready at nine o'clock. I'll pick you up."

"I never want to see you again."

"In Southampton you can hardly help seeing me
again. I'll pick you up at nine."

"No! I can't sneak out with you, Mitch!" And then
she started to weep.

Briney leaned over and tried to kiss her but she
pushed him away. "I can't tell which are the tears and
which is the sweat. Why don't you go in and change
and I'll buy you a drink."

"I thought you liked my smell!" She stood up suddenly and slammed down the piano-key cover, almost catching his fingers in it. "Take one of your fast girl friends to East Hampton!" she said, and she started to walk quickly, sobbing, then running, to the ladies' locker room.

"Nine o'clock!" Briney called to her, but she didn't answer back, and he was alone in the lounge — the damned sunken garden, the place made for comfort and leisure and contemplation, and it seemed for a moment that this black Irishman had no recourse. It did no good to get angry, but he got angry, furious — and he picked up the *Social Spectator* again and flipped through it and cursed the people pictured in it, and when he came to the picture of Millicent Crocker making her entrance into the Beach Club, he ripped out the whole page and threw it on the floor. Then he flung the magazine aside and became angry at everything around him. At Jonathan T. C. Carpenter, at his Uncle Aidan and his old man for trying to screw him out of Princeton — at everyone he could think of. He stood up and slammed out onto the porch, scattering the prep school kids like pigeons in the park.

He pounded down the porch toward where the chauffeurs were clustered about the admissions desk, and spying Herbert, the chauffeur whom Jonathan T. C. Carpenter shared with his daughter Harriet, he headed straight for him. Herbert, seeing Briney coming, tweaked his mustache and scooted behind a pillar, and the others made a wide path for him. Briney pretended to follow Herbert around the pillar, leering at him, and Herbert quaked. Briney hated Herbert because Herbert had once exposed himself to Midge when she was a little girl. Midge had sworn Briney to secrecy about it. The other chauffeurs laughed at Herbert, until Briney spun on them and said, "Imagine driving a car and getting *paid* to do it." Then he leaped off the porch and headed for the Phaeton parked in front of the pro shop.

The sight of his car served to calm him a little. He circled it once, as he always did, taking out a handkerchief and flicking away any dust spots, blowing hot breath on the hood and wiping away the moisture to examine his reflection again in the Kelly green enamel job.

The Phaeton was a gleaming piece of machinery with coffee-colored canvas top, modestly swept back chrome-plated grill and bright engine ventilators running alongside of the tapered hood. She had whitewall tires, polished headlamps and flowing fenders and running boards with rustless steel moulding. There were two taillights flanking the spare tire, mounted rakishly on the rear. Her front and back seat cushions and backs were genuine leather with piping, which Briney saddle-soaped every week. There was a cigar lighter and ash-tray of the tipping type in the center of the instrument panel, with the glove compartment on the right side, two sun visors and a windshield cleaner of the vacuum style with speed control.

Briney Mitchel truly loved this green steel animal of his. And her power, her V-8, "L"-Head engine, her 85 horses, her dual carburetors, her syncromesh gears of second and high. He took care of her like a baby. The tool kit had a lubricating gun; he lubed the Phaeton himself, not trusting a grease monkey to find all the fittings. He had the oil changed every five hundred miles at George O'Connor's Irving Garage; George had a man who knew how to do it well. He rotated the tires himself, too, using the jack and handle provided in the tool kit. Sometimes he allowed the Mitchel chauffeur, George Bohan, to help him with this.

Indeed, the Phaeton was entirely the car for this unreconstructed Irishman, this phantom of Southampton, who now patted her body as he went, almost as he would a piece of livestock or a whore. The spotlight attached to the left-hand side of the windshield was sparkling, but he got the chamois out of the glove compartment and polished it anyway; he might need the spotlight tonight. He polished his "mascot" — the hood ornament, too — the gleaming, solid bronze head of a leering devil, horns and all. He replaced the chamois and then he mounted — he never climbed in — he mounted himself in behind the driver's wheel, and took full possession of his automobile as he would a woman. Not any woman. But a woman like Millicent Crocker.

He rolled off the lawn in front of the pro shop on to the bluestone, gunned the engine and churned through the porte cochere, roaring away down the broad driveway like an express train behind schedule. At the Meadow Club, on the courts, on the porch, even in the bar — they could hear the phantom's engine a good many moments after the car disappeared into First Neck Lane.

6

"I WANT YOU TO FOLLOW THAT CAR, HERBERT," said Jonathan T. C. Carpenter through the speaker attachment in the back of the Pierce-Arrow, after Herbert had held the door for him under the portico of the Meadow Club.

"Yes, sir," said Herbert, shifting into gear and spinning away down the drive to follow the green Phaeton that was rapidly disappearing in the distance. "But I'm not at all sure I'll be able to catch him, sir."

"I don't, for God's sake, want you to catch him," said Jonathan T. C. Carpenter. "I just want to see where he goes. I'd like to catch the goods on him at Aunt Margaret's, for example."

"Yes, sir." Herbert, whose voice crackled through his end of the speaker, had to hold the instrument with one hand while he steered with the other. He drove the big limousine hard and well, just barely keeping Briney in sight.

"You're a good driver, Herbert," said Jonathan T. C. Carpenter into the speaker.

"Thank you, sir."

"In fact you're a damn sight better driver with one hand than you are with two."

"Yessir."

"And I'll bet you something else, Herbert," said the old man.

"What's that, sir?"

"I'll bet young Dennis Washington is a damn sight better tennis player with one arm than he ever would have been with two. And golfer, as well."

"Really, sir?"

"Yes. It's my feeling that people try to excel twice as hard with a handicap as they would otherwise."

"Yessir."

"Why, even that son of a bitch in Washington. I'll bet you he never would have made President if it hadn't been for his infantile paralysis. God damn the rotten luck anyway!"

"Yessir."

"Did you vote for the bastard in the last election? Did you? I'll bet you did. No, wait, don't answer that question, Herbert. It's none of my damned business who in the hell you voted for, is it?"

"I suppose not, sir." The chauffeur said it reluctantly. But then he turned in his seat so that Jonathan Carpenter could see his smile. "But I'll tell you a secret, if I may, sir."

The old man began to feel uncomfortable; he hated a sycophant like Herbert to confide in him. Still, he was anxious to know more about what made a servant like Herbert tick. "What's that?" he said.

"I cast my vote proudly for Mr. Landon."

Jonathan T. C. Carpenter dropped his speaking instrument, leaned forward in his seat, and rolled down the window that separated them. "You *didn't!*"

"I did indeed," said Herbert. "I voted for the man from the Sunflower State. I do think Mr. Roosevelt's gone a bit far, don't you, sir?"

Jonathan T. C. Carpenter leaned back in the seat again, took off his Panama, and fanned himself with it. "Well I'll be damned!"

"Yessir," said Herbert, puffing with pride. "I cast my vote proudly for Mr. Landon."

"Well I'll be damned," said T. C. again.

"Oh, I'm a man full of surprises," said the chauffeur.

"You certainly are," said T. C., who had begun to think, in the time since the election, that there had been a lower class, Communistic conspiracy against Alf Landon. There was a silence between the two men for a few moments, and then T. C. said: "Have you ever been to Aunt Margaret's, Herbert?"

"Oh, *no* sir!"

"No, I didn't think you had."

"What's that, sir?"

"Nothing, Herbert, nothing."

They followed Briney Mitchel across Great Plains and Ox Pasture Roads, and when they began to draw close to Hill Street, Jonathan Carpenter said, "All right, Herbert. When we get to the Southampton Club, turn around and you can take me to my daughter's house. I don't think the boy is going to Aunt Margaret's. If he were, in a way I wouldn't blame him. He's very angry."

"Yessir." Herbert made a skillful U-turn between the Southampton Club and the Irving Hotel.

"I wonder why it is," said Jonathan T. C. Carpenter,

"that when men get angry they always seem to want a woman."

"Why, I wasn't really aware of that," Herbert said.

"Well, it's true. I suppose making love to a woman when you are angry is a safety valve for your frustration. Remind me to ask Dr. Anderson about it sometime."

"Yessir."

Jonathan T. C. Carpenter waited for a moment before he said, "Are you sure you've never been to Aunt Margaret's, Herbert?"

"Oh, no sir."

The old man could see the color creep up the back of the chauffeur's neck, above his stiff white collar. "Well, you should go there sometime. Maybe we should both go there. Right now, I'm very angry. Don't you ever get lonesome for a woman, Herbert?"

"Yes, sir. But I have my work." There was some ice in his voice.

"I mean on your day off."

The chauffeur said nothing more, and thereby made the old man uncomfortable, much to the old man's chagrin. But he knew little enough about this pale, thin, pseudo-British, mustached keeper of his daughter's garage, and he thought he owed it to her — and Midge — to find out more.

Especially if Herbert were a sexual deviate.

They drove back the way they had come, along First Neck Lane, and turned left at Meadow Lane into Dune Road. They rolled past the Beach Club; there was no flag to be seen on the pole above the roof of the public section. No flag meant that it was too dangerous to swim in the ocean, and Jonathan Carpenter commented on this to Herbert.

"I saw the ocean at lunchtime, sir, and it's a *fright*."

As they circled the south edge of Dune Road between Lake Agawam and the club, Jonathan Carpenter suggested to himself that if people — like the Beach Club flagpole indicating the state of the ocean — signaled their own moods with a flag displayed outside their houses, there would be very few flags flying in Southampton this afternoon.

7

HARRIET CARPENTER CROCKER'S SUMMER "COT-tage" was called Ferry Slip. It had been named for the site of the landing the little ferry boat made on its round trips bringing bathers from the foot of Lake Agawam in the village, to the beach many years ago. The house stood almost on this site, in the southeastern corner of Lake Agawam, very near its edge. It was a huge Queen Anne with a Victorian hangover — direct and overstated — with steep gables and towers and turrets and pinnacles and dormers and an odd cupola here and there; everything but gingerbread and gargoyles. It even had a portico containing a porch with a Chinese railing that ran halfway round its bottom floor. Some of the summer people who were not fond of Harriet Crocker called her place The Monster; most of the natives called it Fairy Slip, after Herbert, the chauffeur, while Briney Mitchel, with magnificent simplicity, called Harriet Crocker's place The Crock.

Herbert helped the old man out of the car when they got to the house at the end of the long bluestone drive that led from South Main Street. Jonathan stood and looked at the view across the lake for a moment. The other houses, Gothic, Georgian or whatever, with their hipped and mansard roofs, stood oddly fuzzy against the ugly sky. Jonathan Carpenter always thought of Southampton as being "jungle architecture," drawn up by "monkeys on strings," he often said. There were even two identical French Provincial cottages across the lake, built by a couple who lived separately in each. They were called, respectively, East of the Sun and West of the Moon, and had their own kitchens and serving staffs for lavish, quite separate, entertaining. The man had made his money in cotton futures, and had met his wife in a speakeasy: she was a singer who fancied herself another Helen Morgan. It was true that she sat on a piano, but the lady was a terrible singer, and married the cotton futures man the first time he proposed. Now, here in their separate houses on the lake, they went their own ways. However, they made it quite clear when they had had too much to drink at cocktail parties, that they did do one thing together, because they did it very well together: they made love together.

Jonathan Carpenter often wondered who called who, and in whose house they chose to sleep. Perhaps they took turns visiting.

"Hello, Daddy," Harriet called from that part of the porch that was screened and comfortably furnished. She was reading a novel and having her iced tea laced with rum.

"Hello, Harry."

She put down the book. "Did you win?"

"Of course we won," said her father, climbing the steps and finding his favorite chair and fidgeting with his Panama before he crossed his legs and put it down.

He looked down at his white buckskin shoes. "Damn it, you ask that locker room man at the Meadow Club to clean your shoes — look at them!"

"They look all right to me."

"Well, they're not all right to me, and I'm wearing them, and it seems that ever since the crash you can't seem to get a decent job out of anybody, when the opposite ought to be true."

"Daddy, what's really bothering you? You seem so agitated, darling. What is it, this awful weather?"

"Well, I am agitated, and it's not the weather and it's not the damned shoes. No. I had a terrible row with the Mitchel boy."

"Oh, dear."

"My, what a young smart aleck he is!"

"Midge is going to East Hampton with him to-night."

"No, she's not. I forbade her."

"Oh, Father. But why punish poor Midge for something she had nothing to do with?"

"Harry, I had to. You can't believe what this kid Briney Mitchel said to my face." Jonathan gave his version of it to his daughter and Harriet said, "You'd think Briney would have had a little more consideration for Midge. This is going to take some getting over for her. She was looking forward so to going with him."

"Well, she'll be far better off going with someone else. Or she can tag along with Denny and Carley Harris."

"No, she won't, and you know it. Anyway, it's too late for her to get another date."

Harriet, visibly annoyed by the whole thing, picked

up some knitting she had been working on. The old man was thoughtful for a moment. Then he said: "Do you want me to countermand my order, Harry? You can, you know. After all, I'm not her father."

"You're practically her father."

"But I don't want to be responsible for breaking a child's heart."

"Briney Mitchel is responsible, not you. No, darling, you were right. What a shame it had to ruin your afternoon."

"I just don't understand how a nephew of Aidan Carew —. Well, it didn't ruin my afternoon. We won."

"Good."

"We always win with Denny Washington. Why do you think I call the poor boy up to play every weekend? I hate to lose. You know that."

"It's not really quite fair, is it?"

"He can always say no. No, I think, Harry, that he rather enjoys playing with an old duffer like me. It gives him, well, a chance to excel even beyond his handicap, if you know what I mean."

"I think he'd much rather be playing with Carley Harris." She poured his iced tea.

"He has all the week to play with Carley Harris."

"I hear Denny is absolutely mad for Carley. Sugar today?"

"Yes. My blood could stand it after the tennis and Briney Mitchel. And this weather!"

"Ghastly, isn't it? Well, the radio says we are going to have a storm of some kind. Maybe it will clear things up and the sun will come out again."

"Yes. Well, I don't know who Denny's mad for.

Except that I rather suspect any relationship with Carley Harris would have to be, well, an athletic relationship."

Harriet Crocker put down the sugar bowl and began to laugh. "Now, what in the world, Daddy, do you mean by an 'athletic relationship'? If you're talking about indoor athletics, it sounds like the best kind."

He took his glass and stirred, ignoring the spicy innuendo. "It's the worst kind. It's based on mutual competition. The best tennis player marries the best tennis player, the best golf player marries the best golf player. Ad nauseum. And if they belong to the River Club, they can even play squash against each other." He gulped his iced tea with an unsteady hand, overtired from the match. "Good Lord, a woman playing squash! Almost as bad as a woman playing court tennis at the Racquet Club!"

"Well, at least they have mutual interests," said Harriet, trying to get him off the subject.

"Mutual interests, hell. All they do, if they're of the wrong temperament, all they do is destroy each other. I've seen it happen to couples. They have fights that are almost as bad as those that take place over bridge tables."

"Denny and Carley don't seem to have the kinds of temperament that would destroy each other."

"Carley has a very sharp tongue."

"She should learn to control her tongue," said Harriet.

"Yes," said Jonathan T. C. Carpenter. "It's unattractive in a woman."

"I don't see how Denny stands for that, somehow."

The old man smiled. "Maybe he puts up with her because of her tennis."

"Oh, dear, the athletic relationship."

"I once told Denny," and T. C. made himself more comfortable in his chair, "I once told Denny that marriage is like a small corporation. There are only two members of the corporation, and guess who is the majority stockholder?"

"I suppose you're going to tell me that the woman is," Harriet said.

"Yes, the woman is the majority stockholder. She runs the show even if she owns only fifty-one percent of the stock. But mind you this: if she's smart, she doesn't let her man know that she controls the stock. Even the mousiest woman is the majority stockholder in a marriage."

"You mean I was the majority stockholder in my marriage with Dan?"

"In more ways than one," he said.

"I'm afraid I wasn't very smart with Dan Crocker. I'm afraid I let him know who ran the show."

"I think perhaps you had to let that so-and-so know who ran the show. He chased every good-looking skirt on the Main Line and he was a damned waitress pincher, that one, and when he got out here to Long Island it was the same thing."

"Maybe it was my fault," she said. "Maybe I was too much of a manager or something."

"Well, I don't know why you ever married him."

"I was fascinated by him, Daddy. And besides, no one in my set would ever have dared marry a professional football player."

"Or an FBI man."

"Well, later he was an FBI man, and a very dashing one at that."

Jonathan T. C. Carpenter took a sip of his tea. "Harry, are you still carrying the torch for that so-and-so?"

"Of course not."

"Why don't you marry Charley Anderson?"

"He hasn't asked me." Harriet smiled, making a dimple. She was an immensely attractive woman, and her father was often afraid that he was in love with her. This made him feel terribly guilty and uncomfortable, and he prayed against his feeling in church, and he wished that Sigmund Freud had never been born, the damned Jew, though he only knew about Sigmund Freud through the conversation of others. If Jonathan Carpenter had his way, they would burn all his books, just as Hitler was doing in Germany.

"Daddy, I needed a man like Dan Crocker," Harriet was saying. "When I was coming out, all the boys were going into Wall Street and becoming stuffed shirts."

"Shirts stuffed with money, you mean."

"Never mind, I didn't need the money. But I wanted a *man*." Harriet leaned forward in her seat and dropped her knitting. "Daddy, do you realize how many *men* really exist? Maybe that's why I don't mind Briney Mitchel so much. That boy has the makings of a *man*."

"That young man has the makings of a troublesome, difficult husband, if you're thinking in terms of his marrying Midge."

"Listen," she said with great eagerness. "I once saw

Dan play football, and out there on the field he was the complete master of himself, even in those silly uniforms they wear, and he used his elbows and knees in pileups, and chewed tobacco and spat and scratched himself where men aren't supposed to scratch themselves, and I loved him for it. And he growled at the referee when a decision went against the Yellow Jackets, yes, he yelled at the referee. Now, Daddy, can you imagine any of the young men I knew then doing *that?*"

"There was a fellow from Dartmouth who played —"

"I needed Dan, Daddy, he was everything I wanted, and I got exactly what I wanted."

"You got an irresponsible idiot. Maybe that's why you and Charley Anderson haven't gotten married yet. I wouldn't say that Charley Anderson was exactly an irresponsible idiot."

"Oh, I like Charley Anderson enormously," she said.

"But if he performed illegal abortions," said Jonathan T. C. Carpenter, "you'd probably like him even better."

"That's not true!" But Harriet smiled, showing her dimple again.

She had a nice smile, this good-looking divorcee in her late thirties, and she had the kind of figure that made men turn around and lust after her when she displayed it at the Beach Club, and Jonathan Carpenter laughed then, appreciating the beauty of his daughter and not feeling guilty about it as she sat there clicking her needles, this older man beset by age and young whippersnappers. "That young Mitchel, that troublemaker, was watching Midge play tennis as though he owned her."

"Well, he doesn't own her; she's told me."

"But she's vulnerable to young fellows like Briney Mitchel — not, thank God, that there are many around like him. What I mean is, he strikes me as being the kind of fellow — now I don't mean to alarm you — but he seems to be the kind of fellow that might just run off to Greenwich, Connecticut, some night with a girl and marry her."

"Well, we don't have to worry about that tonight, do we?"

"Listen, countermand that order, Harry." Jonathan Carpenter shifted uncomfortably in his chair. "She's your daughter. And I'm beginning to feel remorseful."

"Don't. Anyway, Midge is too smart to run off with some guy. And as I said, I'm rather fond of Briney. Don't forget, praise God, ours is the only lawn in Southampton he hasn't torn up with the wheels of his car. And that's, ah, somewhat symbolic to me, if you know what I mean."

"No, I don't know what you mean."

"I think it means, symbolically that is, that he hasn't seduced Midge."

"Well, it doesn't mean he hasn't tried."

"In fact," said Harriet Crocker, "do you know what he did the last time he took out Midge?"

"What?"

"He sent flowers to me the next day *anyway* — without having run over the lawn. With the sweetest note."

"Tommyrot. He's frightened of me, that's why he's never torn up your lawn."

"Are you sure, Daddy? Are you absolutely sure the shoe isn't on the other foot?"

Jonathan Carpenter laughed. "What the hell, Harry! Well, whatever. No, what worries me is that he's just too goddam nice and polite to you and Midge. I wish I could say the same for myself."

"How can anyone be too goddam nice and polite, as you put it?"

"In Briney, it makes me suspicious of his motives. Oh, the hell with it, let's forget it. This is getting us nowhere. Anyway, the boy should apply himself to something besides wrestling and swimming and courting the local belles. He's got a very good pair of hands, like Dan has. I told him that this afternoon."

"Well, he won't be using his very good pair of hands on my daughter tonight."

"Damned troublemaker," said Jonathan T. C. Carpenter.

The people of Southampton said that Briney Mitchel was the only bad apple in the whole Carew-Callaway-Mitchel axis. They were Roman Catholic, they were third- and fourth-generation Irish immigrants, but, by God, they were ladies and gentlemen right down to their toes. There was never a breath of scandal about those five brothers and sisters and their hordes of children who conducted themselves as decorously as children could throughout the summer. No one was ever sure which ones were winning all the blue ribbons at the horse shows, and they could never keep track of their names when they saw them at the clubs. All except Briney Mitchel; everybody knew Briney Mitchel.

And not one of them would have dared to talk back to Jonathan T. C. Carpenter the way Briney Mitchel had.

Harriet said: "Look, Daddy, if this thing is going to keep eating at you, why don't you call Lucian Mitchel and tell him the story and have him discipline the boy."

"A hopeless proposal."

"Then call Aidan Carew. They're scared stiff of Aidan."

"Who's they?"

"Lucian, for one."

But they both knew that Aidan Carew, gentleman that he was, spoke only to Catholics and God. Furthermore, it was evident that should Aidan Carew tell his brother-in-law Lucian Mitchel to discipline the boy, there might be some serious bloodshed in the Mitchel house. Briney was almost always in trouble with his father, and Jonathan Carpenter saw no need to "add any fuel to an already roaring inferno," as he put it.

"If only Brian were alive," said Harriet.

"Brian Carew. Yes."

"He had a way with Briney," Harriet said. "Now there was a lovely man, if you could ever use lovely to describe a man."

"Yes, but in the final analysis it's up to the boy's parents. Edyth Mitchel is far too sweet to do anything. Edyth Mitchel thinks that there is no evil in anybody. And as for Lucian — well, draw your own conclusions."

"Barbara Carew is sweet, too. Brian's widow."

"Yes, I know. What makes you mention that about her?"

"She's coming to dinner tonight. Why don't you come, too, Daddy? A small group."

Jonathan Carpenter smiled. "No. No, thank you. And stop trying to marry *me* off."

"I didn't mention marriage. And guess who's coming in the driveway just now, so be prepared."

The wheels of a saucy English Austin spun to a halt behind Jonathan T. C. Carpenter's Packard. The little Austin was a finely upholstered, black, jewel-like box set upon large, ridiculous platter wheels. It had flaring fenders and a broad basket-weave pattern of black and yellow checkers running around its midriff. It was an impertinent, slope-nosed, sexless little car that befitted a dowager who was no longer interested in men, more than it suited Midge Crocker. But it was Midge's car to get around in, and when she got out and slammed the door close in a fury, the little car rocked on its wheels.

"Damn it all to hell!" she said, slamming her tennis racquet against one of the tires of the car. It bounced back and almost caught her in the leg. She came up to the porch, her body in its tight tennis-playing uniform moist still from the sweat of the afternoon, her breasts taut against the polo shirt. She did not go into the porch, she stepped in the flower bed and pressed her breasts against the screening. She oozed anger, she smelled of anger, and the total effect was highly sexual and both the mother and the grandfather knew it, and were somewhat afraid of it, and for a moment neither of them said anything. Midge said: "I'm going to East Hampton *anyway!*"

"I — I'm afraid not, darling," said Harriet.

"You just wait," Midge said, moving her breasts against the screen and leaving the screen moist with perspiration where they had been.

"Go upstairs and take a bath, darling," said Harriet. "And try to compose yourself."

"And you, Grandpa," Midge said. "Couldn't there have been another way than the way you handled it, Grandpa, couldn't there have been?"

Jonathan T. C. Carpenter, feeling suddenly hopelessly lost, said, "I'm sorry, Midge, but I had no alternative. Tell me one alternative I had."

Midge heaved herself away from the screening, stood partly in the flower bed, her feet planted, and held her tennis racquet like a weapon. "Well, dammit all to hell, Grandpa," she said, and her mother jumped to her feet and ordered her daughter into the house and up to her room.

"How dare you! Swearing at your grandfather."

Midge stamped off and Harriet sat down again.

"She didn't swear at me," said Jonathan Carpenter. "And anyway, I'd have been disappointed if she *hadn't* sworn at me. I wonder if she'll go with Briney anyway."

"Of course not," said Harriet. "She wouldn't dare disobey me, or you, on something like that."

"I'm not so sure," said Jonathan T. C. Carpenter, his eyes falling on the damp spot on the screen where Midge had leaned.

Upstairs, Midge undressed, throwing her clothes around the suite, and when she was naked she threw herself on her bed, reaching for someone beside her, who, of course, was not there. Her hand fell on a pillow instead, a Princeton throw pillow, and she took it and crushed Princeton between her legs, leaving the other pillow to weep into.

8

ALONG THE LOW BRICK WALL, THE WALL THAT
ran all the way from Corwith's Pharmacy on Main
Street, where you could get the best milk shake in town
for fifteen cents, around the corner to the Rogers
Memorial Library on Job's Lane — along this wall on
this late summer Saturday afternoon, the cowboys sat.
They were the caddies and the delivery boys and the
truck drivers and the clam diggers and the hedge trim-
mers and the farmhands and potato pickers and the
driveway rakers and the lawn men and the young
gardeners and the old caretakers and the soda jerks and
the bartenders and the unemployed; yes, the NRA had
been declared illegal, and there were always the unemployed.

They watched the long-legged women emerge from
Bonwit's and Saks and Elizabeth Arden's and Charles
of the Ritz and Foulke & Foulke and Peck & Peck —
places they had never seen the insides of. They watched,
sitting in their cheap, worn-out, tattered but freshly
laundered Saturday night leisure clothes. They
watched and they envied these women their money, and
they lusted after them in their beach pajamas and their
floppy hats and their expensive cardigans thrown care-

lessly over expensive blouses, and though the cowboys never dared whistle at them, they made private, obscene remarks about some of them. If the women had come from the hairdresser, their heads were covered with bright scarves instead of floppy hats. If they had been shopping they carried bundles. Some of them shooed small children along in front of them, herding them home to their nannies for supper. Excited about their new hairdos, satisfied with their purchases, they boarded their Lincoln Zephyrs, Delage Cabriolets, Packards, Chevrolets with Free Wheeling, Ford V-8's, even an old Hupmobile or two, which were parked diagonally along Main Street, white sidewall tires snubbing the curbs on both sides. There were even one or two electric "red bugs" to be seen, operated by youngsters who were old enough to drive.

A few husbands came and went, too, stopping for an item of clothing at Finchley's or Saks Men's Department, or at one of the three or four liquor stores to order a replenishment for a cocktail or dinner party. They wore highly polished moccasins and wildly colored trousers, and big-checked sport coats over polo shirts of various hues. Most of them had come from a round of golf at Shinnecock or The National, and they did not linger in the village.

They acted for all the world as though there were no depression, and the Saturday afternoon cowboys on the low wall hated them for it, and they hated the Saturday afternoon cowboys for reminding them of it, and their wives did, too, and the hate was reciprocated a hundred-fold by the cowboys, who needed the rich people because they depended upon them for a mean living, and hated them more for that than they did for not having their affluence.

They depended on something else, too. They depended on the weather. Most of them worked with their hands out-of-doors, and if the weather was bad they did not work and they did not get paid, and the weather was one thing they could not blame on the rich people. This afternoon they talked a lot about the weather, which served to take their minds off the rich people, and one of them there on the wall was describing how wild the ocean had been the last couple of days, and another was saying that there was something brewing in the rotten, dank, airless day, and another wondered aloud when the goddam sun was going to shine again.

Ironically, the debilitating weather animated them, and it came out in their talk, this animation, and there was an air of expectancy about their dialogue, although all of them were fairly certain that nothing more unusual than getting drunk on beer at Aunt Margaret's awaited them on this Saturday night.

And so they gossiped and smoked and watched the ladies and gentlemen come and go, and when the Saturday afternoon parade of limousines which had met the Cannonball express from the city at the railroad station began to back up at the red light on the corner, they examined Lucian Mitchel's Cadillac with more interest than usual. "A new one," Birdie Hawkins said. "A new maid for the Mitchels, and a beauty."

"Maybe she's another girl friend of Briney's," said Harry Jablonski, who was a veteran of the Civilian Conservation Corps and now wheeled the Railway Express truck around Southampton.

"Riding in the front seat with George? And with that hat?"

"That's right," said Roy Strumpf. "She wouldn't be riding up there with George."

"No, she'd be down on the floor in the back with her step-ins down and Briney on top of her," said Jabbo.

"I can just feel her," said Roy Strumpf, the blind man, flexing his fingers until the knuckles cracked. Roy had lost his sight drinking wood alcohol at a Polish wedding in Riverhead during Prohibition. Now he clammed with his toes for a living, occasionally worked in a gas station, and could tell the year, model and make of any car on the road simply by listening to its engine idle.

"No," said Birdie Hawkins, "I don't even think on top of that one in the back, because I think there is something quite serious going on between Briney Mitchel and Midge Crocker."

"Briney is screwin' Paula Kalinski," said Jabbo.

"Don't mean nothin'," said Birdie, a sometime caddy. "I looped for Midge twice this week at Shinnecock, and when she found out me and Briney was old buds, she asked me all about when we was kids and played ball together and served mass and all that."

"And went to Aunt Margaret's together, did you mention that?"

"Up yours," said Birdie.

"Midge Crocker," said Jabbo. "I seen her around her old lady's place up near the beach. Man, would I love to carry her bags around eighteen."

"She plays mostly tennis at the Meadow Club," said Birdie.

"Then I'd be her ballboy. She could hold mine." He slapped his knee, very pleased with his joke. "I wonder if she puts out for Briney."

"Forget it," Birdie said, not because he knew the answer for sure, but he had enough respect for Briney Mitchel to consider it his friend's private business.

"Her old lady puts out, though," said Jabbo.

"How do you know?" said Birdie.

"Stanley Kalinski told me. He has a speaking acquaintance with Dan Crocker over to Riverhead."

"So what?" said Birdie.

"Stanley Kalinski told me, is all."

"Everybody puts out for Stanley Kalinski, according to Stanley Kalinski," said Birdie.

"Just like Paula Kalinski puts out for everybody," said Jabbo.

"The most Stanley Kalinski ever got in this town," said Birdie, "was over to Aunt Margaret's with some Southampton girl. I don't think he ever done anything with a rich girl."

Jabbo spat clear across the sidewalk into the gutter. "I ain't so sure about that, Bird."

"Well, I sure would like to meet that new Mitchel maid," said Birdie Hawkins.

"I can just feel her," said Roy Strumpf, cracking his knuckles again.

"And I got to meet Midge Crocker," said Harry Jablonski, almost under his breath.

The traffic light then turned green, and the Mitchel Cadillac swung around the stanchion and disappeared down Meeting House Lane, ending the cowboy conversation about the new maid. They began to talk about the weather again until they saw Briney's Phaeton coming up Job's Lane from Monument Square, and screech to a halt at the red light at the corner in front of them.

"He's mad at something," said Birdie Hawkins. "When he guns that engine waiting for the light, he's mad."

"Maybe he's just horny to get at that new maid," said Jabbo.

"Who's mad?" said Roy.

"Briney Mitchel," Birdie said, "and I'm surprised you ask, Roy, with the sound of that engine."

Roy squinted his sightless eyes in the direction of the car. "It don't sound like the Phaeton. No, there is something wrong with one of his gaskets. It sounds like a goddam old Marmon or something. He's going to have trouble soon with that gasket."

"Some people," said Jabbo, "think there is something wrong with more than one of his gaskets. Some people think there are a couple of screws loose here and there."

"There is nothing wrong with his gaskets or his screws," said Birdie Hawkins. Birdie was always quick to defend his old friend against the general antipathy the natives had for the summer rich. It had been different when Briney was one of them, one of the old altar boy and nickel-rocket-baseball crowd.

"He's a snot now, too," said Jabbo. "Like the rest of them."

"He ain't," said Birdie Hawkins.

"He's like all them rich bastards, give or take a few. They screw you as soon as look at you. Man, it sure ain't like the 3-C's in Southampton," said Jabbo. "Nobody had a dime in the C's."

"That's why you was in the C's," said Birdie.

"Nobody got a dime in Southampton, either," said Roy. " 'Cept the rich people."

"Screw all them rich bastards," said Jabbo.

"No," said Birdie, "there's nothing wrong with that man's nuts and bolts at all. It's his old man's that could bear lookin' into, not Briney's. Look there."

Briney, looking straight ahead, had dropped his left arm straight down over the door and was extending the middle finger of his left hand in the general direction of the cowboys on the wall.

Birdie returned the semaphore with a compliment of his own: that of placing his hand in the crook of his bent elbow.

Sensing this, Briney turned quickly, saw it, threw them a straight-faced wink, then turned back and gunned the engine.

"There," Birdie said to Jabbo and Roy. "And you call Briney Mitchel a snot?"

"He give you the sign?" said Roy.

"He did. We exchanged the international signs of all time." The light changed and Briney roared away down Meeting House Lane. "But he's mad," said Birdie. "Boy, is he mad."

"He's horny, is all," said Jabbo, and he spat across the sidewalk into the gutter again. "Screw him."

"He'd better fix that gasket," said Roy, "or he's headed for trouble." And the blind man cracked his knuckles again, and thought some more about the angry ocean and the vacuous day that seemed to oppress them all, and his toes began to itch in his soleless shoes — he had not been able to clam for two days, the bays were too rough — and he twitched unhappily on his perch, the low brick wall at the crossroads of South-ampton.

9

THE INN STOOD AT A BEND IN THE MONTAUK
Highway. For drivers it was the dividing line between
Southampton and Water Mill, and it was called the
Twelve Trees, for it had at least a dozen or more large
maples at its back, although some people joked
about it having belonged at one time to the famous
movie actress, Helen Twelvetrees. It was a pleasant,
rambling white clapboard building with comfortable
sleeping accommodations, a large dining room with a
dance floor and bandstand, and a bar just off the dining
room. It was a place where young people went in the
evening to dance and where single men drank at the bar.
It was a place where Briney Mitchel hardly ever
went — except to find Paula Kalinski at an odd hour.

You had to pass the front desk to get to the bar and
the dining room, and Bobby Motley, who was already
half in his cups — although the afternoon was a little
more than half gone — said, "She ain't here yet" when
Briney Mitchel walked in. Bobby Motley had only been
the assistant manager of the Twelve Trees for a month,
and already he was cadging liquor indiscriminately
from the bar. He was a nomad, this man, an eternal assistant manager who drifted from one resort job to the

next. He had worked in many hotels and restaurants on Long Island, and in Florida where he went when the season was over in the north. Once he had dreams of owning his own place, but he had long before given up the idea, since most of his savings went for liquor.

"Who isn't here yet?" said Briney, stopping.

"Paula."

"Paula who?" said Briney, getting very warm again.

"Whaddya mean, 'Paula who?' You come to see Paula, ain't you, Briney? Well, she ain't here yet."

Briney Mitchel took two quick steps and he was at the counter. He leaned over and caught Bobby Motley by the lapels and pulled Bobby's pockmarked face very close to his own. "Listen, you cheap rummy son of a bitch, you guard your ignorant tongue about Paula Kalinski and me or I'll take you out in back and thrash you alive."

"Look out, Briney —"

"*Mr. Mitchel*, godammit!"

"— Mr. Mitchel — you're tearing my coat —"

"You remind me, you jackal," said Briney, shaking him, "of an insurance salesman whom I once found waiting for me in my room in college, sitting in my chair, smoking my cigars, and saying 'Hello, Briney' when I walked in and found him. And do you know what I did with that insurance salesman who had the gall to come out to my room uninvited and sit down and smoke my cigars? Do you know what I did to him, Motley?"

"No, sir. What did you do with him, Mr. Mitchel?"

"I took that jackal by the scruff of his cheap coat, almost the way I have you by the lapels of your cheap coat, and threw him three flights down the stairwell, and I could have had the proctor fired who let him in my house in the first place, but I didn't, even though he hated me and that's why he let the creep in in the first place. No, I threw that man down three flights of stairs and he broke a leg and four ribs and had a mild concussion, and then I took him to the hospital in a taxi I called, and saw that he was taken care of, and then I went up to see that man after a few days and presented him with a check for two hundred and fifty dollars, and warned him never to let me see his face within ten miles of Princeton. And you know what, Motley?"

"What, Mr. Mitchel?"

"I never saw his face within ten miles of Princeton."

"Yessir."

"You're goddam right, yessir." Briney released his grip on the man, and the man with the pockmarks who was half in his cups scurried back from the counter. "Now go back in there behind the bar and make me a South Side."

"Yessir." Bobby Motley fled.

Just as he did, a black Model A Ford pulled into the parking lot out front and a small, well-formed woman in a cheap dress got down from it and hurried toward the door. Briney Mitchel, still enraged, watched her through the screen door. When she opened it, he barred her way. "Around the back."

"What do you mean, around the back?"

"You use the back door. It's bad enough you're using up good parking space with that heap. Now you go around to the back like all good servants."

She said something obscene to him and tried to get past him, pushing, even clawing, but he did not budge, not even using his hands on her. He bumped her with his hard stomach and she pummeled it with small red fists, and he laughed down at her. "You bastard!" she said, her breath coming fast. "You lousy rich bastard!"

Briney Mitchel laughed harder and then suddenly he took one of her slender wrists in his big hand and twisted her arm behind her back until she cried in pain. "I could break this off, you know, right here in the lobby." She tried to scream but he put his other arm over her mouth and slowly released his grip on her arm. Then he bumped her out the front door with his stomach. "The servant's entrance."

She turned, whimpering. "Briney . . ."

He slammed the door and stood behind it, barring her way again. When she started slowly around to the back, he went to the bar and picked up the South Side Bobby Motley had made for him. "Is it okay?" said the assistant manager when Briney tasted it.

Briney grimaced. "Now you go back in the kitchen and tell that wench to come out here."

"Yessir." Bobby Motley disappeared, and in a moment Paula Kalinski appeared in her uniform.

"What's in you today, Briney?" she said, coming around the end of the bar and over to where he was sitting. "Is it the weather, is it —"

"The *weather!* Don't whine dumb questions at me."

She put a hand on his arm but he shook it off. "You got a girl, don't you?"

He spun on the stool to face her. "Of course I've got a girl. I've got lots of girls, godammit!"

"Yes, I know, honey, you got one girl."

"I have *not* —"

"Oh, Jesus, but you hurt me," she said, rubbing the arm he had wrenched behind her back. "You don't know your strength and I'm so little." She put a hand back on his arm and this time he did not move it. "It's about Georgetown, ain't it?" Briney, sullen, nodded. "Well, please don't take it out on me. I'm so little. I'm a hundred and two pounds soaking wet on the Toledo in the bathroom this morning, and you're one eighty-five — eighty-three pounds heavier than me when you're on top of me."

"You're a scrawny, bony little pig," he said to her in the mirror across the bar. The bar was decorated in the manner of a circus tent and was called The Sideshow, while the dining room beyond was called the Carrousel Room, and had a tent over the dance floor. What Briney had just said to the waitress came off with a certain gentleness and affection; he had said it to her before, often. Paula Kalinski was not an unattractive girl. She had had to quit Southampton High School to marry the policeman who got her pregnant, and she was quite puzzled by the rapid turn of events that affect the young, but she was philosophical about them. She was not afraid; she only feared God. She went to Our Lady Queen of the Sea regularly, prayed hard, sang in the choir, was a member of two sodalities, and accepted circumstances as the will of God. She did not consider going to bed with Briney a mortal sin, and she did not confess it; this was because she loved this hulking man on the barstool with all her heart. She did not love Stanley Kalinski, and she had slept with others whom she did not love; she was loyal to Stanley, and confessed her adultery with the others in confession. But she loved

Briney Mitchel so much that any expression of this love was stainless. She also knew that she would never really be able to have him at all, and there lay Paula Kalinski's tragedy. "You got a girl. You got one girl called Midge Crocker."

"Shut up!"

"Jablonski told me. Harry Jablonski."

"Goddam Jabbo!" said Briney Mitchel.

Tears began to well up in her eyes, and Briney, terrified only of this in a woman, slid off the stool and took her by both shoulders and shook her gently. "No, I have no one girl, and don't you cry. Don't you cry or I'll twist your arm —"

"*No!*" she said, her face alight with horror.

"Then *stop!*"

She stopped. He let his arms drop from her shoulders. He wanted to take her right there, right there in The Sideshow. Sensing it, she said: "When will I see you? When can we be together?"

"You'll be here all night?"

"Yes."

"Meet me at Aunt Margaret's later. I have to go to East Hampton."

"With that girl."

"Shut up about that girl!"

Frustrated and jealous, she said, "I'll tell Stanley about you and me. I swear it."

"If you tell Stanley I'll absolutely kill you and throw your body in the Atlantic Ocean and the sharks will get it before they ever find you."

"You would, wouldn't you?"

"You bet your bony little bottom I would."

"Who are you going to East Hampton with?"

"None of your business."

"I know. The One Arm."

"Don't you dare call Denny Washington the One Arm. If you —"

"All right, all right. Something more than Georgetown's got into you tonight."

Briney Mitchel swallowed his drink whole. "When will that jackal learn to make a South Side like they make them at the Meadow Club?" He slammed the empty glass on the bar. "Too much sugar, not enough mint — *Christ!*"

"I got to set the tables for dinner," Paula Kalinski said. "I'll see you later tonight."

"Later tonight."

"Don't be, I mean, don't be too drunk."

"I'll be just as drunk as I please."

She made as if to take his hand, but he pushed it away and placed his own hand gently down on the back of her neck. Then he turned and went quickly out of the bar, leaving the upper parts of her body tingling.

"So long, Mr. Mitchel," Bobby Motley said from behind the desk.

"Put that lousy drink on my bill," was Briney's answer, as he went out and slammed the screen door behind him.

"Yes sir." But before he went to do it, Bobby Motley picked up the phone and asked the operator to give him Southampton 105. "Hello," he said. "Police? Gimme Stanley Kalinski, please."

10

BRINEY MITCHEL ONLY SPED WHEN HE SAW
policemen, and usually only during the vague, mist-
laden, twilight hours around Water Mill and Southampton when it was hard to distinguish forms on the
road far ahead. If he passed Stanley Kalinski coming
the other way on his red Indian motorcycle, Stanley
would invariably make a casual U-turn, and take the
route of the Phaeton, pretending only mild interest.
For a mile or so, Briney would keep the needle of his
speedometer well under the speed limit. Then, without
warning, he would floor the accelerator pedal and roar
away at breakneck speed, disappearing around a bend
or far out of sight before Stanley could bring his Indian up to full speed. Briney would duck up a side road
and bounce into a field, hiding the Phaeton behind a
bush or a barn or an abandoned farmhouse. It was a
game he played with all the police, and so enraged
them, that Briney Mitchel became known among the
constabulary of Suffolk County as the phantom of
Southampton, with which, when he heard it once, he was
quite pleased. The cops simply could not arrest him,
and the judges in the towns in and around Southampton were unhappy about this — not so much be-

cause they could not put him in jail or fine him, as because the bribe they would have accepted from Lucian Mitchel for his release would have been astronomical. They knew that Lucian Mitchel would not suffer his son in jail for one hour if Aidan Carew were to learn about it. And these were depression years, when things were not going well for anybody except the Southampton rich, not even town judges.

But this mood-ridden late Saturday afternoon, Briney Mitchel sped home as fast as the Phaeton would carry him, as fast as he could get away from the wretches at the Twelve Trees and the lousy South Side. He used his Klaxon once as he passed the house of the old crone on Cobb Road, the gray tumbled-down salt-box, hidden from the road by precious boxwood which she sold to the summer people, and kept company by forty-two cats. He hated horns, and had pulled his out and installed the Klaxon when he got the car. He had thought about a siren, but sirens, he decided, were for politicians, policemen, and feeble-minded men who sat in box seats in baseball parks and screamed insults at the players — immune from retaliation by their station and the rules of the game. He could have had the siren too, for Lucian Mitchel, through his late brother-in-law Brian Carew, had known Roosevelt when he was governor of New York State, and had other political connections as well. But Briney chose a Klaxon, resurrected from an old Bulldog Mack truck.

No, Briney Mitchel had no use for a horn; not like Addy Plummer's stepfather, who, when Briney was much younger, honked his horn when Addy Plummer's mother was going to make them late for a dinner party.

Perhaps that was what queered Briney on horns. The stepfather was a teak-faced, red-eyed man who sat fuming in his leather-upholstered, high-slung LaSalle Cabriolet with one hand on the horn, a symphonic horn in those days, which performed best during the still twilight hours when the sun had just slipped into the west, and Lake Agawam was flat and the fish were jumping and the mosquitoes were out, when Briney was mooning about the shrubbery, holding his ears against the orchestral blast of it, as it stuttered back and forth across the lake, stirring the water, frightening the fish, ricocheting off the pink stucco walls of the Beach Club, where the night watchman was locking up, discomfiting the old ladies taking their ease on the porch of the Meadow Club, rocketing along under the eaves of the weathered, gray-shingled Queen Anne and Victorian houses, and finally out to sea to warn all ships.

No wonder the Coast Guard abandoned its old station near the Beach Club, Briney thought, the one Lucian had bought and moved to their place between Mecox Bay and the ocean for a beachhouse, to be used mainly by Briney and the fantastically attractive older girl, Addy Plummer, on whom he had a "crush." They drank Canada Dry and danced in itchy woolen bathing suits to Paul Whiteman records until Briney's throat got dry and his temples pounded when they began to move too slowly and tightly together, and Addy, all-wise, all-knowing, would break away and dash shrieking out the door and over the dunes for the ocean, with Briney following, pants leaden and near bursting, until he caught up with her in the waves and ducked her ferociously for making him feel so agreeably upset.

Then Addy would ignore him for a few days — probably the only girl in the world ever to ignore Briney Mitchel — and he would hide his bike in the boxwood and mope about her big house on the lake after supper, waiting for Mrs. Plummer's third or fourth husband to come out and start blowing the horn of the old LaSalle, until Mrs. Plummer finally did come out, leaving Briney free to go inside and neck with Addy on the couch for half the night, and then pedal home in the dark, the seat of the bicycle no help at all to a terrible case of lover's nuts. He was fifteen at the time and had a somewhat different view of girls than he had now.

The man, the stepfather, come to think of it, reminded Briney of Jonathan T. C. Carpenter.

Lucian Mitchel was a horn-blower, too, but only on Sunday morning assembling his troops for mass. But Briney, the straggler, always made them arrive late, and the pastor's florid face would cloud up, his frown a collision of wrinkles: "You wouldn't be leht for-r-r a Jean Har-r-rlow movie shaw, now would ye, Lucian?" Briney could still hear Dan Regan say it from the top step of Our Lady Queen of the Sea when the Mitchels marched in at 8:05, "r-r-railr-road time," the pastor would add, for the eight o'clock mass. The pastor always held a railroad watch on the latecomers, given to him by his father. "You're damn right I wouldn't, Dan," Lucian Mitchel would say, stepping on his cigarette butt at the pastor's feet and blowing smoke past the pastor's face. "But you see I have this terrible hangover which my brother-in-law Brian Carew and I paid dearly for last night at Canoe Place Inn, and which I will gladly sell to you this morning for prac-

tically nothing." Even if Lucian Mitchel had been nowhere near Canoe Place Inn the night before, his excuse
to Dan Regan was always the same. He never blamed
Briney for making them late, at least not in front of
the priest. Briney smiled to himself; the old man was
not all bad.

Before those days, Lucian Mitchel had taught Briney
to love the ocean, taking him by the hand and leading
him into the surf. He showed Briney how to dive the
breakers and go under the rollers, swooping deep and
resting on the sandy floor while the wave passed over
him, then surfacing for air. It was in those precious
years that Briney came to master the ocean and love the
seashore; he spent many hours on the beach and in the
water and learned to go out beyond the breakers and
swim. He learned to sail, too. Nowadays he sometimes
borrowed a sailboat and went crabbing with some line
and bits of bacon. He always threw back the crabs he
caught, preferring to let the stupid creatures go free.
Sometimes he took a local girl with him and they found
a secluded cove and went skinnydipping. To Briney,
there was nothing like swimming naked and making
love in warm, shallow water.

In those other days, too, Briney Mitchel confessed his
sins of impurity with Adelaide Plummer. His confessor,
Father Dan Regan, pried him for details, but Briney
simply stated that he had been in close physical contact
with the young lady which caused great excitement
within him. Squinting at him through the screen of the
confessional, the priest would urge Briney to give up
the lady, but of course he never did, and he kept having
to go back to confession. Addy Plummer had a good

strong hold on him, and it pleased Briney immensely
that a girl two years older than himself was fond of
him. He did not mind too much confessing his sins of
impurity; it gave Dan Regan and him something to
talk about besides missing saying prayers at night, or
something else of no great moment.

On one or two terribly hot Sundays during the
summer, the pastor would omit his sermon entirely "because of the intoler-r-rable heat," reminding the pa-
rishioners in the same breath, however, that hell was
much hotter. And occasionally he even talked of other
things besides heaven and hell. Even Lucian Mitchel
and Brian Carew stayed in their seats to listen to his
short exercises on the history of Southampton: how it
had been originally settled by Puritans emigrating
from Lynn, Massachusetts, who sailed across Long
Island Sound, stepped ashore at Conscience Point in
Peconic Bay in 1640, and made their way south to a
tract of land bought from the agent of the Earl of
Stirling, and "there," as the story went, "erected the
twenty-third town called Southampton, by the Indians,
Agawam." This fact of history gave the resort its claim
to the title of the "oldest English colony in New York
State." Dan Regan would pause at the end of that pro-
nouncement, a trace of his Irish sour coming through,
and Lucian Mitchel would whisper to Brian Carew sitting next to him: "What a terrible thing it would have
been if Southampton had been settled by the *Irish!*"
They had a private joke between them that if Southampton were Irish, all it would be was churches and
bars strung from one end of town to the other. Now
that they had settled their families here, they had no

use for such Irish watering holes as Westhampton Beach and Spring Lake, New Jersey, originally founded by the English, but overrun with Irish Catholics. No, they liked Southampton just the way it was, and yet they were proud of their Irish heritage and happy to have been accepted into the summer life of a predominantly Protestant colony.

The first summer colonist did not arrive in Southampton until about 1870. He was a New York drygoods merchant who built a summer home and persuaded his physician to do the same. The good doctor was so impressed with the climate that he began to send many of his ailing patients to Southampton for the bracing sea air. Before long there were houses on the shores of Lake Agawam, on the hills of Shinnecock, and along Southampton's historic Necks: Captains, Halsey's, Cooper's and First, which were now the heart of the summer colony.

One summer resident named his home Mocomanto, after one of the Shinnecock Indians who signed with an "X" the deed that conveyed a large part of the Shinnecock Hills to the whites. Another home, belonging to an artist, was called La Malot. A place called Four Fountains soon went up at Halsey's Neck. In 1915, someone moved an old windmill to Shinnecock Hills and made a house called The Dolphins out of it. In that same year, an Italian Renaissance villa called the Port of Missing Men was built on a creek leading to Peconic Bay, not far from where the Puritans had landed at Conscience Point. It was set upon 1,800 acres, and had an oversize Pompeiian-style swimming pool flanked by a solarium with great columns of fluted gold-colored marble. Each room was so lavish that it had its own name. The third wife of the original owner had the approach to the villa changed to a paved French courtyard, so that even in those days Italian Renaissance was not entirely sacred.

Everybody came to gape at what they could see of the Port of Missing Men, even the summer people. The name intrigued them as much as the architecture. In fact, some nannies, out of earshot of their mistresses, struck terror in the hearts of naughty children by threatening, if they did not behave, to drop them at the Port of Missing Men, and they would disappear forever.

The colonists built the first golf club in America on the Shinnecock Hills, and one of the first lawn tennis clubs on the meadows west of Lake Agawam, and one of the finest bathing pavilions at the head of the lake. Dusty cow paths became freshly tarred roads, and pastures were plowed by Polish immigrants and planted with potatoes and picked at harvest by colored people who dropped them into big burlap bags for markets all over America. Around the great houses, grass was planted by native workers, and hedges brought in for privacy, and bluestone for the driveways bearing fine carriages and then gleaming motorcars with shiny brass and white sidewall tubes and monograms and even family crests on the doors, magnificently balky machines of a new industrial age, that rested near the steps of comfortable verandas and great porches that ran around sprawling rambling frame and shingle houses, their style borrowed from England, from where most of the owners' ancestors had come.

The comfortable, pleasant, assuring boom of the ocean was always to be heard. And when there was not the smell of the sea air, there was the smell of honeysuckle on trellises, and new-cut grass and freshly turned earth in the potato fields, and the sound of the tractor the Polish farmer had just bought with his life savings, and the *whoosh-whoosh* of swans flying from one pond to another. And there was no feeling like the clean cool feeling one experienced after bathing, when one got goose bumps in the hot wind after the cold ocean, the hot wind and lovely sun that washed everything disagreeable away.

And so people kept coming and buying and building and living and worshiping. And they loved Southampton, even the few Roman Catholics, who were reminded — much more than the Episcopalians or even the Presbyterians — that all that glitters is not gold.

"Gawld," the pastor, Dan Regan, would put it.

11

WHEN IT WAS CALM, BEATING WITH A REGULAR pulse upon the beach, the night sea whispered permanence and contentment and promises of pleasure, and the promises were heard and spoken from the lips of those in the great houses with their gleaming, polished floors and terraces stretching to great lawns and gardens and shrubbery and hedges beyond. And the promises were passed on to others in Southampton.

But when it was angry, as it was tonight, the sea howled destruction and mortality, and the winds that came with it whined under the gables and mourned, reminding those in the great houses that promises could be broken, and there was no such thing as permanence and very little contentment, especially in those lands beyond the great houses and hedges and potato fields and windmills of Southampton — in those broad stretches of America writhing in the grip of the great depression.

There was a breeze — just the hint of a breeze, but a breeze anyway — springing up from the southwest, shooting out of the alley Denny Washington had talked about, and there had been a raindrop or two on the windshield of the Phaeton tearing along Flying Point

Road. In his anger, Briney Mitchel hardly noticed the change, but others in Southampton and all along the south shore of Long Island that evening noticed it, especially those living on the beach. For the ocean was now beginning to lash at the dunes, the only breastwork the residents had against its winterlike savagery. These people knew about winter storms; winter storms washed away houses. Briney knew it, too. He had seen a winter storm erode away and destroy most of the Ladd house in 1931. The Ladd house, half of it smashed away, half of it teetering grotesquely in the sand, had been an object of fear and curiosity. Briney, as a child, had inspected it with his father. But nobody had seen anything like this fury in late summer. Those who had lost houses in winters past were most fretful; the others simply watched and waited.

Lucian Mitchel, also watching, was already drunk when Briney got to The Wreck, the house that Lucian had built between Mecox Bay and the ocean. Briney could tell because his father and Dan Regan were standing on the terrace having Old Fashioneds with too much Prohibition fruit in them — fruit that was supposed to kill the taste of lousy whiskey. It did not matter that his father drank good whiskey and always had, even during Prohibition. His father loved a lot of fruit. They were watching the surf below, and Lucian Mitchel, weaving ever so slightly, could be counted on never to stay sober when a priest was around. No one in or near the Mitchel family ever quite knew which came first: whether the priest just happened to arrive for dinner on the nights that Lucian Mitchel had had a couple of jolts, or whether it was the prospect of the priest's company that inspired the couple of jolts in Lucian Mitchel. It did not matter which priest it was, either; he got equally drunk with all of them, and had long ago made his peace with Dan Regan. Lucian Mitchel now got to mass five minutes ahead of time and sat in the second row of Our Lady Queen of the Sea behind Aidan Carew and his family, for which privilege he paid one hundred dollars a year. On some Sundays, he even went to two masses with Aidan, which, even Edyth Mitchel, Briney's mother and Aidan's sister, had to admit, was somewhat overdoing it.

Briney tried to escape upstairs when he saw the group on the terrace, but Lucian had heard the screen door slam, and he called his son outside.

"Yes?" Briney said, his head poking through the French doors. "I'm in a hurry."

"Come out here!" his father said. "Come out here and have the respect and good manners to at least greet Father Regan."

"Sure," said Briney, stepping over and taking the priest's hand and bowing elaborately as though Father Regan were almost a bishop.

"You need a shave," said Kathleen, Briney's older sister, who had been standing with them and who should have known better.

"So do you," said Briney. "Especially above your lip. And God knows what's under your arms."

"Now, that's enough!" said Lucian.

"As a matter of fact, I was just going upstairs to shave," said Briney Mitchel.

"Well, there isn't time to shave," said Lucian Mitchel. "Put a tie and a jacket on. Dinner's almost ready."

"How do you know?" said Briney, eyeing his father's whiskey glass.

"Briney —" Dan Regan started to say, but Briney, turning to the priest, raised his hand and his eyes to heaven, shrugging, and the priest began to smile. "Befor-r-re you came, I was saying that I can r-r-remember as a young pr-r-riest there were cattle gr-r-razing out there where the waves are br-r-reaking."

Briney looked toward the ocean, almost as though he were seeing it for the first time. "You can't see the wreck."

"No, you can't see the wreck," his father said soberly, not weaving for a moment.

"You can always see the wreck," said Briney. "Even in the winter you can see the wreck."

The wreck had been there when Lucian Mitchel bought the property. It lay about fifty feet off shore, the stem and ribs of an old sailing vessel, buried in the sand. The story went that some Indians, sailing from Montauk to the Shinnecock Reservation many years before, had foundered and sunk off this beach in Water Mill. To eliminate the wreck as a hazard to his family when they swam, Lucian had hired tractors and cables from the potato farmers in the area, and tried to wrest it from the sand. But they could not budge the hulk an inch. So he left it there, and displaying a sense of humor of which he had an abundance in those days, he christened his new house The Wreck, over the mild objections of Edyth Carew Mitchel.

"Someday even the wr-r-reck will be buried," said the priest.

"Longshore erosion," said Briney, staring at the waves.

"What do you know about longshore erosion?" said his father.

Briney knew about it from the newspapers and from talking to some of the old-timers in the village. He also knew that if the young Bob Moses didn't get his way and wasn't able to put in an ocean highway along the dunes to stop it, someday there wouldn't be any Long Island at all. "I'm thinking about the highway Bob Moses wants to put in along here."

"And if Moses builds his parkway, what happens to our houses?" said Lucian Mitchel. "And our beaches. All the riffraff will come. Hot dog stands . . ."

"If Moses doesn't build his parkway," said Briney Mitchel, "the ocean will wash away the houses and the dunes, and there won't be any place for us or the riffraff or the hot dog stands. So what's the difference? Look how close to the dunes the waves are running now." The ocean was foaming, spuming, crashing, booming, fearsome and furious, every wave smashing into the dune below them seeming to reach for them on the terrace where they could feel its spray.

It was a frightening, dooming ocean, and Dan Regan, his mind suddenly on Eternity, said: "Br-r-riney, when are you coming to see us at Our-r-r Lady? We miss you, son."

"I wish I could say the same, Father, but I'm afraid you shall never have that pleasure; nor I, I might add." Briney liked this fat, red-faced fellow with the collar.

At least he was reasonably honest and did a day's work of comforting the sick and the poor in the Polish quarter without too much conspicuous golf at the Southampton Golf Club, which had become a public course during the depression. Oh, he played a round with Briney's Aunt Caroline Carew on slow afternoons, and some ill-disposed people, putting "a round" together as one word, thought that they might be giving each other carnal pleasures, for Caroline's husband had long since gone to an insane asylum. But such was not the case, and Briney knew it. Briney knew a celibate when he saw one, and this Southampton divine was a celibate.

"How long since your last confession, son?"

"I can't remember, Father, no more than I can remember how many women I've banged."

"Now godammit, that's enough!" said Lucian, stamping his foot.

"How *dare* you?" said Kathleen, who was about to burst into tears.

"So that if I went to confession, I could no more remember the number of women I've banged than I could remember how many times I've seen Pop drunk with priests, and that would be no good at all, would it, because you fellows always want the number of times, don't you?"

The priest and Lucian and Kathleen simply stood with their mouths half open, standing there getting wet from the spray on the terrace, and Briney, the fury again mounting in him, watched the savage waves below, wishing they would somehow rise up and consume his father and the priest and his sister. He stood for a moment and watched the wild water with them. Then he turned on his heel and went inside through the French doors, stopping short at the entrance to the dining room. Janey, his younger sister, who had overheard most of the conversation outside, and had been giggling from behind a couch, came over to him. "Who's that?" said Briney without taking his eyes off the dining room.

"Who?" said Janey.

"That maid, stupid. That new maid."

Edyth Mitchel was instructing the girl in how to set the table. She was a comely, black-haired thing, quite obviously Irish, and also quite obviously frightened out of her wits.

"Her name's Peggy," Janey said. "Peggy something."

Peggy Something had arrived on the Cannonball, and had been the subject of the discussion by the cowboys on the low wall in the village when the Mitchel Cadillac stopped at the light. She had taken a seat somewhere in a rear coach at Jamaica, clutching her rosary beads in a tight wet fist against the imagined lust of her seatmate — a middle-aged, trammeled, indifferent bond salesman on his way to Hampton Bays to tell his wife it would be their last summer out of Brooklyn unless things picked up in Wall Street.

"She's beautiful," said Briney. "Absolutely beautiful."

"And you leave her alone," said Janey. "She's frightened enough as it is."

"What's she afraid of? God knows I won't bite her." He looked down at Janey and smiled. "I'd like to, though." And he thought to himself how much he would like to run his tongue over parts of her body — maybe parts of her that no man had ever touched, let alone licked. Then he left to go upstairs for the tie and jacket while Janey went out to stare at the waves with the others, whose mouths were still open, speechless at what Briney had just told them.

12

"WHAT'S THE WEATHER REPORT?" ONE OF THE maids said in the Mitchel kitchen.

"Whole gale warnings Cape May to Block Island," the cook said.

"What's that mean?" a second maid said.

"Rain and high winds is all," the cook said.

"Where is Cape May?" the first one said.

"How do I know where it is?" the cook said. "Don't bother me. I'm busy with the *potage*."

"What in the name of Joseph is *potage?*" the second maid said.

"It's Gaelic for soup, you fool!"

Peggy Something, waiting for the soup, giggled, and the one who said it, the cook, looked at the new maid crossly.

"I'm sorry," the second maid said. "I didn't mean to bother you. It's just that the weather makes me nervous, living so close to the ocean."

"Don't worry," said the first maid. "We got the Father with us tonight."

The cook, busy with the soup, laughed at this, and the others went on with their own work, saying no more. She was a big, bawdy Norwegian lady from Bay Ridge in Brooklyn, a magnificent cook who never went near a church and who loved to needle the Irishers about their piety.

Out in the dining room where the table had been set and the candles lit, the Mitchels gathered and stood behind their chairs while Dan Regan, his Irish burr soft in the shadows, said grace. All eyes were lowered except those of Briney Mitchel, who stared through the window of the pantry door at Peggy Something nervously waiting to bring in the soup. He was amused and fascinated by her fear — fear was a word that Briney hardly knew the meaning of.

When the priest was finished and signs of the cross had been made, Peggy Something came out of the pantry through the leather-covered swinging door to serve the *potage:* mock turtle soup. She went to Edyth Mitchel first. Briney shifted his gaze to his mother. He loved his mother, birdlike and elusive as she was, because she usually took his side in arguments with his father. When he was younger, his mother had always seemed too busy with other things: this charity or that luncheon. But in the years that had passed in her marriage to Lucian, and as Lucian became more irascible with his only son, Edyth Mitchel, when she was at home, felt an obligation to protect Briney. He loved her; when she was around she was constantly pouring oil on troubled waters. This time, to set a steady course of dinnertime conversation, she asked everybody what their plans were for the evening.

Janey said: "I wish I had someone to play Monopoly with."

Kathleen said, "Herb and I are going to the movies."

"What's the movie?" said Lucian Mitchel, whose right eyelid had now almost fallen closed from the drink.

"*Alexander's Ragtime Band.*"

"Has it to do with Irving Berlin?"

"Yes, Daddy."

"Good. Irving Berlin is a good friend of mine." He took his napkin out of the monogrammed silver ring and patted his lips with it. Lucian Mitchel had met Irving Berlin at The Players once in New York. "Is it an 'A' picture, Kathleen?"

"Oh, yes, Daddy."

"Kathleen wouldn't go to anything but an 'A' picture, you know that, Pop," said Briney.

"Yes, and you wouldn't go either, not if I knew about it."

"Well, I never go to the flicks, or hardly ever, except down at Princeton where you can see the 'D' pictures."

"You go to Condemned pictures at Princeton?" said his father, knowing full well that Briney did.

"Sure, Pop. The 'A' and 'B' pictures are Dick Powell and Ruby Keeler rubbish or Tyrone Power and Alice Faye rubbish. And the 'C' pictures are just 'A' and 'B' pictures with a little more thigh showing, and the 'D' pictures — the Condemned pictures almost never come to Southampton."

"Mike Glynne wouldn't book a 'D' picture," said Lucian Mitchel. Mike Glynne was the manager of the Southampton Theatre.

There was an edge in the father's voice, but the son pursued him: "Don't tell me he takes the Legion of Decency pledge, too," said Briney.

"No," said Lucian. "But some of his patrons do. Like me, for instance." The eyelid that had fallen before was now fully risen to where it belonged.

"Censorship is a curse," said Briney Mitchel.

"I wish to God," said Lucian, with a slight quaver in his voice, "I wish to God I had followed Father Regan's and Aidan Carew's advice and sent you to Georgetown originally, boy."

"Luce," said Edyth Mitchel from the other end of the table. "Let's not start on that again."

"He could still transfer-r-r," said Dan Regan. "Oh my, yes, they'll take a transfer-r-r from Pr-rinceton at Geor-r-rgetown."

Briney Mitchel sighed. Why didn't the priest shut his face? "Well, sirs," he said, "Georgetown might not make me a better Catholic, whatever that is, but it might teach me to say mass."

"What do you mean by that?" said Father Regan.

"One of those Hoyas over in Westhampton was telling me the other night at the Twelve Trees that after one of the promenades at Georgetown, he was walking his date home — to a school called Visitation, I think he said — and on the way they passed a group of drunken sophomores taking turns in saying the holy sacrifice with a beer case as the altar and a beer can as the chalice." Briney paused. "I think they sang the mass. Gregorian chant or something."

"A small, isolated group," said Dan Regan.

"At the Biltmore Bar in New York one night, I ran into a halfback from Notre Dame — or he ran into me. He was catching a train for Bronxville or someplace and the poor fellow ran into me and bounced right off onto the floor. So I picked him up and brushed him off and convinced him that he had missed his train and I bought him a beer. We compared notes about Notre Dame and Princeton, and compared to Princeton he said that Notre Dame was a prison. He told me that they let the inmates out at South Bend every so often, and they go off to Chicago and Detroit and Cleveland and take a suite of rooms in a hotel and get very drunk and they burn holes in mattresses before throwing them out the window, and they break up furniture and start fires in baskets, and they roll up the rugs and play Goodman records and jitterbug all night with expensive whores. For the women, it costs them about —"

"*Stop!*" said Lucian Mitchel.

"What dreadful stories," said Edyth Mitchel. Briney's mother had not been wholly concentrating on what he had been saying; she was thinking about the next meeting of the Catholic Big Sisters. Edyth Mitchel was hard put to recognize life's harsher realities as far as they concerned her own family. She was a sweet and nonplussed person who tried desperately in her own ineffectual way to separate Briney and her husband in their quarrels. She was deeply religious; her ambition was to die a saint. She trusted that God would take care of everything and set things right — if not now, then in the hereafter. She tried to shut her ears against the conversation and think about the Catholic Big Sisters again, but she found it to be very, very difficult.

"Nobody gets drunk at Princeton, I suppose," said Kathleen.

"Oh my, yes," said Briney. "Very drunk and publicly so. Also, there are such things as rape and arson at Princeton."

"*Rape?*" said Edyth Mitchel, not quite sure she had heard it correctly.

"Yes, Mother. Though I doubt that it's physically possible. Of course, I've never tried —"

"I'm cutting off your tuition at Princeton!" said Lucian Mitchel.

Briney shrugged. "I'm sorry, Pop. Kathleen only asked."

"Oh, my dear, let's change the subject," said Edyth Mitchel. "What are you doing tonight, darling?" she said to Briney.

"I'm taking Midge Crocker to Devon, Mother. There's a dance over there of some kind."

"Oh, no, you're not!" said Lucian Mitchel. "I'll be damned if you're taking that Protestant girl out tonight or any other night!"

"Luce," Briney's mother said, a terribly pained expression on her face. "Not at the dinner table, Luce. Can't we wait until dinner is over before we discuss Protestant girls?" Unlike her husband, Edyth Mitchel was more tolerant of the infidel. It suddenly occurred to her that she and Lucian had courted surreptitiously, and she didn't want a repetition of this in Briney's generation. "Don't be too harsh, Lucian," she added. Edyth Mitchel had always felt highly protective about Briney when he was jousting with his father, but she never could quite succeed in placating her husband.

"She's a Protestant girl," he said. "And you know I forbid Brian to take out Protestant girls, just like Aidan Carew forbids his boys. And look at Millicent

Crocker's mother. Harriet Crocker has been divorced from an FBI man who was a professional football player of some kind. Now what kind of a home is that?"

"I'm not taking her mother out," said Briney.

"Are there no attractive Catholic *summer* girls in Southampton?" said Father Regan. "Surely —"

"Not that I know of," said Briney. "All the Catholic *summer* girls are over in Quogue and Westhampton going out and getting drunk with prospective Georgetown priests."

Dan Regan cleared his throat but kept his peace, and Edyth Mitchel said with a quiet fury, "That wasn't necessary," and Briney knew that she was right, and for a moment he was truly sorry for having said it.

The remark cast a pall over the table, and Lucian Mitchel, seething with anger, thumped his fist on the table and said, "I'll cut off your tuition at Princeton and I'll lock you in your room tonight!"

"Go ahead," said Briney, finishing his soup with an ugly slurp and laying down his spoon so that it clattered in the bowl.

"I mean it!"

"I know you mean it."

"Well, what do you say to that?"

"I say it's your privilege."

And then there was a blessed silence for a few moments while Peggy Something retrieved the soup plates and came back with the sole amandine. She had done well, this girl, straight off the boat from Ireland, not having spilled any of the Norwegian cook's *potage* and serving people on their proper sides. But when she got to Briney with the fish course, she began to serve him on the wrong side, and Edyth Mitchel said, "On the left side, Peggy, and hold the plate lower, dear."

"Yes'um," said Peggy, and moved to Briney's other side.

"God watches you, God sees you," Briney said. He took his sole amandine carefully, controlling himself against the fury he felt at his father's bigotry, Aidan Carew's influence on his father, Jonathan T. C. Carpenter's stubbornness, Bobby Motley's lousy South Side, at the fact that he had to eat fish — he hated fish, especially on Friday — and the stupid business about Princeton. He had a measure of tolerance for Lucian Mitchel which did not much waver. But tonight, this Saturday night with the priest and everything else, he hated this surly, drunken sot of the man who was his father. So that when he deposited the sole on his plate, he returned the serving fork and spoon hard down on the Lowestoft platter, and Peggy Something had tilted it just enough to allow some of the lemon juice and butter sauce — even the serving fork — to fall into Briney's lap, smearing his white ducks, before the whole mess, fork and all, fell on the rug.

"Godammit to hell!" said Briney, finally fully angered, and throwing back his chair, almost knocked over Peggy and the serving platter.

"*Brian!*" his father said.

"I'm so sorry, Mister Brian," Peggy said. She was very pale.

"Don't you dare use such language in this house — ever!"

Briney said nothing. He reached down and picked up

the fork, wiping up some of the mess with his napkin.
Then he adjusted the platter in Peggy's frozen hands
so that it was level again before replacing the fork on it.
His eyes fell on her fine breasts pointing smartly at him
from under the starchy black uniform that crinkled
when she moved, only inches away from his tongue and
his teeth, and he wondered what would happen if she
took out one of her creamy, saucy Irish tits — right out
there in the dining room in front of everybody, and he
took the lovely tit between his teeth and sucked it,
making great noises right there in front of the priest
and his father and everybody, and how he would make
the blood run to her cheeks and her juices flow, just as
she had caused the fish juices and sauce to spill down
onto his fly. An Irish bacchanalia, by God.

"Hey, Peggy," he said in a voice barely audible.
"How would you like to go to the movies with me tonight? It's all about one of Pop's best friends, a fellow
he shook hands with once, it's an 'A' picture, so it's all
right for us to see it, and you're a good Catholic girl, so
it's all right for me to take you, and we can even sit in
the loge and neck, and we'll pick a spot right in front of
Kathleen and Herb Johnstone —"

"*Brian!*"

"— and after that I'll show you Aunt Margaret's,
and after a little drinking we can go upstairs —"

"*Brian Mitchel, get out of this dining room!*"

Peggy Something, who had almost let the platter slip
out of her hands when Briney was talking to her, recovered it, and blushing furiously she passed the
amandine on to the next person, Janey, on the wrong
side again.

"Go to your room immediately and stay there for the rest of the night!"

To continue the argument would have been a useless test of shouting, so Briney stood up, threw his napkin on the table and began to leave the dining room, his fly still wet from the sauce amandine.

"And excuse yourself!"

"Go to the left side, Peggy," his mother whispered, trying desperately to think about the Catholic Big Sisters.

"Excuse me," Briney said.

"Apologize to our guest!" His father was at the top of his form now, winning the battle with the son, causing the candles to flicker and the very room to tremble, booming away like the ocean outside, his voice strong and full like the wind whipping about the house.

He had Briney in full retreat and Briney let him have his victory. "I'm sorry, Father Regan."

"Apologies accepted," said the priest.

"And to the maid!"

"Sorry, Peggy." Briney was suddenly amused: apologizing to a servant in the house of his father.

"Q-quite all right, sir," Peggy said.

Then he left the dining room and went upstairs to his room, dripping sauce amandine here and there on the carpets.

"That boy," said Lucian Mitchel, shaking a finger at his wife through the candles at the other end of the table. "That boy —"

"The left side, Peggy," Edyth Mitchel said, still trying desperately to concentrate on the Catholic Big Sisters.

"Yes'um," said Peggy Something, who wondered why she had ever got on the boat at Cobh to come to America in the first place. Or was it God's will that she should meet Briney Mitchel, and perhaps that was her reason for coming to America? She had never met a man like him in all her born days.

13

JANEY WAS DYING TO LOOK LIKE A GLAMOUR GIRL as she took a cigarette out from under some things in her bureau drawer. But the effect was impossible. Though she was wise beyond her years, she was still too impish and perky to even remotely resemble a "glamour girl." She lit the cigarette and opened her window a few minutes after Lucian had locked Briney's door. The wind was so strong coming in that it blew the smoke halfway down her lungs again and she coughed and gripped the sill against it. "Briney!" she called. "Hey, Briney!"

"What?" he said from his bed where he was reading *Studs Lonigan*.

"I wish we could play Monopoly!"

"Thank God we can't."

"I can't hear you!"

"I'm not going to shout. Go away."

"Tell the ocean to shut up," she said.

"Shut up, ocean!"

"Come to the window!"

"No."

"Please."

He got up, went to the dormer, opened the screen and then the casement window. The wind caught him and held him for a moment. He half shouted, leaning out into the black night. "What's your trouble, Little Orphan Annie?"

"What's so bad about Aunt Margaret's?"

"What do you mean, what's so bad about Aunt Margaret's?"

"They were discussing it after you left the table. They were practically spelling things out to keep me from knowing about it."

"It's a whorehouse, child."

"It is?"

"Yes."

"I thought it was a restaurant."

"It's that, too. It's a very bad restaurant and a half-assed whorehouse. You can take a girl upstairs there, that's all.

"Golly day. Will you take me there sometime?"

"Of course not. It's a dump."

"Where is it?" she said.

"In the Polish section near the railroad station. Just off David White's Lane."

Janey took a sophisticated drag on her cigarette. "Golly day. A cathouse right here in Southampton."

"Not really a cathouse, Janey. Anyway, where did you learn about cathouses?"

"In a book someplace. Did you ever take anyone there?"

"Sure."

"Who?"

"Oh, Joan Crawford, Barbara Stanwyck, Janet Gaynor."

"Oh —! Golly day, what a wild night it's turning into."

"Will you kindly stop saying golly day," Briney said. "And now leave me alone."

"The new maid's a cute one, isn't she, Brine?"

"She's a clumsy fumble-finger. And now goodbye."

He started to close the window and Janey said, "Just because she spilled gravy on your nice clean white ducks. It's no wonder, the way you were acting."

"That's enough about that."

"Whatever made you ask her to go out with you right there in front of Daddy and Mummy and Father Regan?"

"I was angry at Father's arrogance, stupidity and bigotry."

"He was potted," Janey said.

"That's no excuse. He could at least be pleasantly potted."

"You must like Midge a lot."

"I like her as well as I've liked any girl."

"I like her, too. She's nice to younger people."

"That's always a good sign."

"Briney?"

"What?"

"Will you invite me to Princeton for a football game?"

Briney looked across the roof at his sister, sweet-faced in the soft light reflected from her bedroom. "No."

"I'll be sixteen next February fourteenth, and I'm not too young, if that's what you're thinking."

"What would they say at Eden Hall, your going to Princeton for a weekend?"

"Who cares what they'd say?"

"The nuns would have a baby." He looked at the black night. "They would all be virgin births, of course."

Janey sighed. "Imagine, a football weekend at Princeton. What are they like?"

"They're terrible," said Briney. "Truly terrible. Everyone gets absolutely stinking drunk in their clubs, and they have dates, and if they don't pass out and get some food in them Saturday night, the odds are they'll deflower a virgin or make someone pregnant. Usually both."

"Oh, goody." Her cigarette had gone out in the wind and she threw it away.

"And how about Pop? Pop would kill you if he found out you went to Princeton for a weekend."

"He needn't ever know. Which club will you be in next year? Ivy? Oh, I hope Ivy!"

"Probably none."

"Why?"

"Because there are a certain number of idiots in all the clubs and I have purposely been rude to all of them."

"You should be more tolerant."

"People should be less tolerant of fools. That's the trouble with this country today. Fools are running it."

"You mean Roosevelt."

"No, I don't mean Roosevelt. Roosevelt is brilliant because his Brain Trust is brilliant. It's Wall Street I'm talking about. Idiots. Dick Whitney. Christ!"

"I thought Dick Whitney and those people were pretty smart."

"Dick Whitney is so smart," said Briney, "he is playing first base for Sing Sing."

"You'd better not let Daddy hear you talk like that."

"I couldn't care less what Daddy hears me say."

"I wish you could take me to the movies tonight, Briney."

"I do, too. It's a crappy picture but you'd like it."

"Damn, if I only had a license to drive."

"A good thing for everyone on the road you don't."

"Next year I'll have a Junior License. I can't wait."

"Why don't you go to the movies with Kathleen and Herb Johnstone?"

"I'd rather not go at all. What pills."

"You could sit in the orchestra while they hold hands in the loge. If they've gone that far with each other."

"No," said Janey. "It's no fun alone."

"*Alexander's Ragtime Band*. You'd enjoy it. Alice Faye and Tyrone Power."

"Do you think they'll get married?"

"Alice Faye and Tyrone Power?"

"No, silly. Kathleen and Herb."

"Of course," said Briney.

"But Herb's not a Catholic."

"Ah, but he's taking instructions, isn't he?"

"That would be awful if Kathy married Herb."

"No, it would be lovely. A perfect match. I can't imagine where either of them would find another duller,

stuffier partner than they've found in each other."
Briney leaned further forward into the night. "You see,
Herb has everything. The only thing more he wants is
to become a Catholic and take Kathleen to bed. But he
will have to pay the price."

"Pay the price?"

"Every man, Little Orphan Annie, has to pay the
price for taking a woman to bed — be it a whore or
someone like Kathleen Mitchel."

"But that sounds so cynical!"

"In Herb's case, he will have to give Kathleen a new
ranch mink — she's already tired of her old one. A big
Park Avenue apartment, although Fifth seems more
stylish nowadays."

"But Herb lives in Cleveland."

"Never mind, he'll work in New York. Trips to
Europe on the *Normandie*. A box seat at the Polo
Grounds every Sunday to see the football Giants, where
Kathleen can wave at all her friends and show off the
new mink and gossip with all the other people who were
at La Rue's last night and will be at the Bird tonight
for the balloons, and —"

"The Bird?"

"The Stork, Janey, where nobody goes to make love
like they do at Aunt Margaret's, the stork brings the
babies."

"Oh, Briney!" She giggled.

"And they'll all be at El Morocco Monday night because Monday night is a dull night unless you stay
home and make love, but it's my hunch that Kathleen
will do everything in her power to get Herb out of the
apartment and minimize that possibility."

"You make it sound as though Kathleen's going to blackmail Herb instead of marry him."

"She is. Our dear sister is also going to want a box at the Horse Show and a box at the Metropolitan Opera and a box for theatre opening nights, and a box —"

"Well, if Herb Johnstone can give it to her, why not?"

"Herb can give it to her, all right, but he'll be giving her every box she wants and not getting the one box *he* wants, and he wants that box right now and he's going to want it very badly after they're married, but I don't think Kathleen's going to want to give it to him very much."

Janey shuddered. "You make marriage sound awful."

"For some people it is. They walk into it with their eyes closed, and they get what they deserve." Briney wished he had a cigar. "Sure. Herb will get every box in the book but the one that counts."

They were silent for a minute; Janey found herself breathing heavily against the wind. Then she said, "I wish I could go to the Stork Club."

"I only went to the Bird once and they wouldn't give me a check, and I went up to Billingsley who was sitting with Winchell and Damon Runyon and tried to get him to take my money, but he refused."

"But why? Why did you want to pay?"

"Because I had a legitimate bill and I wanted to pay it. A man should pay for what he gets. I never went back."

"You never went back? Why?"

"Billingsley had no business not taking my money,"

said Briney. "There are other ways to be a nice guy besides that."

Janey shook her head and her hair flew in the wind. "I just don't understand you, Brine. I'd love to go to the Stork Club. And free!"

"It's too bad the Nine O'Clock isn't in business any more."

"The Nine O'Clock?"

"It was a nightclub for kids a little older than you. If you got there at nine o'clock you got free drinks. Or there was no minimum charge or something like that. I got a Singapore Sling in there one night that was a beaut."

"How old were you?"

"I don't remember. But they served me. They must have lost money, that place. The kids wouldn't drink, I guess. They only lasted a couple of years. We used to go there after the Mets and the Get Togethers and Throw 'Em Ups."

"And the Gotham," she said. "You forgot about the Gotham."

"So I did. The one at Thanksgiving for the high Irish."

"Is the Gotham bad?"

Briney viewed the Gotham as no worse or no better than the others, except that everyone was conspicuously Catholic, and they all went to Catholic schools, and it was a wonder, he thought, that they didn't break out the rosary in the middle of the Big Apple or the Lambeth Walk. There were BIC among them, too — Brooklyn Irish Catholics — and these, in his view, were the worst of all.

They listened to the ocean for a little while longer, and then Janey asked Briney if he were going out to-night, and Briney said, "Yes, even though the warden has the keys."

She told him to be careful on the roof, for it was getting wet, and that she would close her window all the way so he could crawl by.

He looked at his younger sister and marveled at how different she was from Kathleen. If only everybody's sister could be like Janey. He closed the window then and went away to shower and shave and get into his tuxedo. When he was ready, he put his patent leather pumps and socks into the side pockets of his white linen dinner jacket and listened for a minute to hear if the maids were still doing the dishes below his room. Nothing; they had finished and gone up to their quarters at the other end of the house. There was only the thunder of the waves pounding against the dunes below the terrace and the drone of his father and the priest in the library drinking port. So he turned out all but one light, opened the screen and window again, and crawled through the casement of his dormer to the broad edge of the gambrel slate roof. Then he began to make his way on all fours toward the steel trellis at the far end. When he passed her dormer, Janey came to the window. "Be careful!" she whispered. She was naked to the waist. "Look how big my bust is getting!" Briney glanced at her small breasts and said, "Magnificent. I wish you weren't my sister." Then he inched his way onward. The windows of the old playroom were closed and he went past them quickly, glancing at the dimly lit terrace below. The window of the next dormer was swung open, so he pushed it gently with his shoulder and it squeaked, causing Peggy Something to rush to the opening, terrified. The maid had been temporarily assigned this big guest room on the top floor. Her own room was being painted. "Jesus, Mary and Joseph, I thought you were a thief!" She was in a slip, both hands clutched across her breast.

"No such luck. Close your window," Briney said, "and keep quiet."

She opened her screen and pulled her window toward her. "What if you should fall?"

"Then I'll be killed and go straight to hell."

"You're going to see the Protestant girl, aren't you?"

"Now how in the world did you ever guess that?"

"Is she pretty?"

"She's beautiful." Briney began to move past her dormer.

"Oh, dear God, if they should find out."

He glanced at her over his shoulder. "You tell them and I'll crawl into bed with you when I get back tonight."

"Oh, you wicked man!" she said, crossing herself.

He watched her white-skinned, black-haired beauty, momentarily forgetting that he was crawling on the wet roof, the wind pinning him against the Vermont slate shingles. "In fact you'd better lock your window."

"Indeed!" She pulled the window tight and locked it, and Briney crawled on, making his way past the other, darkened guest rooms. When he was almost to the trellis, Peggy Something opened her window again, and shouting into the wind, said, "Do be careful, Mister Brian."

Briney got a bare foot on the wet trellis and glanced back at her. For a moment, he thought it might really be more fun to stay home with Peggy Something. But Janey was looking at him from her window, too, so he descended out of sight, after a last lingering look at the gorgeous new Irisher. When he landed in the garden, he padded swiftly across the soaked lawn to the back of the four-car garage and opened the door leading to the chauffeur's quarters upstairs and the cars below. George Bohan, hearing him, came to the head of the landing with a flashlight. "Who goes?"

"John Dillinger."

"No need to be smart, Mr. Brian."

"I'm taking the Ford."

"The boss has took the keys, you can't."

"Then drive me over to Crockers'."

"I can't do that. I hear tell in the kitchen the boss locked you in tonight."

"Then I'll take the Plymouth."

"What will I tell the boss if he sees it gone?"

"Tell him it's being fixed."

"He'll fire me if he knows I lied."

"Tell him I took it then."

The chauffeur came down the stairs. "You shouldn't run with the Protestants, boy." George Bohan could get away with this sort of thing with Briney, where no other servant would dare. For Bohan, next to Birdie Hawkins, had been Briney's closest childhood companion, having been in the Mitchel service for years. At one point, Lucian, afraid the Irish chauffeur might corrupt

Briney, had hired a tutor for his son, but Briney had
made life so miserable for the man, a boxing champion
at Fordham who later became a policeman, that the
companion left howling in two days when Briney got
into a dispute with him and kicked him in the groin.

"Who the hell are you to tell me I shouldn't run with
Protestants?"

"Listen," the chauffeur said. "It isn't all that. It's
your ballsin' it up with the old man."

"What do you mean?"

"Well, you been a pretty good lad since you went off
to college, better than your Priory days, better than
you've been since I've known you when you was a squirt
chuckin' sand in the pool at the Beach Club. Maybe it's
because you're growin' up, I don't know. Whatever it is,
why balls it up now?" George sniffed the air. "And it's
turnin' to such a rotten night."

Briney, impatient to be off, said, "He's a drunken
fool."

George Bohan shook his head. "Tonight he's drunk.
But he's no fool, your Dad. No, I'm dead serious, lad.
And look at you with your shoes and socks off, and your
feet covered with grass. Wait. I'll get a towel." George
went away, came back with a towel, bent down and
wiped Briney's feet, which made Briney very uncomfortable. "You got the boss on your side for the first
time in years," George Bohan said when he was finished.
"And now you want to go off and balls it up."

"To hell with the boss," said Briney, taking out his
pumps and socks. "Anyway, he won't even know I'm
gone. Unless, for God's sake, you tell him. And if you
tell him, George, I'll —"

"Oh, I ain't sayin' nothing, don't worry about that. I got enough on me mind as it is, with the old woman and all. But be careful tonight. It bodes ill tonight, Briney Mitchel." Briney smiled at the chauffeur's old-country vernacular; he suddenly wanted to throw his arms around George Bohan and hug him. "And be quiet when you come in. Not only so the boss don't hear, but the wife is poorly."

"I'm sorry to hear that, George," Briney said, straightening up, his shoes and socks on. "Remember me to her."

"That I will," George said, sniffing the air again. "She gets the asthma you know. It's this blinking sea air, and it's worse than ever tonight."

"Sure, I know." He patted the older man on the arm, then he jumped into the Plymouth, released the brake and let the car roll out onto the bluestone turnaround. George watched him for a moment, then went back upstairs. Briney started the motor quietly and ran it at a murmur, letting the car move slowly down the driveway away from the dunes toward Mecox Bay, not turning on the headlights until he was out of sight of the house.

George Bohan put out the stairway light, went back upstairs and closed and locked the door to his apartment. He went into the bedroom.

"It was Briney, wasn't it?" said Clara Bohan, wheezing.

George hooked his thumbs into his suspenders. "Ay, he sends his regards."

"He's ballsing it up again, ain't he?"

"I told him he was, but he don't listen. How do you feel, luv?"

"Misery, misery, this bleedin' climate."

"Ay, and it's worse tonight. But so many of them takes to it."

"Like ducks to water, these rich. Did you ask the boss about the rise?"

"I haven't had a chance, luv."

"Damme, you've had a whole week, George!"

"You know how I am about those things," he said, sitting down on the bed and taking her hand.

"Fifty dollars a month is not enough, George, even with room and board."

"I'll ask him tomorrow."

George Bohan hated to ask Lucian Mitchel for anything, because Lucian had been so good to George. George was that kind of a man. He was loyal as hell to Lucian; he suffered his wife's asthma when he could have got another job in a drier climate. As far as George Bohan was concerned, there was no other family in the world to work for than the Lucian Mitchels of New York and Southampton.

14

JANEY MITCHEL KNOCKED ON PEGGY SOME-thing's door.

"Oh, it's you, lass."

"May I come in?"

"I'd be complimented. But is it permitted?"

"Not really. At least Daddy doesn't like it."

"Well, then —"

"Oh, but it's all right. Daddy's potted and Mummy's in her room reading."

"Me Mum warned me; it's that way the world over."

"Not all over, I hope," said Janey, coming in and closing the door. "Can I help you unpack?"

"No, thanks," said Peggy. "I'm all but finished."

"That's a lovely slip you have on," Janey said.

"Why, thank you," said Peggy Something, blushing. "Me Mum give it to me for a going-away present."

"But you mustn't roll your stockings."

"Roll my stockings?" Peggy said, her hand falling to just above her knee.

"No," Janey said. "You must get a garter belt and let your stockings rise up to their full length, up to here." Janey pushed her nightgown halfway up her thigh and described how a garter belt worked.

"My, what a good idea," said Peggy Something. "But is it not uncomfortable?"

"It's very comfortable when you get used to it. And you can get one at Hildreth's, the drygoods store in the village, on your day off. Or I'll get you one Monday."

"You musn't spend your money on me," Peggy said.

"They're cheap. And anyway, I can charge it. I'll make it a welcome-to-the-Mitchels' present." Janey sat down on the bed.

"That's sweet. I'm grateful to ye."

"You're beautiful," Janey said. "Do you have lots of beaus back in Ireland?"

Peggy Something smiled and blushed again and sat down beside Janey on the bed. "I live in the remote hills of Kerry, and don't see many lads. And, oh, my goodness, the lads in Kerry don't come a-courtin' till they're near thirty-five or even older. It's a, well, a . . ."

"Yes?"

"It's a poor country, lass, and with the work and all, there seems to be little time for *luving*."

"*Luving?*"

"Yes, luving. And one must take what one can get. And sometimes . . ."

"Yes?" Janey was all ears.

". . . sometimes that isn't often very much."

"Oh?"

"And besides."

"Yes?"

"Luving outside of marriage is very sinful."

Janey looked at her toes. "I suppose. But Ireland sounds awful. For a girl, I mean."

"It's not so bad, really."

"No wonder you came to America."

"I marvel at this country!"

"What do you think of my brother Briney?"

"Oh, I really couldn't say about Mister Brian, really."

"You don't have to be polite," Janey said.

Peggy Something smiled. She had a lovely smile. "Well, now, he is a one now, isn't he?"

"He's a one, all right. He wasn't always this way, you know," Janey said.

"No?"

"No. Mother says he was very shy when he was little. He even stuttered."

"Stuttered?"

"Yes. Or so Mummy tells me."

"He made Mr. Mitchel very angry tonight, didn't he, Miss Janey. And I feel a good deal of the fault was mine."

"Yes. But you mustn't take the blame. Briney's always getting in fights with Daddy. You just gave him an extra excuse tonight."

"Oh?"

"Yes. And you can call me Janey when we're alone together like this."

"Very well. You wouldn't prefer that I called you Miss Janey, even when we're alone?"

"No. I'm not really old enough."

"And how old is that?"

"Fifteen."

Peggy Something looked at the black night through the window for a moment, and listened to the wind and the surf. "His girl friend must be very beautiful for Mr. Brian to take such risks."

"You saw him on the roof?"

"Yes."

"She's pretty," Janey said. "And Midge Crocker is sweet. So unlike Briney, really. Her mother married an FBI man."

"FBI man?"

"Federal Bureau of Investigation. Federal police, I suppose you would call them. There was a big scandal when it happened."

"Ah, I suppose," Peggy said. "When people of quality . . ."

"Are you homesick?" Janey said.

"Not yet. But I suppose I will be. I've really been too busy with the employment agent and the traveling to be homesick, but I suppose . . ." And then Peggy Something began to weep quietly, and Janey said, "Oh, my goodness," and put an arm around her and patted her shoulder. When the girl was finally quiet, Janey said, "You have the nicest breasts."

Peggy sat up sharply and looked at Janey.

"Well, I was only trying to say something to cheer you up."

"I know. It's just that you startled me a bit."

"Oh, I didn't mean it in the wrong way. I know all about lesbians and those things. I was flattering you. I hope I have as nice a bust as yours someday."

Peggy Something, fearing the compliment and wondering if all young American girls talked this way, said: "That's sinful talk, Janey, for one so young." She folded her arms across her breasts.

"It's not sinful talk, at all. You sound like some of the nuns at school."

"Well, I don't mean to sound like a nun. It's just that —"

"It's natural talk, perfectly natural talk, for me anyway. I grew up almost four years ago."

"Four years ago! When you were eleven?"

"Sure." Janey said it with great pride.

"Gracious!"

"Yes, I was way ahead of time." Janey hugged her knees and grinned. "And do I like it!" Then she stood up from the bed and said, "Well, you must be tired, Peggy, so I'll leave you alone now."

"Very well."

"Some night I'll teach you to play Monopoly. It's a very good game where you can win a lot of money and own a lot of property."

"I'd like that, I think."

Janey went to the door and opened it. "Otherwise, the evenings can be awfully dull around here."

Peggy Something smiled. "This evening hasn't been a very dull evening, though, now has it?"

Janey laughed. "Good night, Peggy."

"Good night, Miss Janey. Oh, I mean Janey." When she had put on her nightgown and finished her prayers kneeling by the bed, Peggy Something went to the window. Rain was beginning to drum on it. Nonetheless, she unlocked it, opened it just a crack, and screwed it tight with the fixture at the base. The night was wild, like those she had heard about on the Connemara coast. When she was finally in bed, she wondered if all rich American men were wild like Briney Mitchel. Tired as she was, she could not sleep for the warmth in the lower part of her belly. She was sorry that she had not asked Janey to tell her about Aunt Margaret's. Then, to put the sinful thoughts out of her head, she took her rosary out from under her pillow and started to say a decade. Before she had finished eight Hail Marys, the prayers, or the pounding surf below her window, lulled her to sleep.

15

"YOU GOT TO STOP THIS, STANLEY," SAID POLICE
Chief Sam Drover to motorcycle policeman Stanley
Kalinski on the steps of the Southampton Post Office.
They were standing in the shelter of the roof, wearing
yellow slickers. The chief rocked on his heels when he
talked. "You got to stop this or I'll have your wheels
and put you in Krabowski's job." He nodded in the
direction of Saks Fifth Avenue where Krabowski, whose
father had hung himself after his potato crop failure in
Wickapogue last year, was sullenly checking the doors
of the village shops to see if they were open or had been
tampered with.

Stanley, who had been stewing over the phone call
from Bobby Motley about Briney Mitchel and Paula
Kalinski, was nursing a growing load of injured pride.
Yes, he was proud, and that's what hurt about Briney
Mitchel screwing his wife. He was proud of his carefully softened peak cap, proud of his shiny black puttees that glittered in the streetlights on the wet, and he
was proud of his red Indian motorcycle which snorted
him around town when it wasn't in George O'Connor's
garage being fixed. Stanley hated it when his wheels
were out of commission. Well, maybe next year he could

talk Sam Drover into a new Harley-Davidson. He was even sometimes proud of Paula when they went to Bingo Night at Our Lady Queen of the Sea. He hated to hear that a rich kid like the phantom was screwing Paula; especially to hear it from a rumpot like Bobby Motley. And now this; the chief picked the damndest times to lecture him.

"Well, you got no proof," Stanley said.

"You always say, 'I got no proof,' " said the chief. "But I hear stories, oh, I hear stories. Maybe they originate with you, I don't know, but I hear them, and someday, I hope to God it never comes, but someday I will have proof like you've knocked up one of those fancy young boarding school ladies, Stanley, and there'll be Jesus and hell to pay, and you know it, so —"

"I don't fool around with the rich girls, you know that, Chief."

"— so I wish to dear God Himself that you would please keep your pants buttoned. And you, a married man."

"A shotgun, remember, Chief?"

"For if you don't mind yourself, Stanley, surer than God made little green apples, I'll have your wheels and give them to Krabowski over there, who, poor fellow, carries the world on his shoulders, and you'll have his beat every night, checking doors and stepping on Pomeranian shit in the dark."

"You wouldn't do that, Chief."

"And if you persist with the ladies, I'll throw you off the force altogether and you can go pick potatoes for all I care."

"A fine choice you give me."

"It would make you look bad, would it not, Stanley? The young ladies would laugh at you, wouldn't they, watching you bending over in filthy overalls picking spuds out of the dirt?"

"No broad laughs at Stanley Kalinski," said this proud man.

"Well, I'll say it once more: when you pinch the ladies for speeding or making a wrong turn, confine yourself to the issuing of a summons."

Stanley kicked a step. "The other night I got invited to take another ride back in Shinnecock Hills. Just to beat a ticket."

"By whom?"

"I ain't sayin'."

"There's a good boy. I don't want to hear."

"She'll be in traffic court next Wednesday."

"There'll be a lot of ladies in traffic court next Wednesday."

"Well, take your pick; I ain't sayin'."

Chief Drover wet his lips. "Was she pretty, Stanley?"

"She was an older broad, Chief, but real stacked."

"Ah, by an older broad, you mean about twenty-eight or twenty-nine, I gather."

"No, she was a good forty."

"Oh, doddering."

"Well, young or old, they do that to me once in a while. Even the rich ones. They invite me up to Shinnecock just to beat a speeding fine, and some of them got gin on their breaths."

"God help us," said Sam Drover.

The truth of the matter was that Stanley Kalinski had not been invited up to Shinnecock Hills by a woman at all, but by a man in a tuxedo driving a Duesenberg. Stanley was so appalled that he might be attractive to men that he had to fabricate the story about the woman to Drover. "And Chief, I ain't made of wood."

"No, certainly not. But then you do have a wife, haven't you?"

"Some wife."

"And isn't it more comfortable in your own little bed on Moses Lane than in the back seat of a — you must tell me sometime how you manage to — no, forget it. Stanley, you must start going back to church regular." The chief was rocking quickly.

"Oh, my God, Chief, the last time I went to church I got Costigan in the confessional and you could hear it all the way out in the street, never mind the church."

"Costigan the deaf one. Why did you go to him?"

"It said 'Father Regan' on the door, but it was Costigan all the time in there and I felt as though I had been ambushed. I couldn't very well leave once I was kneeling down in the booth and saw Costigan through the screen. I had to holler at him. You could hear it all the way out in the street."

"You shocked him, boy."

"Shocked him? How could anybody shock Costigan, in Southampton for thirty-two years, or whatever it is?"

"Well, you must have shocked him. What did you tell him?"

"All I did was tell him I took a girl upstairs at Aunt Margaret's."

"Which girl?" said the chief, wetting his lips again.

"I ain't sayin'."

"You sure it wasn't in the back seat of one of them fancy cars and not Aunt Margaret's?"

"It was Aunt Margaret's."

Chief Drover often felt fatherly toward Stanley Kalinski, and he had to know all the details; at least that was his excuse. "And you a married man," he said.

"Well, he give me terrible hell and twenty-five decades of the rosary. I told him, 'that's pretty steep,' and he says fornication is a terrible sin, and then he says, 'besides, it ain't legal.' Then I tell him there is no such thing as fornication in the State of New York, and he says, it's not legal for Aunt Margaret to run that place, and I says, 'render unto Caesar what is Caesar's,' and why I thought of that I'll never know. I'm hollering all this, mind you, so he can hear. Well, anyway, I got him conned into thinkin' that it ain't me, Kalinski, there in the confessional, but some fresh high school kid. And then I guess he notices my badge or something through the screen and he says, hollering right back at me, 'don't try to fool me, you adulterous young whippersnapper, you're Kalinski the bike cop who is married to Paula O'Neil, married right here in this church,' and then all hell breaks loose, and when I finally get out of the booth, people waitin' to get in have their ears covered. I was lucky to get out of that place alive." Stanley kicked the step. "And I ain't been back since."

"That's what you get for trying to fool a priest," said the chief. "Well, you must go back. Go back to Father Regan or go to the one in Hampton Bays. I understand they have a nice young man in Hampton

Bays this summer. A Jebbie. Brian Carew used to take his family over to Hampton Bays every Sunday; he couldn't stand Regan's or the deaf one's sermons. 'The forty-minute commercials from hell,' he called them. But then he took sick, poor man, and stopped going over to Hampton Bays. The last time I saw him in Regan's church was in the vestibule at the eleven o'clock. He come in with his brood ten minutes late as usual. Regan is in the back, holding his blasted railroad watch on everybody, looking for the latecomers, Costigan is saying the mass, and Regan spies Brian, and he says to Brian like he says to Lucian Mitchel and everybody else: 'Do you think this is a continuous performance like the movies, Br-r-rian?' And Brian says, 'I wish it was so I could miss the goddam sermon, especially on this day,' he says, 'when I got such a terrible hangover from drinkin' Aunt Margaret's bootleg gin last night.' And he says it right there in front of the children and everybody."

"What happened?" said Stanley, who was doing something he almost never did: smile.

"Why, he just pushed on past Regan, leaving the priest struck dumb, and goes in and sits with his brother-in-law Lucian Mitchel and his son Briney, who are waiting for him with a space in the pew, while his missus and the kids march themselves up and plant themselves behind his sainted brother Aidan and his brood in the front pew."

"Brian Carew was a fine gent," said Stanley Kalinski.

The chief was laughing. "Him and Lucian Mitchel:

what a pair! But somehow I don't picture the Carews or the Mitchels or the Callaways for Southampton. Somehow, they seem to belong more to Quogue or Westhampton with the rest of the lace curtains. And yet," Sam Drover said, squinting at the dirty weather in the streetlights, "they're not really lace curtains at all, they go far beyond the lace curtains . . ."

"A different breed of cat?" suggested Stanley.

The chief glanced at his motorcycle cop, surprised at the sudden articulation. "Maybe. For they are fine, good-looking people who never give anyone a bit of trouble. All except for the phantom, of course, but there has to be one black sheep, I suppose."

"Yeah," said Stanley, feeling suddenly obtusely proud that someone in the Carew Mitchel Callaway family had chosen his wife to screw among all the ladies to be screwed, rich and poor, in Southampton. "Yeah, and they ain't snotty like a lot of the other rich people."

"That's the reason I said they seem to belong more in — speak of the devil."

In spite of the growing wind and rain, they heard the car long before it got to Job's Lane and Main Street, and they were sure, without saying it to each other, that it was the phantom, for only the phantom would be foolish enough to go full blast past the corner near where San Drover and Stanley Kalinski stood. But when the Plymouth began to take shape in the streetlights, Stanley said, "No, it ain't the Phaeton."

The car went blasting right through the caution signal on the stanchion, and kept on going like an express train down Job's Lane. "Jesus," said Stanley, running down the steps to his machine. "Whoever it is," said the chief, "go get him but don't risk your neck. It's too slick tonight and he's not worth it, whoever the dimwit is. I'll call Maguire in Hampton Bays in case you lose him. Maguire has a new Ford V-8 with a supercharger."

Chief Sam Drover descended the steps of the post office and walked slowly up the street toward the station house, while Stanley Kalinski, siren screaming, began the chore of closing the distance between his Indian and the red needle point that was the taillight of the Mitchel Plymouth, far up Hill Street. He rode his wheels with enormous glee, hugging the saddle with his thighs, punching it along with his pelvis, the throttle full out under his right glove, both hands pushing the handlebars hard ahead into the night, as though he had a woman half under him, the wind screaming past his ears her voice in pure ecstasy. Across Monument Square he flew, stopping traffic, turning heads: it was Kalinski after another one. Up Hill Street past George O'Connor's and the movie house, where people lined up in the rain and waited for the second showing of *Alexander's Ragtime Band* and wondered who the cop was after tonight. Some of them knew; even Stanley knew by now. It could only be one. He begged his Indian on, banging the hot hoarse engine under him with the insides of his shiny puttees, scarring them. There goes the Indian, someone said in the Irving, and up at Our Lady, Kalinski's machine and his siren for a full minute drowned out Costigan, who was holding a Forty-Hour Devotion. Stanley had the taillight in sight until the end of Hill Street, until the taillight swung into St.

Andrew's Road; then he lost it. He lost it not because his Indian lacked speed, or that the Plymouth was faster, or because the car had got too big a jump on him. No. Stanley knew that he had lost it because he knew the car had bumped off into one of the old Shinnecock Indian trails that wound through the hills, and was now hiding someplace, crouched in the wet and the dark.

He brought his hot, sizzling-in-the-rain wheels to a slow halt. Siren dying, he slumped in the seat, no longer a dick or a bull, but a cop, and he found that he was perspiring under his slicker, his heart thumping fast, like just after he had screwed somebody. He took a cigarette out, as he did after making love, and his hand shook lighting it, as it often did after making love, and he sat there astride his horse, drained, in the dark, the rain pelting around him, sizzling off the hot engine. He smoked the Camel for a few moments. He had lost the phantom again. It burned him terribly, like the cigarette burned his lungs. He threw the cigarette away and pushed off. There were going to be a lot of other things to do tonight. But he would get the Mitchel son of a bitch yet.

16

THE BIG CREAM-COLORED CLOCK IMBEDDED IN layer upon layer of dark green paint near the peak of the roof of the public bathing pavilion at the Beach Club facing the ocean, struck nine. The big black hands, carved of wood and attached to the face many summers ago, now rattled at their moorings, as if they were trying to break loose of the old building and bath-houses that shuddered in the wind and rain. Off at the other end, in the new section, the private section that had been erected in 1927, and whose clubhouse and bathhouses had the solid look of Moorish pink stucco and Mediterranean red-flute tiles about them, the watchman, smelling of gin, made his flashlighted way around the pool and the peristyle that bordered it. The watchman noticed that there were waves in the pool, rather large waves, and if there were waves in the pool, what was the goddam ocean like? He did not dare go up the steps that led to the beach to look. He wore a heavy black raincoat, borrowed from one of the lifeguards, and an oilcloth sea hat stolen from one of the bath-houses. He was sweating — as much from the heat of the raincoat as from fear of the storm. He had been in Southampton as a young man in 1916 when another bad storm went through. A hurricane, they called it now. But then, in those days, it was just another bad "line storm," one of those three-day blows that came every late summer when the sun was about to cross the equator. Leaning into the wind, he went out of the pool section and made his way along the rows of private bathhouses to where Max, one of the bathboys, who taught ice-skating at Rockefeller Center in the winter, kept towels marked "Bathing Corporation of Southampton" and which cost ten cents to use. With one of his own master keys, the watchman opened the door of Max's office and got Max's master key to the bathhouses. He closed Max's door, locked it again, and began to walk down this particular aisle playing his light on the rain-swept metal nameplates on the doors. When he came to "H. C. Crocker," the watchman stopped. He opened H. C. Crocker's door with Max's master key, went inside, closed it behind him, and sat down on the couch, grateful to be out of the weather and back with his woman again. The bathhouses had two rooms, one for changing and one for lounging. The watchman was sitting in the room for lounging. It had wicker furniture with cushions and a dressing table with a mirror. There was a lamp on the dressing table, but the watchman did not dare turn it on for fear someone would see it from the Dune Road. He played his flashlight around the room. It was painted red, bright Chinese red. H. C. Crocker liked red, whoever he was. Henry C. Crocker? Harold C. Crocker? Strange. He had heard once that people who lived in red rooms often went crazy.

He brought the light around the bathing suits on the

wall until it fell on the two-piece Hawaiian job. It hung
dry and lifeless from a wooden peg. Max always put it
in the same place every night, having dried it outside
along with the jocks and other bathing suits in the late
afternoon sun. The watchman had never seen a two-
piece bathing suit in his life, until this summer, let
alone a girl wearing one. Although he did not like girls,
he wanted desperately to see the owner of the two-piece
Hawaiian job wearing it. He hated girls. He was, in
fact, afraid of them. The reason was that one of them, a
French girl, had given him gonorrhea in Paris after the
Armistice. He remembered her, small and black-haired,
in a *Les Chambres de la Nuit* hotel in Pigalle, taking
his penis out of his uniform pants, pulling the foreskin
back and washing it with soap and cold water over the
sink. She led him to the sink by the penis. Then she got
on the *bidet* and washed her own parts. She did not
want to get fully undressed for the watchman, then a
Lightning Division rifleman. But the watchman made
her get undressed. He let her keep her stockings on, and
that may have been the reason he came into her so soon;
stockings excited him. At first she had been dry, trying
to lubricate herself with her finger and her own saliva.
But she was quite wet when the watchman finished, and
she wanted more from the watchman, having been fully
aroused in spite of his fast ejaculation. But the watchman would not give her any more. Embarrassed about
his premature ejaculation, he pointed to his division
patch, a white streak of lightning on a half circle of
red, and he tried to make it clear to her with what little
French he knew, that the lightning was the reason that
he had come into her so fast. The girl was not amused.

And the watchman was remorseful and disgusted with himself as he got off the bed and pulled up his pants. He paid the girl with money thrown on the floor, and took himself immediately to a priest at a little church in Pigalle to confess his sin. The priest spoke only French, and the watchman had a terrible time making him understand what he had just done. Finally, in desperation, he used the splendid four-letter Anglo-Saxon word for copulating, and the French priest knew immediately what the sin was, and he sighed in relief and smiled, and gave the watchman a mild penance and absolved him. The watchman made his Act of Contrition and went out into a pew and kneeled down and said a great deal more penance than he had to.

He tried to hide his gonorrhea so that he could ship home with his own outfit and march like a hero in the parades up Fifth Avenue. But they gave everybody a short-arm inspection on the pier at Le Havre, and when pus came out of the watchman's urethra the Jewish doctor who was making the physical inspection cursed him and his Christian foreskin, and sent him packing to a hospital. The cure was agony: they pushed that big closed metal spider up inside of him to irrigate the infection, and pulled it out like an open umbrella to carry it away. The watchman came home eventually, attached to a quartermaster laundry outfit, and did no marching up Fifth Avenue. The only thing he had to show for his war in the Argonne, besides his dose, was that he had later got his name chiseled in granite on the war memorial at the foot of Lake Agawam, right along with the rich people and the rest of the Southampton Yanks who had fought in the war. But the memory of his dose would remain with him forever, as though it, too, had been chiseled in granite.

No wonder the watchman hadn't been near a woman since France.

Holding the flashlight with one hand and shining it on the two-piece Hawaiian job here in the Crocker bathhouse, he closed his eyes. The watchman had a trick: he closed his eyes hard and created a marvelous picture for himself in his mind's eye. He made the bathing suit on the wall begin to come to life for him, dancing it off the peg and filling it with a woman, a faceless woman whose breasts were so big they almost spilled out of the halter, and whose thighs and buttocks were enormously voluptuous. She danced for him, at first swaying in the light from the flash, captured in the closed eye. He would not let her come too close. He made her roll her hips and shake the upper part of her body, so that her breasts undulated. The watchman kept time for her with his fist. She turned around and undid her halter as he had seen them do at the Gaiety in New York, where the watchman, on his day off, had once been. She turned around, this faceless woman, slowly, teasingly. The big breasts rolled in front of his face. She threw the halter so that it caught on the peg by itself. Then she began to wiggle out of her pants, grinding as they did it in New York. When they were low on her hips he reached out for her with his free hand but she pulled away from him and turned her back on the watchman and let the pants drop down around her ankles, trapping her legs so that she could not spread them apart. When she turned around she had no genitalia at all. It was a cruel joke the watchman played on himself.

Now the watchman was fine, strong, young and full again, his heart racing with the sweet joy in his mind, racing like the clock on the wall outside, racing like the wind, thundering like the waves on the beach, and he was a young Yank again, and he came, like the rain had come, and then his love for himself, not the faceless, naked woman he had produced within his own mind — no, his love for himself was unspeakable, and he poured more sweat, and looking at the mirror he could see himself and loved himself even more, for he had full mastery of himself.

At that moment, the minute hand on the big cream-colored clock near the peak of the roof of the old public bathing pavilion facing the ocean blew off its mooring and flew away into the night.

17

BRINEY MITCHEL LOVED THE WILD NIGHT; HE
laughed all the way from Shinnecock Hills to Ferry
Slip. The phantom had lost the motorcycle cop again
— and on a night like this. The driveway was crowded
with cars for Harriet Crocker's dinner party, so Briney
parked the Plymouth in South Main Street and, turning up his collar against the weather, hurried along the
service driveway toward the kitchen door of the big
house. He made his way through the catered bustle in
the kitchen unnoticed, but when he was about to ascend
the back staircase, Eckshaw intercepted him. Eckshaw
was an old Carpenter-Crocker retainer — an English
nanny whose job of minding Midge had long since
given way to occasional cleaning, cooking, laundering
and making up marketing lists. "She's getting ready
for bed," Eckshaw said to Briney. "She's forbidden to
go out with you tonight."

"Get out of my way, Eck," Briney said, trying to
push past her. But there was no bumping the for-
midable Eckshaw out of the way. "No, she won't see
you." Eckshaw established herself firmly in his path. "I
told you, she's not —"

"Move, please."

"No, you don't," Eckshaw said, remaining planted.

"I'm going up or I'll squeal to her old lady you're taking kickbacks from the butcher."

"You go up and I'll get Herbert after you. I'm not disturbing the madame, thank you."

"Who, the fairy chauffeur?" said Briney, laughing. "Go ahead." He finally bumped her hard enough with his stomach and she gave just enough so that he was able to push past her and climb the stairs. Eckshaw went away, crying, "Herbert! Herbert!"

Harriet Crocker, hearing Eckshaw call, put down her wineglass with a crack. "Dear God, what's that?" she said.

"Probably nothing," said Dr. Charley Anderson.

"Well, with due respect to you, Barbara," she said to Barbara Carew, "if it's Briney Mitchel in the house at this hour, I'll call the damned police. I'll even call Dan over in Riverhead!"

"Go right ahead," said Barbara Carew.

"Briney Mitchel," said Charlotte Potter. "The Mitchel who brought the native boy, Birdie Hawkins, into the Beach Club as a *guest?*"

"The same," said Harriet, getting to her feet.

"Sit down, Harry," said Charley Anderson, but Harriet got up from her chair and marched determinedly out of the dining room and into the kitchen.

"What is it, Eckshaw?" she said to the woman calling out the back door toward the garage for Herbert, her voice carrying off in the wind.

Eckshaw, turning, started to say something, then caught herself. "Oh, it's nothing at all, Madame. Only that I thought I heard a prowler out there by the maze."

"In this storm?" Harriet said. "How could you hear a prowler in this storm?"

"Well, I just thought I did."

"I wonder if we should call the police."

"No," said Eckshaw. "Herbert with a flashlight should be enough."

"Herbert, with or without a flashlight, is hopeless."

"Well, I'm sure it's nobody, Madame."

"Is Midge in her room?"

"She's taking a bath, Madame."

"Another bath?"

"Yes, Madame."

"And if Briney Mitchel shows up I want you to tell me immediately."

"Straightaway, Madame."

Harriet Crocker went back to her party. "Eckshaw thought she heard a prowler." She sat down and drained her wineglass. Her dinner guests understood her apprehension about prowlers. Since the Lindbergh kidnapping, some Southampton parents had received threatening notes about their own children, and not a few of them kept bodyguards.

Barbara Carew helped Charlotte Potter finish the story of how Briney had once signed the native boy, Birdie Hawkins, into the Beach Club. "Why, my dear," said Charlotte Potter, "I could take my chauff*euhh* there as a guest!"

"I've seen your chauffeur," said Harriet, "and he's absolutely stunning. Be careful, or *I'll* take him in as a guest."

Charley Anderson laughed with the others. They needed something to ease the tension that the storm was bringing.

"Eckshaw's baby turtle ran away," said Harriet Crocker, suddenly. "Or at least she set it free." Her guests looked up at Harriet, puzzled. "I mean it was one of those little painted turtles that comes in a box from West Palm Beach."

"Oh, yes," someone said.

"Well, anyway, a couple of weeks ago, Eckshaw's turtle, I think she called him Timothy, got very agitated and tried desperately to climb out of his bowl — you know, one of those little shallow bowls, and he kept falling back on his shell, and Eckshaw kept having to turn him over. So she finally took the poor thing outside on the grass, and let him go off."

"I haven't noticed any rabbits or birds around in the last few days, have you, Harry?" said Charley Anderson.

"No, I haven't, Charley."

"Maybe Eckshaw's little turtle was trying to tell you something, Harriet," said Barbara Carew.

"The end of the world, I suppose," said Harriet.

Barbara laughed. "Not quite. It's just that there's something about this storm. Maybe it's really a bigger storm than the predictions have been saying."

They were all silent for a moment, listening to the wind outside and watching the candles flicker in the subtle drafts that came through the door thresholds and under the windowsills.

"It's eerie," said Henry Meadowgold, another guest

of Harriet's, who had inherited a seat on the Stock Exchange from his father.

"Poor Eckshaw's Timothy," said Barbara Carew. "Out there somewhere in all of this."

"*I* know why Eckshaw's Timothy ran away," said Charlotte Potter.

"Why?" they all said.

"Because Father Divine is moving to Southampton. Haven't you heard?" she said, looking at everybody. They shook their heads. "Well," she said proudly, "Father Divine is looking for a place for his flock right here in Southampton."

"Good Lord," said Henry Meadowgold. "And I don't mean to make a pun. I thought all we had to worry about in Southampton were the Jews."

"I'd say the report was highly exaggerated," said Charley Anderson. "Would anyone like more wine?" he added. "Harriet, why not ring for more wine, darling?"

Harriet Crocker pressed the buzzer under the carpet near her foot.

Henry Meadowgold finished his glass and set it down on the table. It was a vintage Pouilly Fuissé; Harriet had an excellent wine cellar, filled mostly by her father when her mother died. "I'd say that Franklin Roosevelt was responsible for a great deal of what we've been talking about."

"You know what Franklin Roosevelt's been a great deal responsible for?" said Charley Anderson.

"What's that?"

"Flying."

"Flying?"

"Yes," said Charley Anderson. "When he flew to the Democratic Convention in Chicago in that Ford Trimotor in 1932. That gave a big boost to commercial aviation."

"I wouldn't be caught dead in one of those contraptions," said Henry Meadowgold. "Especially one that Roosevelt flew in. I'll take the streamliner, thank you, the Broadway Limited."

"I'll take the Twentieth Century Limited," said Charlotte Potter. "Don't all the film people take the Twentieth Century, Henry?"

"Yes, but those *Hollywood* people," said Henry Meadowgold, patting his lips with his napkin, very much the way Lucian Mitchel did it.

"I beg your pardon," said Barbara Carew with spirited good nature. "How about Gary Cooper? He comes to Southampton every summer and he sometimes has people like Clark Gable stay with him."

"That's because he married a girl who was brought up here."

"What's that got to do with it?" said Barbara Carew. "Gary Cooper is a perfectly lovely man."

Even Henry Meadowgold made no attempt to deny that. And so the conversation went back to the favorite topic in Southampton that night: the weather.

Midge Crocker's second-floor living quarters were more or less a suite of two rooms supported by the front porch of the house on Lake Agawam. Briney could hear her splashing around in the tub when he opened the door to the smaller room, which had been turned into a dressing room. So he closed the door gently, sat down in one of the chairs and picked up a copy of *Town Tat-tler*. Someone knocked on the door and Briney got out of the chair. "It's Herbert, Miss Midge," Herbert called. "I'm, ah, looking for Mr. Brian Mitchel."

"Well, good heavens, Herbert, he's not in the tub with me!"

"No, ma'am, of course, I didn't mean to imply . . . I thought perhaps he might be in the dressing room."

"Well, is he?"

"No, ma'am. It's just that Eckshaw told me he's somewhere upstairs."

"He is?"

"Yes, miss."

There was a pause; Midge had been feeling much better since she'd got back from the tennis and exploded at her mother and her grandfather. Now she said, giggling slightly, "Well, if you see him, throw him out."

Herbert cleared his throat and stared at Briney Mitchel with great fear and respect. He would not dare expose Briney Mitchel, and Briney knew it; he almost sneered at the fairy chauffeur. "Yes, of course, Miss." Then he closed the door softly and Briney went and sat down in the chair again with the magazine to await his golden girl. She was all of that and more, and he cared for Midge very much, and the idea disturbed him that a woman should get such a hold on him. He heard her get out of the tub and let the water drain with a marvelous deep-echoing belch only old pipes could make. She began to hum, and then in a few moments opened the door and came into the dressing room, drying her hair in such a way that she could not see Briney sitting in the chair. She let the towel fall on the floor beside the dresser and sat down in front of the mirror, still humming. Briney watched her body, stripped of tan where her two-piece Hawaiian bathing suit had covered it; Midge had been the first one to dare wear a two-piece bathing suit at the Beach Club. Then, after a few moments of relishing this delightful sight with his eyes, he leaned forward and snatched the towel away from where she had dropped it on the floor. It was a big, wet Cannon, and it made a heavy noise when he grabbed it. "Hello, Midget."

Midge froze, then groped furtively in the mirror with her eyes, not daring to turn around. She reached down, felt for the towel, squirmed in her seat, found that it was gone, then quickly stood up in all her naked glory. "You — you unspeakable —!" she said, finding him in the mirror. Then she fled back into the bathroom and slammed the door. "Now give me my towel and get the hell out of here!"

"You're going to East Hampton with me!"

"No, I'm not!"

"Listen, I risked my goddam neck to get here. And I don't risk my goddam neck for every girl in the world."

"You're always risking your goddam neck." Only Briney could bring out blasphemy in Midge. "Now get out of here or I'll scream for Herbert." But she said it without much conviction, and she knew that Briney was laughing at the ridiculous remark.

"Yes, and you'll disrupt that dinner party, won't you?"

"I'll scream for him through the window."

"Well, cover yourself or the poor bastard will run a mile."

"I swear to God, I'll —"

"You scream, Midget, and I'll go in there and knock you on your golden brown ass."

"I'll scream for Mummy."

"No, you won't, you're too smart for that because you know we're going to East Hampton tonight, so why prolong the agony?" He stirred himself from the chair and went to the door of the bathroom. "Listen, Midge Crocker, I'll give you exactly ten minutes to get dressed. Or do you want me to drag you out of there and dress you myself?" Silence. "I'll wait for you in the bedroom. And if Herbert shows up again, or your mother instead of you . . ."

There was another silence, and then she said very softly: "Go into the bedroom, then, and wait. But give me my towel first. And don't *look!*" She opened the door and he pushed the wet Cannon through it to her. The steam and her lovely smell came out to him from the bathroom and he wanted very much to go in there and dry her off himself. But instead he went into the bedroom and lay down on the silk bedspread with his pumps hanging over the edge. He looked at her bookshelves full of Yale bulldogs and Princeton tigers and broken plaster-of-Paris Popeye dolls that he had won for her at a carnival that came through Southampton. He had won them knocking three rag dolls off shelves with three baseballs. Nickel rockets, they were, and the barker had given him a hard time, because he was a rich kid. They had ridden the Chump Twist, too, the merry-go-round, and he had won a brass ring for her, a damned wedding ring, Briney thought suddenly.

In nine minutes she came out fully dressed and made up with lipstick.

He got off the bed and took her by the shoulders. "That's very good."

"We'll have to be awfully quiet, Mitch." She called him Mitch occasionally; she was the only one in the world Briney allowed to call him Mitch. "I hate Briney," she told him once. She slid softly into his arms and he held her gently; he was really a very gentle man when he wanted to be. "What am I going to do about you?" she said.

"Kiss me with your tongue."

"That's a soul kiss, isn't it?"

"You bet it is. It's an application upstairs for a job downstairs." He rammed his slim pelvis into hers.

"I'll bite yours off," she said.

"No. Just suck it," he said.

They kissed, and she sucked his tongue and bit it lightly, just enough to make him draw away. "Gosh, that was *swell*," she said, with all the little girlness that remained within her.

"Let's stay right here," he said.

"That's *all* we need."

She broke away from his strong arms, leaving him momentarily, oddly, drained, and she went and got a raincoat out of the closet, and they went out, then, and down the back stairs, and were confronted by Eckshaw at the bottom. "Oh, there's going to be trouble," Eckshaw said, wringing her hands almost in pleasure.

"Not unless you make it," said Briney.

"March right back upstairs, young lady," she said to Midge.

Midge leaned over and kissed her. "Sure, darling."

"Well, then, have a nice time."

"Good night, Eck."

"Good night, Mr. Brian. Good night, Miss Midge. You look beautiful." Midge squeezed Eckshaw's hand. "Don't get too wet." The old Crocker retainer returned Briney's wink as they went out the back door. It had begun to rain and blow harder. They ran down the driveway to Briney's Plymouth, holding hands so that they wouldn't stumble and fall on the bluestone.

At Harriet Crocker's dinner table, they had been talking about rude and independent men, and Briney's name was somehow placed in juxtaposition to that of Franklin Roosevelt.

"I tell you," Charlotte Potter was saying, "besides being diabolical and paranoic, that man in Washington is a rude man, he has no sense of good manners. Why, he never even stands up when a lady comes into the room."

Charley Anderson said: "Maybe it's just simply too difficult for him to stand, Charlotte."

"No, it isn't," said Henry Meadowgold. "He can stand, just as easily as you or I or Briney Mitchel can stand. I know he can stand. It's a lot of hogwash about his braces and not being able to stand up by himself. He stood up when he accepted the nomination in 1932, didn't he?"

"Helped by his son Jimmy," said Charley Anderson, "and with a great deal of difficulty."

"Oh, those *dread*ful Roosevelt boys and all their wives!" said Charlotte Potter. "I'm sorry, Barbara, but

I can't help placing Briney Mitchel in the same category as they are."

"No apologies necessary," said Barbara Carew.

"It's a lot of rubbish!" said Henry Meadowgold, plunging his stubby fingers into a fingerbowl so hard that their tips stung.

"Have you ever worn leg braces, Henry?" said Charley Anderson. The doctor smiled. "I don't think you ever have."

"Of course not. But — godammit, Charley, what are you, a *Democrat?*"

"I don't have any party affiliations, Henry. Being a doctor, I suppose I should be a Republican, but —"

"Charley's a Roosevelt-lover, Henry, and come to think of it," said Harriet Crocker, "so is Briney Mitchel, and I don't know why the hell I invited him here tonight. Charley, I mean, not Briney. Oh, yes I do," she said, smiling.

They laughed. Even Charley Anderson laughed. They laughed long and hard, for people had fun at Harriet Carpenter Crocker's dinner parties.

18

NOT EVERY SUMMER FAMILY IN SOUTHAMPTON enjoyed the privileges of oceanfront living during the depression. Some of them just got by, renting a small house on Meeting House Lane near the center of the village from a local merchant who went to live with relatives or took a trip to Ausable Chasm, using the rent money to pay for it. The sent their sons and daughters to St. Mark's and Fermata, and they joined all the clubs "for the children," but at home, at least, they lived frugally, entertaining little, taking a dingy bathhouse in the sprawling, wooden public pavilion of the Beach Club where they were much cheaper. It bothered them to change into bathing suits in bathhouses next to those rented by the natives. But their anguish was salved by the fact that they could swim in the pool of the private section and use the bar and restaurant and bathe in the ocean between the ropes that led to the barrels separating the private part of the Beach Club from the public part. Between the ropes made all the difference in the world; dogs, society photographers and natives were not allowed.

These people lived on the fringes of Southampton social life; just knowing they skirted this edge was enough to keep them reasonably content. The husband cut the lawn with a hand mower found in his landlord's garage, and when he took his family to the movies at Mike Glynne's, they sat in the orchestra seats instead of the loge, which was really the only place to sit at the movies in Southampton in order to be seen. When President Roosevelt appeared in the newsreel, they booed him just as loudly as those who could afford to sit upstairs, but there was a certain spiritlessness about their booing. After all, you couldn't blame *everything* on Franklin Roosevelt, could you?

They were careful with charge accounts, too, for the consequences of cutting loose and going on a spending spree in the marvelous shops of Southampton could be disastrous. The drugstore bill at Corwith's, alone, could throw a whole summer budget completely out of whack; one even had to be careful at Holden's, the stationer. Then the bills would have to be paid piecemeal, over the next winter, and the local merchants would wait patiently, knowing the money would come, probably after Christmas from stock dividends, before these families would return for yet another summer, to run amuck in their stores again.

Such a family was that of Carley Harris. Eilene Harris devoted most of her time to fussing over her daughter and worrying about her someday getting a husband. "You're so long and angular, darling, I don't know what to do with you." And Carley would say, "Yes, Mums, but don't you worry your little head over Carley. Carley knows just what she's doing."

"Do you, darling?"

"Yes, Mums, I do, and I'm going right out that door

one of these mornings and take the next train to New
York if you don't for Christ's sweet sake leave me
alone!"

"Oh, mercy!"

"I promise you, Mums, I'll move out and quit college
and get myself a garret in Greenwich Village and find
me a nice Jewish Communistic boy from CCNY to live
with and I'll sculpt. Yes, I'll sculpt."

"Oh, mercy!"

"So leave me alone, Mums, and let me play my tennis
at the Meadow Club and get my tan and gossip at the
Beach Club and let me finish up at Bryn Mawr. Instead
of me, why don't you worry about poor Daddy who is
going broke while we're trying to keep up appearances
down here?" And then Carley would bounce away from
this fretful woman who was her mother. And her father,
a Wall Street customer's man, pushing the lawn mower
but hearing it all from the kitchen, would sigh and mop
his brow and inwardly curse the present administration
for this lousy little house on Meeting House Lane in the
incorporated village of Southampton.

"Yes, or worry about Jimmy," Carley would say,
coming back to remind Eilene Harris of her difficult
son. Jimmy was Carley's younger brother, a problem
child who had, several times, just avoided being kicked
out of the Buckley School in New York.

"Oh, Jimmy will grow out of it," Eilene Harris
would say. "But you, Carlotta, you're fully grown and
I worry about you."

"What, Mums, do you really worry about?" Carley
would say, sometimes saying it in her bra and step-ins.
"My mosquito bites, Mums?"

"Oh, Carley!"

"Well, do you?"

"No, darling, of course not. You really have, ah, quite a lovely figure."

"Oh, bull, Mums. And anyway, I hear they get bigger when you have babies."

"What's that about having babies?" David Harris would say, coming in from the yard.

"I was just telling Mums I think I'll have a baby and get a big bust."

"Now stop that kind of talk!" David Harris would say.

"Okay, Pops."

"And don't call me *Pops!*"

Then Carley would go over and kiss her father and he would pat her gingerly on her ribby back and tell her to, for God's sake, go put something on. When she went upstairs, David Harris would say, "Who is it tonight, Denny Washington again?"

"Yes, Dennis," Eilene Harris would say, with a certain sadness in her voice.

"Well, she could do worse. He's a nice boy and I think he's going to be a successful lawyer someday."

"But she never goes out with anyone else but Denny."

"What's wrong with that? He's got money. My God, has he got money!"

"But David, the arm. I can't help but be bothered by the arm."

"Well, it doesn't seem to bother Carley," David Harris would say, going in for a beer. "When's dinner?"

"Soon."

"Where's Jimmy?"

"Playing with those native boy friends of his. The good Lord knows what goes on, what those wretched, smelly little people are doing to him."

David Harris said, "You mean what *he's* doing to those wretched little smelly people, don't you?" He brought his bottle of Pabst Blue Ribbon back into the living room. "What terrible furniture the Harwicks have. How do they stand to live in this house all winter? There's not a decent chair to sit in."

"Here, darling, sit here by me on the couch."

"All right, if you call that horsehair divan a couch." He sat down; the couch prickled. "No, it isn't Denny's arm that bothers me about Denny. What bothers me more about Carley going out with Denny Washington is that they always seem to have to double-date with Briney Mitchel and some girl he's dragged up from someplace."

"I wouldn't exactly call Midge Crocker a girl he's dragged up from someplace."

"Briney's taking Midge out tonight?"

"So Carley says. And apparently he's *been* taking her out."

"That's an interesting combination."

"Why?" said Eilene Harris.

"Well, Midge Crocker doesn't seem to be exactly Briney's type. I'd say, for example, that Carley was more Briney's type."

"God forbid. Do you know where Lucian Mitchel went to college?"

"No, why?" said David Harris.

"Well, I just happened to be looking through the Hampton Blue Book —"

"Oh, sure, you dog-ear that stupid thing, Eilene."

"Well, I just happened to be looking through it, and — don't be mean — I keep it for phone numbers, you know that. Well, it says in there that Lucian went to Holy Cross College in Worcester, Massachusetts."

"So?"

"Well, I mean really, David, who ever heard of Holy Cross College?"

"Oh, the Pope and a few others. What the hell's the difference, Eilene? Lucian's done pretty well, hasn't he? And look at me. Harvard and the PC, and I can't even afford a decent place for my family for the summer."

She took his hand tenderly. "Now don't say that."

He squeezed it. "Lucian Mitchel. Listen, if I had one third of his money . . ."

"It's probably why Briney's so spoiled and wild."

"I hope he's not driving tonight. It's a terrible night." They listened to the gathering storm for a moment, absently, although it was getting nearer to them.

"No. Apparently Denny is doing the driving."

"Good."

Carley came down then, in her father's beach robe, and said, "Briney's not even coming tonight, and I guess Midge isn't either." She told them about the row with Jonathan T. C. Carpenter.

"Serves him right," said Eilene Harris.

"But I'll miss him," Carley said "He's fun. Say what you will, but he's a swell guy. A killer-diller."

Feeling his Pabst, David Harris said, "He's a wencher and a boozer and he drives too fast, and if he ever tries to rip up this lawn —"

"It might improve it," said Carley, laughing. "You call this a lawn, Daddy?"

"Well, you just stay the hell away from Briney Mitchel."

"Daddy, you hardly know Briney Mitchel. And that's the trouble. People don't know him. Therefore," said Carley, in her perfectly logical, ordered mind, "they don't understand him."

"You sound as though you're going out with *him* tonight instead of Denny Washington," David Harris said.

"Thanks but no thanks," said Carley, not really meaning it, but at least ending the discussion.

They sat down to dinner; Eilene had prepared a roast. Jimmy came in, surly and dirty, and was told to wash up in a hurry. "You know," said David Harris when the boy was gone, "I'm going to take that kid out of Buckley; it's hardly worth the expense. He's a tramp. The money we spend and what we have to show for it!"

"Darling!" said Eilene, terrified. "But where would you send him?"

"There are plenty of damned good public schools right in the city of New York."

"Oh, mercy, not that again!" said Eilene Harris, about to weep.

"Why not?" Carley would say, grinning.

And Eilene Harris would say a silent prayer that the stock market would start trading heavily again — maybe even give David a couple of two-million-share days a month — so that he could swing the Buckley tuition for yet another year.

19

DENNY WASHINGTON'S STUMP STILL ACHED, AND he felt uneasy and fumbly with his one hand. He usually did very well tying bow ties with it, but this one which he had just recently bought at Finchley's was giving him trouble, and he was irritable. Finally he dropped his hand and worked his fingers, which were getting cramped. His mother, watching him from the shadows of the hall, poked her head in the door and said, "May I come in?"

"Of course, Mother," Denny said, knowing full well she had been out there watching him all the time.

She was carrying a red carnation for him and she went over and stood with him in front of the mirror and said: "Why don't you get one of those new snap-ons, darling? It would be much easier for you."

"No, these look better. And anyway, I like the challenge."

"I understand," she said. "But this one is satin and it's probably too slippery."

Denny sighed, his hand still cramped. "It's new." He let his hand drop. "Okay. You can do it, Mother."

"Good!" She did it for him expertly and took a step back. "Oh, you look so handsome!"

"Thank you. And you look beautiful as usual."

Heather Washington was wearing a long black ruffled gown with a lace mantilla over her graying head. "You must have left a string of broken hearts after Father died."

She laughed. "Hardly." And it was the truth. Denny Washington had never known his father, who had gone down with the *Lusitania.* Heather Washington had never married again, nor had she encouraged suitors. She had lived in sublime celibacy for two decades in a huge apartment in New York, and in the house on Ox Pasture Road in Southampton. Occasionally she took a side trip to visit friends in Dark Harbor during the summer or Hobe Sound during the winter. But mostly she presided regally, and with dedicated interest, over the bringing up of her only son. She had coddled him at first, but after the accident under the streetcar she had been wise enough to do quite the opposite of what most mothers would have done: instead of overprotecting Denny, she fired the nurse, took care of him herself, and put him more on his own. Growing up, he attended Buckley, St. Paul's and Harvard, and she saved all the clippings from the school papers about him, and had his Old Hundred football and hockey photographs especially framed in black for the little alcove that was his study in New York. He played those sports and others very well with one arm, but he played tennis best, and two years before had gone to England with the combined Yale-Harvard tennis team to play Oxford-Cambridge.

"Yes, I'll bet you left a string of broken hearts."

"Well, I didn't." Heather Washington had had many men who were interested in her. But somehow she could never be sure they weren't just after her money. Some of them were quite well off themselves. But she never felt that she could fall in love again after her husband died. They had been married such a short time, he was perfect in every way.

"I understand," Denny said when she explained it to him.

"Of course he wasn't perfect, nobody is. But we had such a love. Oh, my God, how I loved that man!"

Her eyes filled for a moment and Denny took her hand, cold in his. She suddenly began to scrutinize him. "Your hair, Denny, you're losing more of your hair."

"Oh, *Mother!*"

"If you'd use that cream on your scalp that I gave you . . ."

"Mother, if there were a cure for baldness — oh, forget it!"

"Who's driving tonight?" she said, jumping around the way she did.

"I am."

"Good. Not that I'm not very fond of Briney Mitchel. I am, you know, genuinely."

Denny looked in the mirror, grim. "Sure."

"Well, you never believe me, but I am. No, darling, but I'm glad you're driving."

"I don't have very much choice," said Denny, putting on his white linen dinner jacket. While Heather Washington slipped the red carnation into his lapel, he said: "Briney had a run-in with Jonathan Carpenter this afternoon after tennis, and Jonathan forbade Midge Crocker to go out with Briney. So I don't know whether he'll be along or not. I'm not sure about Midge, either. I'll just pick up Carley and see who's waiting there with her."

"Darling?"

"What, Mother?"

"How much do you like Carley Harris?"

"I like her, that's all. She's amusing. And she plays one hell of a game of tennis." He glanced at his mother. "I think she's really rather swell."

"But you're not serious about her?"

"No." Denny checked himself in the mirror. "No, it will be a long time before I become serious about any girl. I've got my eyes on a target, you know. I don't play tennis with Jonathan Carpenter just for my own amusement." He half turned toward her. "And you and I are the only ones who know that. Not even Briney Mitchel knows that."

"That sounds so cynical and cold-blooded."

"It's not a bit cynical and cold-blooded. It's simply being pragmatic."

"You and your big words," she said.

"All right. *Practical* then."

"You know you'd never have to do a day's work in your life if you didn't want to."

"Of course I know that. But it's a terrible thing not to work a day in your life. You and I know some men right here in Southampton who 'retired' after college." He turned around to face her. "Good Lord. That's decadent."

"I don't agree at all."

"It's decadent. They're totally useless. Oh, they play impeccable bridge and golf. And they're charming dinner companions, and they're knowledgeable and they have good minds, usually, but they contribute absolutely zero to the, well, to the social order."

"Dear heavens, you sound like a New Dealer."

"Thank you."

"Darling?"

"Yes, Mother."

"Have you ever slept with Carley Harris?"

He looked at his mother with pity, with ice-cold compassion. "That's an unfair question, and you know it."

She lowered her eyes. "I know it is," she said.

"But, if it will set your mind easier, the answer is no."

Then she was back at him again. "But you do, as they say, fool around with girls when you're out with Briney, don't you? I mean, not-nice girls."

She was beginning to tire him; he looked at his watch. "I have to go."

"Darling, I'm sorry. But a mother worries about those things."

"Give me *some* credit for discretion, won't you?"

"Of course, my darling Denny." She kissed him on the lips, wetly, as she had when he was a small boy, and had ever since. And when he was finally away from her and downstairs in the big house on Ox Pasture Road, she called to him and told him not to forget his raincoat.

He was furious; he disobeyed her. He went out the front door, slamming it behind him. It was beginning to rain and his balding head was getting wet and his stump hurt fearfully, and he ran to the garage, stumbled once, lost his eyeglasses, recovered them unharmed on the wet bluestone, and cursed in the black night.

20

"WHAT IN THE NAME OF GOD ARE YOU DOING here?" David Harris said to Briney Mitchel when he and Midge rushed up to the porch of the house the Harrises had rented on Meeting House Lane. "I thought you were quarantined tonight, Briney."

"I was. But I busted out. He locked me in, the idiot, for taking out Protestant girls, so I —"

"You shouldn't call your father an idiot."

"— so I got out a window and crawled the length of the roof."

"You're crazy," David Harris said. "And in this weather." He turned to Midge. "Are you sure you're doing the right thing going out tonight, young lady? I don't mean to pry, but —"

"Well then, don't!" said Briney Mitchel.

"You're a fresh kid, Brian Mitchel," said David Harris. "And you never call me sir, do you? You never once in your life have ever called me sir."

Briney smiled in the half dark of the porch. "No, sir."

"Where's Carley, Mr. Harris?" said Midge.

"She'll be down, don't worry." He wanted to tell Midge how pretty she looked, but he didn't think it was his place. Instead, he said, "Who won today? I forgot to ask Carley."

"Mexican standoff," Midge said. "One set apiece and then nine-nine in the third and then we quit."

"Too damned hot and humid for tennis today."

"Yes, it really is," she said.

"You kids." He automatically fanned himself with the evening *Sun* while Briney watched him. "Too damned hot in this house. I'll bet it's cool up on the ocean, eh, Briney?"

"It's blowing up," said Briney. "But it was hotter than hell inside the house there for a couple of hours tonight."

David Harris forgot about his heat and smiled a smile of pure satisfaction in the half dark. For all his money, Lucian Mitchel probably had more trouble than David Harris. "You want a drink, kids?"

"No, thanks," said Briney. "We can wait."

"Sit down then," said David Harris, sitting himself down in a porch rocker, one of the few comfortable pieces of furniture in the whole house.

Midge sat down, but Briney said, "I'll stand."

"Stand then," said David Harris. The Mitchel boy was getting his goat. "And be careful driving over to Devon."

"I'm not driving," said Briney.

"It's sixteen miles from here to Devon, and don't forget when you get to the flagpole in Amagansett —"

"I'm not driving," Briney said again.

"—turn left at the flagpole and go over the tracks, and — you're not driving?"

"No, I'm not driving, but I'm sure Denny knows the way."

"You're not driving," said David Harris, his eyes glazing a little. "Of course, Denny's driving," he said, recovering. "Well, you'll get wet in the rumble of his Studie. I wish I could loan you my Auburn for the night, but Jimmy let air out of one of the tires."

"Never mind," Midge said, "I just love the rumble, even in wet weather," and the two men had to laugh at what she said, and Briney was glad that she had said it, even though it would have made more sense to take the Plymouth, and glad that he hadn't brought a raincoat and didn't want David Harris to offer him one.

"Where is the rascal?" Briney said, still grinning.

"Jimmy's in the cellar," said David Harris, "with his chemistry set or some pulpy trash magazine, I don't know which. Nor do I care, as long as he doesn't blow up the house or render pregnant one of the local girls." When he said this, he gave Briney a piercing glance that did not go unnoticed by either Briney or Midge.

"*David!*" said Eilene Harris, coming out on the porch. "How could you say such a thing! Why, Jimmy's not old enough to —"

"Like hell he's not old enough," said David Harris, beginning to laugh, Briney watching him stolidly, his legs spread, his hands in his hip pockets.

Midge laughed, then cut short her laugh when she saw Briney.

"Oh, stop it, Eilene," said David Harris.

Eilene did stop. But she fumbled for a handkerchief and David Harris groaned as if he were very weary and got up from his comfortable rocker and went over to where she was standing. "Now, Eilene . . ."

Denny drove up, and then Carley appeared, and Briney noticed how smartly put out she was, how good she could look in an evening dress, and sizing up the situation, Carley said, "God, let's go. Good night, Mums and Pops."

"Don't call me —!"

"Dad. Daddy. Da da da Daddy!" Then, with a raincoat caught around her shoulders as though she were going to a party next door, she skittered off the porch into the dirty night, Midge, Briney and Denny following, Briney having politely accepted an old umbrella David Harris offered him.

Jimmy Harris had not been in the cellar at all; Briney caught him letting air out of one of the tires of the Plymouth, just as he had done to his father's Auburn. Now they *had* to take Denny's Studebaker. He picked the boy up by the front of his shirt and held him a foot off the ground while the others, even Eilene and David Harris from the porch, watched with fascination. "You ought to know better than to do that, Sonny," Briney said, shaking him so that the boy's shoes banged together.

"Yes, Briney."

"Yes, Mr. Mitchel!"

"Y-yes, Mr. Mitchel."

"Yes, Mr. Mitchel, *sir!*"

"Yes, Mr. Mitchel, sir."

He dropped Jimmy in a heap at his feet. "Now you march your little ass off into the garage and get that hand pump that must be in there someplace, and bring it out here in the rain and start pumping."

"Yessir." Jimmy scampered off in the dark.

Briney stood and watched him for a moment. Then he turned to rejoin the others, dark shadows in the vague porch light coming from the Harrises' rented house on Meeting House Lane where the Studebaker stood.

21

KATHLEEN MITCHEL, BRINEY'S OLDER SISTER, could sit in the sand at the Beach Club and tell somebody she was "going to Long Island" for the weekend, and the person she was talking to knew exactly where she meant. Kathleen could be dancing with someone at a coming-out party at the Ritz in New York and tell him the same thing, and unless her partner were a Black Shoe from Brooklyn who had probably crashed, he knew she didn't mean Shelter Island or Montauk or even East Hampton or Southampton. No, "Long Island" meant Locust Valley and Oyster Bay and Cold Spring Harbor and Glen Cove and little places within their townships such as Muttontown and Lattingtown and Brookville that only the people who lived there in comfortable luxury knew about. For the most part, they were summer commuting towns; the houses were closed down for the winter when their owners went back to the city.

Yes, that's where "Long Island" was; all the old money was in that pocket of wooded, hilly towns on the North Shore. Most of the big parties took place there, and that's where many of Kathleen Mitchel's friends had been born, were coming out, and would die. You were never born in Southampton; you might get married in Southampton at St. Andrew's Dune Church, and you might die in Southampton, simply by accident. But if you weren't born in New York, you were born in "Long Island," and that's where everything happened to you that was traditionally important in your lifetime.

Briney's older sister met Herb Johnstone at one of these elaborate coming-out parties on Long Island. He cut in on Kathleen because she was beautiful — not thinking that she might be nice to talk to, as well. "Hi. I'm Herb Johnstone."

"I'm Kathy Mitchel."

"Where do you go to college?" he said, asking the standard question.

"Rosemont."

"Rosemont," Herb said.

"It's in Philadelphia. On the Main Line."

"Is it a college?"

"Of course it's a college."

"Oh, I'm sorry, I've never heard of it."

"It's a *Catholic* college."

"Oh, I see."

"Where do you go?" she said.

"Cambridge."

"Harvard?"

"No. In England."

"Oh, how wonderful."

"I think I'm going back to Harvard next year, though. I'd like to spend at least two years in an American college."

He smiled down at her, and she reminded him of an

Eddy Duchin record called "Moonlight and Shadows."
"Where did you go to school?"

"Sacred Heart Convent in Noroton."

"Oh."

"Yes. Always Catholic schools."

"I went to Exeter. I never met a Catholic girl in my life."

"You thought we were all cooks and maids I suppose."

He had patience and some humor, and he smiled at her and said, "Now, wait a minute, Miss Mitchel, I —"

But Kathy laughed and Herb Johnstone was glad she laughed; she had a nice laugh. "Indians where I come from," he said. "Cleveland, Ohio." And they danced and talked of Cleveland and Cambridge, Noroton and New York.

She put her head on his shoulder and relaxed more in his arms, and she let him press the lower part of his pelvis against her, and she was quite pleased to discover that he was hard down there, and she wondered if Herb Johnstone wore a jockstrap to these dances like she had heard about other boys from gossip in the ladies' room at these parties. It was fun and she tingled, allowing herself to be pressed by him, but then she suddenly remembered that Herb Johnstone wasn't a Catholic, and so she had to stiffen in his arms, and as she did so, his hardness melted, and he, too, stiffened, his body stiffened, and she had to say something stupid to him and she had to smile mechanically, and she remembered something one of the nuns at Noroton had told them all once about dancing too close to boys, or dancing at all with boys, "it leads to other things," the nun, a sweet

nun in her black bonnet, had said, and she had told
them to always take their rosary beads to dances, if
they had to go to dances at all, and Kathleen Mitchel
smiled, remembering this, the words of the sweet nun,
and remembered also that she had left her rosary beads
back in the room at Brookville, and the moment she
remembered this, she was cut in on.

Herb Johnstone thought that Kathleen Mitchel had
meant her last smile for him, so he gave her the rush
that night, even more than the others on the stag line,
some of whom were drunk and happy or sullen from the
champagne, and he finally got her away from the dance
floor and sat down with her and drank some champagne
with her and got her laughing about some of the things
he told her about Cambridge, and he found where she
was staying in Brookville, and the next day and the day
after that he pursued her, and fell in love with her that
weekend.

When she had to go back to Southampton, he drove
her in his Cord Sportsman 812, stopping at Roth-
mann's on Route 25A for a sandwich and a last late-
summer goodbye to old friends she wouldn't see until
the parties at Christmas.

When they got to Southampton she took a taxi from
the village to the Mitchel house on Mecox Bay so she
wouldn't have to go through the pain and derision of in-
troducing a Protestant beau to Lucian Mitchel. And
Herb took a room at the Irving so he could be near her.
She wouldn't date him at night, but she would sign him
in at the Beach Club, meeting him on the steps and making sure that Brad Horton, the photographer stationed
there, who was an old friend of the family, did not snap

their picture for the *Social Spectator* or the society pages of the newspapers. They went horseback riding at Aylward's and played golf at Shinnecock, where Herb insisted on teeing up her ball for her, and they were seen so much together that it was inevitable that Lucian Mitchel would hear about it. He heard about it, quite naturally, from the brother-in-law he feared the most: Aidan Carew. "Say, that daughter of yours gets more stunning every day, Luce. She's even more beautiful than when she came out a couple of years ago," Aidan told him one day at the Carew-Callaway pool.

"Thank you, Aidan," said Lucian, suddenly feeling nervous all over.

"I saw her playing golf with a tall, good-looking stranger."

"Oh?" said Lucian, wondering what was coming next.

"Yes. A fine-looking fellow."

"Well, she hasn't told *me* about him."

"She hasn't?" said Aidan Carew, and Lucian Mitchel felt like a child about to be in for a scolding.

"She hasn't told me, either," said Aidan's sister Edyth Mitchel who had been busy thinking about the Catholic Big Sisters. "And I don't see why there's any reason that she should." Edyth, who was doing crewel work, glanced at her older brother. She almost never got her back up, but when she did, she could be as firm as Aidan. "It's her business, Aidan. Kathy's my most sensible child."

"Of course," said Aidan Carew.

"What do you mean, 'of course'?" said Edyth Mitchel.

"You know darn well what Aidan means, Mother," said Lucian Mitchel to his wife, delighted for the chance to shift the burden of guilt to her. "Aidan means that the boy's probably not a Catholic, that's what Aidan means, and Kathy's afraid to show him to us."

"Well, I don't think it's any of Aidan's business," said Edyth Mitchel, with a flourish of her needle.

"*Edyth!*" said Lucian Mitchel, appalled.

Aidan Carew knew better than to trifle with his sweet, innocent, tough-minded sister, and his expression remained benign. "Edyth's perfectly right, Luce. It is none of my business. It's your business entirely. I just thought I'd mention it. It was really quite innocent. All I really wanted to say was that your daughter Kathleen is quite stunning." Aidan Carew, the self-appointed patriarch of the family, was not passing out compliments just for the sake of pleasing his sister and brother-in-law. He had got his main point across, and everyone around the pool knew it, including Father Regan, fat and white in a hot, black, one-piece woolen bathing suit, and Willard Callaway, fat and red in solid black woolen trunks and candy-striped top, and all the children who were splashing around them.

Kathy Mitchel, of course, was quite stunning, and Lucian Mitchel, in a rare display of tact, reminded her of this that night at the dinner table. "Which makes you quite vulnerable to the wiles of unscrupulous men," he said at the end of his rather self-conscious little speech.

"Oh, Daddy," said Kathleen, coloring.

"What Daddy means, darling," said Edyth Mitchel,

"is that he'd very much like to meet that new beau of yours."

"*What* beau!" said Kathy Mitchel.

"Herb Johnstone," said Briney, who had not said a word through the whole meal.

Kathy spun on her brother. "Oh, *you!*"

Briney put down his fork. "My dear sister. It's plainly evident, except to a deaf, dumb and blind man, that you are being wooed by one of the richest guys in Cleveland."

"She is?" said Lucian Mitchel.

"Yes, Pop, she is," said Briney, turning toward his father. "But you know what, Pop?"

"Shut up, Briney!" said Kathleen.

"What?" said Lucian Mitchel.

"Herb Johnstone is a dirty black Protestant."

"Still —"

"I don't care," said Edyth Mitchel. "I for one would like to meet him."

"Me, too," said Lucian Mitchel.

"You would, Daddy?" said Kathy, touchingly pleased.

"Of course he would," said Briney Mitchel. "The richest guy in Cleveland? Christ, if Herb Johnstone were a Jew, Pops would like to meet him."

"You shut up!" said Lucian Mitchel, sensing that Brian was teasing him, as, indeed, he often had done to Briney when Briney was a child.

"All right, I'll shut up," said Briney. "But you know what I say is true." He looked around the table at the others. "In this house, money talks, just like it does in every house." Then Briney went back to his former silence. He was curious about what kind of a fellow would be attracted to such an unbearable sister as Kathleen.

So Herb Johnstone came to dinner and made a favorable impression. Briney was on his best behavior, so much so that Kathy came up to him after dinner and thanked him for not starting anything disagreeable.

"Forget it," said Briney. "I'd really like to see something come of this." And he winked at her, and Kathy went away wondering what Briney had meant by that. The next Sunday, Herb Johnstone went to mass with Kathleen, sitting up near the front with Aidan and his family, and started instructions in Catholicism the following Monday evening. Father James Costigan was assigned to teach Herb Catholic Faith and Morals, and though Herb had to shout to be heard, he got his questions reasonably well answered by the old priest with the ear machine.

"It seems like a very sad kind of religion," he said to Kathleen, driving her home in the Cord.

"A *sad* kind of religion?"

"Well, I mean it seems so sure of the inevitability of heaven and hell and purgatory. It seems so sure of itself. It seems to have all the answers, without any doubts."

"Oh, I'm glad you feel that way," she said. "Except for the sad part. It can't be sad if it holds the promise of heaven."

"A friend of mine who went to Groton remembered one of your famous priests, James Keller, coming up to talk to the school, and this fellow was actually embarrassed at some of the questions his chums put to Father

Keller. Simple, fundamental questions that they should have known the answers to without asking a Catholic priest."

"That's because they never went to Catholic schools."

"Maybe we all should have gone to Catholic schools."

Surprisingly, Kathleen took his right hand off the steering wheel and squeezed his fingers. She had never made such an overt gesture to a boy in her life before. They held hands frequently after that, and the night that Briney Mitchel sneaked out of the house to take Midge Crocker to East Hampton, Herb Johnstone not only took Kathleen Mitchel's hand while they were driving through the building storm to the movies in the Cord, but he put an arm around her shoulders, dangling his hand just an inch from her right breast, and she let it stay there, and even let her head rest on his shoulder. But then she had to say: "We must never do this in the movies, darling. It's so cheap. Doing this in the movies is for Southampton natives. Cheap people. I mean I hate it when people display affection in public places. Especially in the Southampton Theatre and in the *loge!*"

Herb Johnstone took his arm away and smiled. "Don't worry."

"But it does worry me a little, because I know how men are. At least I know they're different from women in this respect, and I don't want to lead you on so that, well, we might lose control of ourselves or something." She shivered, and it was not cold out.

"I understand," he said, patting her left thigh where

he could feel a girdle, and he wondered why a girl like Kathleen Mitchel with such a stunning figure thought she had to wear a girdle. Well, maybe it was sexier.

"I don't want to be late for this movie," she said. "I mean we'd be missing seeing who's in the loge when the lights go on after the first show."

Herb looked at the radium dial on his watch. "We won't be late."

"I suppose," she said, "it would be much easier if I had the scruples of Briney, who has the scruples of a jackrabbit. Or the habits of a jackrabbit, I should say." She giggled, in spite of herself.

Herb Johnstone laughed. "You'd hardly know you came from the same family." He took out a Chesterfield and lit it with the dashboard lighter. "I like Briney, though. Yes, I like him and I think he likes me."

"I know he does. He told me so."

"He did?" said Herb, very pleased with the news.

"Yes. He wants something to come of us, as he puts it, and I can't quite understand why."

"Maybe it's because he thinks you're a difficult person and it would get you out of the house."

Kathy Mitchel said, "Oh, the mean, selfish —! I never thought of that!"

But Herb Johnstone was laughing again. "I don't find you difficult at all," and he started to put his arm back around her shoulders again, but as he did so, a car's headlights came up behind them and shone through the rain-spattered rear window on the back of their heads, and Kathleen moved over to her side of the car. "No, darling. Someone might see us."

22

BRINEY MITCHEL'S BEST FRIEND AT PRINCETON
had been a senior, a Rhodes Scholar, who was kept
company by a girl from Boston with a lot of money.
The girl lived at the Nassau Inn for weeks on end, just
to be near — not necessarily to sleep with — the Rhodes
Scholar. The Princeton senior fascinated her, just as he
did Briney Mitchel; the girl from Boston would hold
salons for the three of them at the Nass; if she ever were
inclined to suggest a *ménage à trois*, the subject was
never brought up. Anyway, that sort of thing was
distasteful to Briney. He had no use for it anymore
than the sexual exhibitionism in France, where, he had
heard from the Rhodes Scholar, *pars tous* was common:
a veritable daisy chain of sex all in one room.

The Rhodes Scholar liked Briney's mind and his
extreme heterosexuality. He was a brilliant, passive
man, also heterosexual, but given to moods of deep
depression about women whom he thought had used him
poorly. The girl from Boston did her best to palliate
this, and Briney Mitchel cheered him up with his aggressive maleness, while at the same time the Rhodes
Scholar bore him no jealousy about the girl from Bos-

ton who, he was sure, exercised visions of making love to Briney.

But Briney would have none of it. The girl from Boston belonged to the Rhodes Scholar, just as Midge Crocker belonged to him and even Paula Kalinski, in her own way, belonged to him.

This possessiveness began to show itself in the rumble seat of Denny Washington's Studebaker. Unlike his sister Kathleen, Briney Mitchel wasn't a bit worried about anybody seeing him—not even with his arm around Midge Crocker. But he was getting wet; the umbrella had collapsed in the wind and he had flung it away miles back. Huddling in the rumble, he shouted to Midge: "Give me some of your raincoat!"

"I will not. You should have borrowed Denny's. And get your hand off my leg."

"I need something to hold on to." He let his hand go and slid up in the seat and nestled against her.

"I love rumble seats!" Midge said to him.

"I do, too!" And he gave the lobe of her ear a good bite.

"No, I mean I love rumble seats because when I was younger and Daddy worked that one summer in Wall Street and hated it so, Mummy and I used to meet him on the train at Hampton Bays."

"He got off at Hampton Bays?"

"He got off at Hampton Bays, and the reason he got off at Hampton Bays was so he could race the train to Southampton. He used to let me ride in the rumble seat. We had a Hupmobile then. Seventy-six miles an hour under a full head when it hit Shinnecock Hills. The train, that is. We always beat it."

"A great car!" Briney shouted.

"What?"

"The Hupmobile. A great car!"

"Oh, yes. Well, it was more fun, and we always beat the Cannonball."

"Sure you did. I've seen your old man drive."

"He drives almost as fast as you do," she said.

"No, never that fast."

Briney straightened up and turned her chin toward him with his hand and tried to kiss her, but she wouldn't let him. She pulled her raincoat up over her head and shoulders to protect herself, and he kept running his left hand down the front of it, pretending he was making sure it was buttoned.

"Stop that!"

"Stop what?" he said.

"Stop fooling around with my front. I'm a *nice* girl, remember?"

"I'm getting wet. All I want is a piece of your raincoat. Anyway, who'd want to fool around with *your* front?"

She was silent for a moment, and then she said, "It's not so bad!"

"What's not so bad?"

"It's not as big as Paula Kalinski's, but it's not so bad!"

"Who's Paula Kalinski?" he said.

Midge poked her head through the top of the raincoat like a turtle and looked at him with great seriousness. "Don't kid me."

"I'm not kidding you. Who is she?"

"Don't play dumb!"

He smiled then and leaned over very close to her lips. "You're jealous."

"I am not. Oh, I could kill you, Briney Mitchel!" and Midge Crocker snapped her head back under the raincoat.

No, Briney Mitchel had decided long ago, Midge Crocker's front was not bad at all; better than Carley Harris's, and he wondered how she and Denny were doing in the front seat. He had always felt genuinely sorry for Denny Washington, that he could never drive one-armed with a girl. Briney could only tell, through the back window in the silhouette of lights from an oncoming car, that Carley was sitting very close to Denny.

"Can you drive with your knees and pinch the wheel with your forearm, Dennis?" she was saying to him. She often called him Dennis when they were alone; Carley liked its British stuffiness.

"Why, I've never really tried," he told her.

"Well, try."

"Why?"

"Because I want you to put your arm around me."

"Why, you know in all my years of taking out girls in cars, I've never really thought of how I could do that. A brilliant suggestion." He raised his knees against the steering wheel, pinched it with his left forearm, and put his arm around her. "I don't need the knees," he said, finding that the elbow pinching the wheel was more than enough, "but I don't feel terribly secure."

"I'll help you." Carley rested her hand on the steering wheel.

He kissed her hair once, that straight, black, tennis-playing hair, and they drove in silence for a few moments. "What an extraordinarily good idea," he said.

"Yes but it's dangerous especially on a wet road at night. You must only do it when Briney Mitchel can see us."

Denny began to be annoyed. "Why?"

"Because I want Briney to find out that we can be just as hot in the front seat as he can be in the rumble."

"What the hell's the matter with you, Carley?" he said, withdrawing his arm. "Don't you have any feelings at all? I mean, for me?"

"Yes, of course I do, Dennis, and I'm sorry, it was a mean, bitchy thing to do and forgive me." She leaned over and kissed him on the cheek, and he was quite touched, but he did not put his arm back around her, they were coming into some Bridgehampton traffic. He only wished, really, that Carley Harris didn't have such a sharp tongue.

"My God, he put his arm around her!" Briney was shouting to Midge in the rumble seat.

Midge poked her head through the raincoat. "We'll crash!"

"No, she's steering! Or doing some of the steering!"

"Maybe she should be driving so she could put *her* arm around *him!*"

"That's a bitchy thing to say!"

"I know it is!"

"Why did you say it, then? Because she tied you in tennis today?"

"Maybe. It's just that she gets so uppity with Denny sometimes."

"That's Denny's fault for not slapping her down."

"It just makes me mad," Midge said.

"Just like I do with you," Briney said, his left hand finding a way through the buttons on the raincoat and under her breast.

"Oh, you're bad, Mitch!" she said, but she let his hand rest there, and he hardly noticed the rain that was getting him wet, and after a little while he said, quite softly, but so that she could hear it through the rush and howl of the wind: "Beautiful. Absolutely beautiful."

It was about sixteen miles from Southampton to Devon and they made it in the rain, so that Briney felt disagreeably wet by the time they had parked the car and gotten into the clubhouse. He hardly ever smiled when he met strangers, but when Midge Crocker introduced him around the table to her East Hampton friends, he gave them a restrained greeting. "So that's the great Briney Mitchel," said Billy Wrenn, sitting with his old Andover and Yale buddies at one end of the table.

His date said, "Yes, I haven't seen him in years and I think he's rather super-duper looking."

"You would."

"Now don't get grumpy, Billy," said Adelaide Plummer. "And don't you and your groupie make any trouble tonight, for Christmas sake." The Andover gang were thick as thieves. Briney knew some of them, and how they had all gone down to New Haven to-

gether, all roomed in Vanderbilt when they were freshmen together, all broke up Haunt Clubs, the post-foot-
ball drinking parties, on Sunday together, and they
had all had sexual intercourse with the same taxi dancer
from the Orpheum Ballroom in New York together.

Or rather, one at a time.

Billy Wrenn had invited her up for a football weekend, but instead of going to the game with her, he persuaded her to stay in Vanderbilt and take on the gang.
Billy going first, while one or two stood lookout for the
campus cop, they had all summarily taken turns
coupling with her until people started coming back in
the open-air trolleys from Yale Bowl. Then they had
zipped up and got out the ice, and switched from beer
to whiskey drinking. The girl got drunk very quickly,
and threatened them all that she would run to the police
or to the Dean of Yale College or several other authori-
ties about mass rape, but Billy dissuaded her with a
large check, and hauled her grumbling down to the railroad station, where he put her on a Boston express for
New York.

Briney also knew that Billy Wrenn could not be
wholly blamed for these carryings on. His father had
abandoned his mother when Billy was very young, and
had taken to beachcombing along the length of the
Atlantic coast; nobody had seen the man for years. He
lived in a shack near Myrtle Beach and reportedly had
one of the most extensive seashell collections in the
world.

Briney knew about Billy's mother, too. She lived in a
dreamworld of alcohol and narcotics, which she ob-

tained through an old physician friend of hers who had
long since given up rehabilitating the woman. She had
been a belle of Boston and New York society. Now she
took a cottage every year near the railroad tracks in
Amagansett, and every late afternoon would wave a
silver shaker of martinis at the engineer of the Cannonball, hoping someday that he would stop and join her
in a drink. But he never did, this dashing Casey Jones,
this Lothario of the Montauk Branch who had a wife
and six children in Mastic. He was unfamiliar with
silver cocktail shakers, and he thought the woman was
trying to present him with a trophy of some kind. But
he was amused by it all, and gallantly waved his cap at
her, and sometimes even slowed his steam engine. Then
on to Montauk he clattered, with his load of drunken
fishermen from Brooklyn in the rear smoker, having
disgorged the summer weekenders at waystops. So Billy
Wrenn ran with his gang, a handsome-looking if sullen
bunch of boys with good minds and wrong motives, who
just got by at New Haven. "No, there won't be any
trouble tonight," said Billy, looking around the room.
"There are too many of them here tonight."

"Too many what?" said Addy Plummer.

"Too many cheap Catholics. We're outnumbered.
Look over there at all those Aidan Carews and all those
Callaways at one table."

"Only two Callaways."

"And there must be some from Westhampton, too,
those fellows with the white dinner jackets and maroon
bow ties and maroon cummerbunds interspersed among
the white men in this place where they don't belong."

"Oh, don't be so grim about it."

"It's Roosevelt, that's what it is," said Billy Wrenn. "Pretty soon Devon will be full of Jews."

"Dance with me and let me cheer you up."

So Billy Wrenn danced with his date, Addy Plummer, who knew the formula for calming her man, and soon she had him smiling, glowingly so, and then he wanted to take her outside, but she said, "No, darling, it's too early. Later."

So for a while, at least, Billy Wrenn was content to watch Briney Mitchel dance with Midge Crocker, and the one-arm Denny Washington dance with Carley Harris, who placed her right hand lightly on his shoulder in a most natural position. No competition there, thought Billy Wrenn, but he did want to meet the little one, Midge Crocker, and he stood up, roughly.

"Where are you going?" said Addy.

"I'll be right back," said Billy Wrenn. He went over and cut in on Briney and Midge, and Briney came back to the table, a puzzled look on his face.

"Sit here," said Addy Plummer, and Briney picked up his drink and went over to where she was sitting. "How long's it been?" said Addy Plummer.

"Since we danced in the beachhouse? Maybe too long."

"Maybe. But you've changed. I used to lead you, remember? I'll bet you don't let that happen anymore."

He smiled slowly, a lopsided grin, and said, "You can bet your boots I don't." She smelled good, and she looked good in her organdy, this girl, and she was quite a pretty girl who seemed to have some sense, and he wondered how she had happened to be the girl friend of a troublemaker like Billy Wrenn.

Billy Wrenn, at that very moment, was thinking the same thing about the relationship of Briney Mitchel to Midge Crocker. "Why do you do it?" he was saying as they danced, Billy holding her tightly. "Why do you go out with a guy like Briney Mitchel?" And Midge, bristling, said, "What do *you* have against Briney?" and Billy Wrenn said, "He's a Carew, isn't he, even though his name is Mitchel? And the Carews just got off the boat."

Midge wanted to hit him across the face, but instead she said, "You're talking nonsense, Billy."

"And I don't see why in the hell you're out with him." He looked at her with his insipid smile. "Are you sleeping with him?"

And then Midge Crocker gathered her dignity about her, covering her sense of outrage, and left Billy Wrenn standing on the dance floor, and went back to the table, furious. Addy Plummer, sensing what had happened, went to find Billy in the bar, and Briney rejoined Midge, not knowing she had left Billy Wrenn in the middle of the dance floor. "I think maybe we made a mistake coming here tonight," Midge said.

"Why?"

"Billy Wrenn is just dying for a fat lip."

"And I'm just the guy who can give it to him."

"I know you are," she said. "That's why I think we ought to be going pretty soon. He's getting drunk. And Devon really isn't our territory, is it?"

"Like hell it isn't," said Briney Mitchel. "Anyplace I go is my territory." Briney took a sip of his South Side, a good one. "What did he say to you?"

"I won't tell you because it would make you mad."

"You'll tell me."

"No, I won't."

"Then I'll get it out of Billy."

Briney started to get up, but Midge said, "Mitch, please don't. Please don't spoil the night. Because that's the way it will end up. I'll tell you what he said later."

"You promise?"

"I promise."

Briney Mitchel sat down again, and Denny came back with Carley, and Briney, looking in the direction of the six-piece band, said: "Mickey Mouse."

"Who's Mickey Mouse?" said Carley.

"The band," said Briney. "The band plays Mickey Mouse music. Dopey foxtrots all in the same time. Why don't they *swing?*"

"This is not exactly Glen Island Casino," said Denny.

Briney turned back to the table. "I wish it was. I wish it was Glen Island we were sitting in and listening to Glenn Miller, whose music, I'm sorry, I can't help it, gives me a spiritual erection."

They laughed, the other three, and they said that they understood what Briney meant. "Miller makes that marvelous sound with his saxes by using a hybrid." They all asked Briney what he meant by "hybrid," and Briney said, "It's a clarinet playing a whole octave higher than the saxes. Other bands have used clarinets with saxophones, but none of them like Miller does. Dorsey has the clarinet and Johnny Mince, but Johnny Mince plays it mostly during solos." Carley asked Briney why he was such a smartie pants about the big

bands, and Briney said that he read *Downbeat* magazine and talked to musicians. "Yes, it's sexy music
Miller plays all right," Briney said, "and I wish we
were sitting and listening to it at Glen Island."

"Well, we're not," said Carley Harris.

"No, it's Devon Yacht Club in East Hampton, isn't
it, and in spite of that, and in spite of the goddam Big
Apple and they'll do that tonight and maybe even the
Lambeth Walk, I'm going to ask that frustrated Larry
Clinton over there if he can swing a little." Briney got
up and made his way to the bandstand, and the leader,
a genial trombonist, said, sure, he could swing a little,
and he did, he started to play "Martha," and Briney
went back to the table and took Carley out onto the
dance floor.

The band played "Song of India" and "Marie," but
Briney was not with it, and he merely two-stepped with
Carley. He was thinking about what Billy Wrenn had
obviously said to Midge.

"I wish I could lindy," Carley said to Briney.

"Hmmm?"

"I said I wish I could do the Lindy Hop. Can you
lindy? I've never seen you jitterbug."

"Sure."

"You can not."

"Sure I can. I'm a killer-diller."

"Then lindy with me."

"No."

"Why?"

"I'm pissed off."

"You've never in your life used that expression with
me."

"I'm burned up at what that son of a bitch Billy Wrenn said to Midge."

"What did he say?"

"I don't know what he said, but I've got a pretty good idea what he said."

"And you're going to ruin Midge's evening over it, I suppose."

"No, I won't ruin Midge's evening."

"Then you'll let the Carews and the Callaways and the Westhamptons take care of Billy Wrenn."

Briney looked at her sharply and smiled crookedly. "Why not? Everybody seems to be dying to get his block knocked off around here, so they can do it to each other."

"Yes, and don't you get involved, Briney. You're liable to kill Billy Wrenn." Unconsciously she held him tighter, and he pressed his face close to her hair, watching the Carew-Callaway table, and wondering how much trouble his idiot cousins and their friends from Westhampton were in for tonight. "All right. But one thing is certain. I'm not going to start anything, remember that."

"Yes, and see that you don't," Carley said. "I think I know what Billy said to Midge."

"How would you know?"

"Because I know Billy Wrenn. And I know you, too, Briney Mitchel."

As they were going back to their table, Briney did some small wondering about this girl Carley Harris. Midge was already there with Denny, and when she saw Billy returning from the bar with a drink in each hand, she said, "Let's go. Let's go to Twelve Trees or Bowden or Aunt Margaret's. Mitch, I've never been to Aunt Margaret's, take me to Aunt Margaret's!"

"Not for a million dollars," said Briney, meeting Billy Wrenn's stare at the other end of the table.

"Well, let's go to Twelve Trees," said Denny. "I've about had it here. How about you, Carley?"

"I'm ready."

Briney said nothing. They got their drink check, and when it was paid they all got up, all except Briney, who kept glancing at Billy Wrenn, who was muttering things to his friends at the other end of the table.

"Come on, Mitch," said Midge, pulling him by the sleeve. Briney stood up, slowly, and turned around to leave with them, but he saw Billy Wrenn coming at him over his shoulder, and he said to them, "Remember, I didn't start anything," and Billy Wrenn grabbed Briney by the sleeve and spun him around.

"You are not welcome at Devon!" Addy Plummer, pulling at Billy's sleeve, was trying to get him away from Briney.

"That's why we're leaving," said Briney.

"Well, you can take your friends with you — over there," Billy said, pointing to the Carew-Callaway table.

"They may be my cousins, dear boy, but they are not my friends." Briney Mitchel had very little use for Chip Callaway, or any of his cousins for that matter. He disliked them because they were prissy and pious and stuck to each other like glue. They would have no part in any congress that was not totally Catholic. Nonetheless, Briney felt a certain loyalty toward them — a blood kinship if nothing else. "Suppose you go over there and tell them what you just told me," he said to Billy Wrenn.

"You're the cheapest Catholic of them all."

"But you wouldn't dare, would you?" Briney Mitchel said. "No, there are too many of them even for the Andover gang, aren't there?"

"How's Midge Crocker in bed, Briney?" Billy said.

Without batting an eye, Briney said, "Now why don't you go back and sit down like a good little boy and drink yourself into your normal state of stupidity." Then, showing great control, he turned on his heel and started to follow the others out the door. Whereupon Billy, grabbing a carafe of water from a table, pursued them, caught up with Briney, and dumped the contents of the carafe over his head.

Briney stopped, wheeled and caught Billy Wrenn a mash in the midsection, and a sharp slap in the face, and he picked him up, squirming and cursing, threw him over his shoulder, and carried him through one of the French doors that led to the club's landing dock. Denny Washington, seeing the Andover gang rise in a body from their table, told the girls to get themselves to the car, then rushed over to rouse the Carew-Callaway table. His friend was going to need some help. Both tables poured through the door and the band played on. They arrived at the edge of the water just in time to see Briney Mitchel, who had slipped in the mud under the high rising tide and fallen with his burden, pinning Billy Wrenn in the mud and sand of the water, half covering Billy, the rain coming down on them, and asking Billy did he have enough. But Billy Wrenn, cursing, got one arm free and ran his hand full of nails down the side of Briney Mitchel's face. Then he spat at Briney Mitchel, and Briney, enraged, tried to spit back at him but he could not raise enough spittle, his mouth was so dry. So he took Billy into a half nelson and made him yell with pain, and then he picked him up like a child again, kicking, and raising him the full length of his arms, he spun him around like a professional wrestler, carried him to the end of the pier, and, while both groups watched, dumped him into the inky black waters of Gardiner's Bay.

Then the two groups fell upon each other: the Andovers versus the Carew-Callaway-Westhamptons. In the melee, Chip Callaway, his waist-length white dinner jacket a mess, and one of his front teeth missing, came up to Briney and said: "I owe you something and I'm going to pay you back," and Briney thought Chip was going to take a swing at him, but instead, Chip turned and rushed back into the fight.

At least Chip Callaway had gumption, Briney thought. In fact, enough gumption to sneak over to Water Mill one night and break windows and furniture in Lucian Mitchel's beachhouse. His motives were unknown, unless he wanted to bring trouble down on his head, or he was jealous of Briney for something. To avoid a feud between the families, Edyth Mitchel kept the incident a secret from Lucian, who was away, but when Briney got it out of George Bohan what had happened, he went over to the Callaways' one night and invited Chip to come outside and settle it. But Chip told the maid who answered the door to tell Briney that he was sick and couldn't fight. And now here was Chip, trying to make up for it, and Briney was glad to let him go and do his will on the smart-ass East Hampton crowd.

Then Briney quit the fight. He quit the fight because it wasn't his fight anymore. No, now the fight really belonged to Chip Callaway and the other Hoyas. Briney Mitchel's run-in with Billy Wrenn had only served to start it, and now Briney Mitchel, not spent, hardly tired at all even though his face had been scratched, still had this blood lust in him, and he wanted to turn it on a woman, and he went back through the dark with Denny toward the parking lot to find Midge who would be waiting for him.

He found her huddled in the rumble. He vaulted in beside her and Midge threw her raincoat over him, and put her arms around him and drew his head, blood and all, down to her bosom. He kissed her, and she wept some salty, reactive tears to all the goings on at Devon.

"Let's go, Denny," said Briney, calling into Midge's bodice. "There will be cops here pretty soon, and let's for Christ sake go to Aunt Margaret's, where there is at least a little peace and quiet."

"Oh, goody," said Midge, as Denny started the motor. She immediately stopped crying, but she wouldn't let go of Briney's bleeding head at her bosom until they were in Bridgehampton.

23

AIDAN CAREW HAD AN ELABORATE HOLY WATER font inside the front door of Rosscommon, his house in the Agapogue section, from which Briney Mitchel filled his water pistol when he was very young. When Aidan found out about this from one of his own children, who were carbon copies of their father, he was ready to kill his nephew for the sacrilege. But Lucian, displaying some of the fire that was characteristic of him in those days, told Aidan that whomever Briney sprayed with the water would thereby be blessed, and Aidan found himself hard put to argue with the logic, try as he might. Nonetheless, he was angry, and Lucian, fearful of Aidan's wrath, took Briney's pants down when he got home and whipped the boy with his own belt.

As a matter of fact, Rosscommon had been designed by an architect who specialized in ecclesiastical structures: churches, schools, a local bar and grill, even a cathedral or two. The house had several tall steeples and a living room similar to the nave of a church, with a soaring ceiling and high narrow windows that faced the ocean, but which were difficult to see through. There were two broad wings, one for Aidan Carew and his family, and the other for the servants and a garage. "If

Aidan Carew's house looks like a church," said Lucian Mitchel once, "then Willard Callaway's house should look like a stock market ticker."

"And ours," said Briney Mitchel, "should look like a bottle of Johnny Walker Red," whereupon the father had chased the son out the door, hurling invectives.

They lived fairly close together, this Irish Catholic cantonment — their houses wedged into the dunes and jutting high over the Atlantic, which was a constant threat to their tenure in spite of their footings driven deep in the sand. The late Brian Carew's and Lucian Mitchel's houses, farther away in Water Mill, were quite ordinary compared to the standards of the others — substantial but unpretentious, and more comfortable than most. Willard Callaway's, on the other hand, was built in a huge semicircle with big windows facing the ocean. And Aidan Carew had his quasi-church. Indeed, mass had even been celebrated in the house of Aidan Carew.

Mass had never been celebrated in the rude mud hut of Brian Carew in County Rosscommon seventy-five years before. No, Aidan Carew's grandfather had had to walk nine miles to church every Sunday, if he wasn't lucky enough to attend a "section" — a visiting priest celebrating mass in a neighboring farmhouse. He had prayed hard for his potato crop, but the crop had failed and there was terrible starvation in the land. So one day he packed his mean belongings and he and his wife trekked all the way to Cork by foot to make a fresh start in the new world. After a few weeks they embarked on a packet for Boston, coupling tenderly every night of their passage in stowage, while the other Irish immigrants turned their heads in horror and told their beads.

A fierce, lusty man with snapping blue eyes and a flaming red beard, Brian Carew settled his bride and went to work on the Boston & Albany Railroad which was a-building. But Brian hated the squalor of East Boston and made off again, moving to Five Points in New York City. He could find no work in New York, and he got suddenly caught up in the excitement of the recruiting for the Union army. Leaving his wife and small baby born of the union aboard ship, he went off to fight the Northern cause, and fell, carrying the Irish colors at the Battle of Fredericksburg.

Back in Five Points, his grieving widow took in wash, never married again, and brought up a bawdy, roistering son who had to quit school and go to work at the age of twelve. He studied by candlelight, and by the same candlelight he tinkered. He started to invent things, this brash youth still in his early teens. He was fascinated by electricity, partly because of his job as one of the young gaslamp lighters of the streets of Five Points.

He began to explore the means to control and feed electricity, and soon he was inventing switches and panelboards and other devices that would make electricity safe. Though he never cared a whit about money, he began to get rich; he invented a great many more safety devices for the workingman in the factory, and he built a plant in which to manufacture them.

Yet he did not confine his inventions completely to safety devices. A lover of the good life he had been so deprived of in his youth, he even invented a perfectly serviceable winebottle opener.

In the course of making his fortune, he took a lass, a lace curtain by the name of Margaret Mulligan, for a bride. From this marriage were born Aidan, Junior; Brian and Edyth and Rita and Caroline, all of whom, upon the urging of Aidan, Senior, came to make their summer homes in Southampton, after the manner of Aidan, Senior, who in the early twenties began to enjoy life and established himself in solitary splendor on the dunes of eastern Long Island. When the depression came, nobody seemed to be able to support the clubs, and the Carews, Callaways and Mitchels were invited to join them all, which they promptly did.

When Aidan, Senior, died, Aidan, Junior, bought the house from the estate, and while the others built their houses around him, he commissioned the ecclesiastical architect to remodel the house of his father to resemble a church.

Aidan, unlike his father who mistrusted them, was very thick with prelates, and had them as frequent weekend visitors. He was also a Knight of Malta and a Knight of St. Gregory, and so it came to pass that permission was ultimately granted from Rome that one or two selected priests could celebrate the holy sacrifice in the living room of Aidan Carew, Junior, very much as "sections" took place in the old country.

Briney had been to these masses when he was younger, and he rather liked them because there was no sermon, and yet he hated them, too. It was something about being in his Uncle Aidan's house that made him uncomfortable; Aidan Carew disapproved of Briney wholeheartedly, for Briney was already showing signs of independence beyond Aidan Carew's control. Aidan Carew ran his sisters and their children like a fist in a glove of mail. There was no defying him; when Briney challenged him, he put his foot down, usually through Lucian, as in the incident of the water pistol and the holy water. But as time wore on and Briney became bolder, beatings proved insufficient to dampen the spirit of this young, unreconstructed Irishman. He took great joy in disobeying his father and Aidan, and pretty much went his own way.

The situation got worse as Briney grew older; and tonight was perhaps Briney's boldest stroke of all.

24

THE WIND WAS RISING AND THE RAIN BECOMING heavier as Stanley Kalinski rolled his Indian motorcycle around to the back of the Twelve Trees. He turned off the engine, sizzling and steaming in the wet, pushed down the kickstand, and dismounted. He took off his big black leather gloves, hefted his revolver on its heavy bullet belt, walked into the kitchen, took off his dripping slicker and hung it up on a hook.

"Hallo, office-ah," said the Greek chef, who always spat in the *soup du jour* for good luck. "You look' for Paula? Paula's inna fron' serving."

Stanley grunted, grabbed a dishtowel to dry himself off, and paused at the celery bowl to pick up a heart and chew on it. "Get Bobby Motley, Greek."

"Yeah, sure," said the Greek. "You stir da soup, I get assis' manager." Stanley went over and took the wooden ladle from the chef and stirred, and in a moment Bobby Motley appeared through the swinging doors. He was reasonably sober.

"You seen the phantom tonight, Bobby?"

"No, Stan, not since I called you."

"Well, you see him, you call me, you understand?"

"I understand, Stanley."

"Now get Paula."

"She's very busy, Stanley, and I'd rather —"

"Get Paula, godammit, Bobby!"

"Sure, Stanley, sure," and he went back through the swinging doors.

Paula came back in a minute and said, "Now, what the hell do you want, Stanley?"

"I want you to come right home tonight after you're done work here," he said, still chewing on the hearts of celery and pointing at her with a stalk. "I don't want you going to no Aunt Margaret's with no Briney Mitchel, you understand?"

"You go screw yourself, Stanley," she said, knowing she had a hold on this brute of a man.

The Greek chef stifled a laugh and forgot to stir the soup. Stanley moved over very close to Paula, stuck the stalk in his mouth and crunched it off between his teeth. He threw the stalk on the floor and took Paula by both arms and squeezed, and she let out a short squeal of pain. "Listen, you, I don't mind your shacking with every son of a bitch in Southampton. But you don't shack with the phantom, you understand?"

"Who says I'm shacking with the phantom?"

"Never mind who says," and he began to shake her.

"It's a lie!"

"At the phantom I draw the line. If I ever catch you in bed with the phantom, I'll kill you — and him, too!" and he shook her till her teeth rattled and she cried out. He dropped his arms then and went to the door, finishing another piece of celery he had picked up on the way. He took the slicker off the hook and put it back on, took out his revolver and brandished it, and the Greek chef scooted to the other side of the stove. "And if you see Briney Mitchel, you just tell him what I said!"

Then Stanley was out the door and off with a roar in the terrible night, and Paula rushed back into the bar to find Bobby Motley, who was helping the regular bartender. She grabbed him by the sleeve.

"Go back to work," he said, trying to brush her off.

"You told him, didn't you, Bobby. You told Stanley!"

"Told Stanley what?"

"Told him about me and Briney Mitchel."

"Honest, I never said a word. Anyway, it's all over town about you and Briney Mitchel."

"You're a lying bastard."

Bobby Motley shook his arm free of her. "Now wait a minute, baby. You watch your tongue."

"Nobody knew."

"Everybody in Southampton knows."

"No, nobody knew, only Aunt Margaret knew. But you told Stanley, Bobby, you goddam *pansy!* Yes, you dirty, lousy, stinkin' pansy."

Bobby Motley slapped her across the face. Whereupon Paula Kalinski took an Old Fashioned cocktail from in front of an amazed customer and threw it, fruit, ice and all, full in Bobby's face. Then with a flourish, she undid her apron and threw that in his face, too. "Now, you keep your mouth shut or I'll spread it all over town about you cornholing with the chef, and you cornholing with the Crocker chauffeur, Herbert, and you cornholing with this one and you cornholing with that one!"

The bar customers began to smile and one or two of

them laughed, and Bobby Motley's face, free of the apron, began to be very sad, and Paula thought he might cry, and she began to laugh, a coarse shrill laugh, and the people at the bar who had been watching, amused, turned away embarrassed, having heard it all, and understanding it fully. Then Paula left this wretched, pock-faced man and walked straight through the bar called The Sideshow and out the front door with all the dignity she could muster. But when she got outside in the black wet, she ran all the way to the Model A in the parking lot, breaking into tears, and sat for a full fifteen minutes behind the wheel crying before she could bring herself to turn on the key and feel for the starter high on the floorboards with her foot, stretching down in the seat, for she was a small woman. It was a shame that Stanley really cared about her sleeping with the one man she had ever really loved. She should go home, she knew, first picking up her baby at her mother's, but when she had got the Ford rolling, it was as though she had no control over its mechanics. Like a horse heading for its favorite stable, the old, faithful Model A simply took her through the storm toward Aunt Margaret's and Briney Mitchel.

25

MARGARET MARINELLO RAN A SEEDY-LOOKING place off David White's Lane near the railroad station in Southampton. She and her husband Nick had bought it during Prohibition and immediately opened a speakeasy with rooms upstairs for couples who liked to do their drinking lying down. For a long time, business flourished, until one night Margaret found Nick himself relaxing upstairs beside one of the waitresses, half undressed, when he should have been minding the cash register, and she threw him out in the street, along with some cheap glassware.

Nick Marinello did not immediately disappear from Southampton. No, Nick Marinello made his own deal with a torpedo in New York to run illicit booze in from the ocean and truck it into the city. But he needed a road from the beach, and the only road remote yet accessible enough ran past Brian Carew's house. So Nick went to Brian one night and said, "Mr. Carew, I pay you a t'ousant a mont' to turn the ot'er way when my trucks run the stuff in off the beach." Brian Carew, knowing Nick's troubles with Margaret, and being on friendly terms with Prohibition liquor himself, said, "Sit down, Nick." And Nick Marinello, feeling terribly uncomfortable in the grandeur of Brian's modest library, sat down across from the man. "You know what would happen to me if they caught me taking that money letting you run booze?"

"What would they do?"

"They'd throw the book at me, that's what they'd do."

"How can they catch you?"

"How can they catch me? Well, I'll tell you how they can catch me. So far, only two people know about this proposition, you and me, right?"

"Right."

"All right. Suppose you got drunk some night and spilled the beans to a very close friend. Say a girl."

"Now wait a minute. I don't drink, or I don't drink much, and I don't tell nobody, Mr. Carew, I swear on a stack of bibles."

"All right. But you know what?"

"What?"

"I drink."

"So?"

"Sometimes I drink a lot. Sometimes I talk too much. One slip, and there goes the old ball game."

"I never seen you drunk, Mr. Carew."

"And you never will. But yes, Nick, I use the stuff pretty well, or pretty badly, depending on how you look at it. And one slip — I tell a buddy, for instance — and then this buddy of mine has a few himself, and goes and tells another buddy of his how Brian Carew is picking up a grand a month for simply turning his head one hundred and eighty degrees West when the trucks go by on the other side of the hedge. And then that buddy tells another buddy, and pretty soon there isn't any secret anymore, and guess who gets indicted for a felony?" Brian Carew leaned back in his chair. "No, not for a thousand dollars a month, not for anything."

"Five t'ousand a mont'."

"Not five million a month."

"Jesus."

"Yes, Jesus." Brian Carew lighted a Lucky Strike. "There is one thing you guys will never get through your heads. When you want to break the law you must do it all by yourself, because if you let a buddy in on it, or a sweetie, or even a wife, forget about it, because sooner or later somebody's going to sing. And why do people sing, drunk or sober? They sing because they want to be big shots, and the reason they want to be big shots is because they're little shots, with a dot over the *o*, and the fastest way to get to be a big shot, and also maybe get your head blown off or get thrown into jail, is to sing secrets to friends that you are breaking the law."

"Listen, Mr. Carew, I ain't no little shot, remember that!"

"No, you are not a little shot. You are a little shot with a dot over the *o*."

"Goddam you!" Nick Marinello said, knowing the truth when he heard it and starting to rise out of the chair. Brian Carew simply smiled at him through the smoke of the cigarette.

"Now please don't raise your voice," he said. "I have children in this house. And sit down. You're learning something tonight."

And Nick Marinello did sit down, and he listened to

what more Brian Carew had to say, but he did not
learn; for what more Brian Carew told him was lost on
him.

When Nick left, properly respectful and character-
istically morose, Brian went upstairs to Barbara and
told her the story while they undressed, and Barbara
said, "Prohibition is a terrible, terrible thing," and
Brian said, "Prohibition of any kind is a terrible, terrible thing. But give it this: it does give the Nick
Marinellos of this world a chance to be big shots, and
that fellow with that wife of his throwing him out of her
place like she did, that fellow needs to be a big shot very
fast. But you know what?"

"What, darling?"

"I don't think he'll make it."

And Nick Marinello did not make it, even after finding another road from the beach. For one night, a few
weeks later, while waist-deep in the surf and signaling a
rum runner with a flashlight, Nick Marinello disappeared forever. Some said he swam out to the runner to
get away from Margaret once and for all. Others said
he was gunned down on the beach and thrown in the
ocean. But in fact what happened was this: Nick simply
could not swim a stroke and had been caught in the
powerful undertow off Southampton. He had simply
been washed out to sea, and trucks marked FURNITURE
waiting behind the dunes went back to New York on the
Sunrise Highway empty that night.

And Margaret never batted an eye. She ran her joint
twenty-four hours a day, paying off the police and
letting some girls come in and hang around the bar.
But there was never really any scandal about the place,

and there was plenty of reason to be, like the night a New York Circuit Court judge was caught upstairs during a routine raid by Drover and one or two of his boys. The jurist, panicking unnecessarily, since he was afraid his name would leak to the papers, grabbed his BVD's, and interrupting his monthly coitus with his favorite girl, jumped out of the second-story window, broke his ankle, and was carried howling with pain and rage to his Delage by his chauffeur, who more or less took care of this man in such situations.

With the repeal of the Eighteenth Amendment, however, Aunt Margaret's — and that was the only name it ever had — took on a more subdued personality, and it stuck pretty much to the law, keeping proper hours and even refusing to serve kids under eighteen once in a while. Aunt Margaret still paid protection, for you could still relax with a lady upstairs, but it was a far more respectable place than it had been in the rowdy days and nights of the twenties. Mostly it attracted the younger group of Southampton local boys, such as Birdie Hawkins and Harry Jablonski, who came to drink beer slowly and ogle the girls, and Roy Strumpf, who drank beer with them and cracked his knuckles when a girl clicked by. "I can just feel her," Roy would say. "I can just feel her."

Paula Kalinski came, too. She met Briney Mitchel at Aunt Margaret's, but usually it was during the off-hours. She would wait for him with just her bra on in one of the rooms upstairs, instead of in the bar where the genuine tarts loafed. For Paula was no real tart, but a foolish youngster who had got herself with child, been forced into a marriage with a man she did not love, slept around, and had fallen hopelessly in love with one of the rich summer guys.

Briney Mitchel knew that she would be waiting for him upstairs at Aunt Margaret's, and as Denny Washington's Studebaker drew closer to the place, Briney had some second thoughts about taking Midge in there. "Maybe we shouldn't," he told her in the rumble seat of the car. They were huddled under her raincoat, his arm around her waist.

"Maybe we shouldn't what?" said Midge.

"Go to Aunt Margaret's."

"What are you suddenly changing your mind for?"

"We ought to go someplace where there's a fire and we can dry out. The Post House, maybe."

"But Paula Kalinski won't be waiting for you at the Post House, will she?"

Briney sat up straight. "What do you mean?"

"Don't kid me, Mitch. Paula Kalinski's waiting for you at Aunt Margaret's."

"Now what in the hell ever gave you that idea?"

"Never mind."

"Well, I don't think we should go to Aunt Margaret's." He started to rap on the window to get Denny Washington to stop at the Post House, but Midge Crocker began to cry softly — he could feel it in her shoulders, though he couldn't see her — so he leaned back and took her chin in his left hand and said, "What?"

"You know what."

"No, I don't know what."

"I love you."

"That's a mistake." Briney felt uneasy.

"I love you. I've never told another man in the world that I love him."

"Don't love me." He felt stupid saying it, but he said it.

"The way you handled yourself with Billy Wrenn."

"You love me for the way I handled myself with Billy Wrenn."

"You know it's not just that." She turned her face and brought her lips against his, and she was soft and damply warm and delicious in his arms. When they were finished kissing under the raincoat, she said: "I don't care about Paula Kalinski. Take me to Aunt Margaret's anyway. I don't give a damn who all your girls are." And then Midge Crocker nestled against him and put her head on his shoulder, and they tucked the raincoat in around them and they held hands with the utmost contentment all the way to the Polish section near the Southampton railroad station.

26

MARGARET MARINELLO, WHO DID NOT SHOCK easily, was genuinely appalled when she saw Briney and Midge hurrying through the storm toward the steps of the porch. And who were the two behind them?

"Hello, Maggie," said Briney. "This is Millicent Crocker."

"What in the name of sweet Jesus are you bringing Millicent Crocker into my place for? You're Harriet Crocker's daughter, aren't you, dear?"

"Yes, Ma'am," said Midge, who had not used "Ma'am" since Chapin's.

Aunt Margaret looked hard at Briney. "I thought you had more sense." She could not see in the darkness of the porch that Briney had been in a fight. "My, this is a sweet-looking child and you bring her —"

"This is Carley Harris, Maggie," said Briney.

"Hello, Aunt Margaret," said Carley.

"Well, I don't know Carley Harris, but good God, Briney —"

"And you know Denny, of course."

"Yes, I know Denny, and how are you, Denny?"

Denny Washington said, "Just fine, thank you."

"Well, I might have thought that at least Denny

Washington would have better sense than to bring two lovely —"

"They dragged us here," said Briney Mitchel, smiling a lopsided smile that he sometimes used. "They said they wouldn't put out for us later unless we brought them here."

"You're a fool, Briney Mitchel," said Aunt Margaret, and took him by the sleeve and drew him against the wall, near the porch light. "Look at your face and your clothes. You been fighting?"

"Yep." Briney smiled again.

Aunt Margaret shook her head. "She's up there waiting for you, you know that, don't you?"

"Sure I know it, and so does Midge, so what the hell are you worried about?"

"Trouble, that's what I'm worried about. You already had trouble tonight, I can see. Now trouble with Paula, trouble with Stanley when he comes in here later."

"Paula will be home by then. He'll never see her."

"You'll send her home?"

"Yes."

"Do it right away."

"All right. But get us a table first."

Aunt Margaret took them through the front room, which had the stale smell of urine — the universal smell of beer parlors — and where there was a jukebox and some tables around an empty center of the room for dancing. You couldn't tell who was at the tables in the big room, it was so dimly lighted, but when they followed Margaret into the little barroom in back, Birdie Hawkins, the native boy who was Briney's old friend, gave him a big hello and a lesser one to Denny and the girls. "Does your old man know you're here tonight?"

"Does yours?" said Briney Mitchel.

"Hell, mine came with me. He's right over there in the corner fast asleep, or passed out, I can't tell which."

Briney turned and looked at Big Ed Hawkins, now gray and grizzled, slumped over a table in the corner, a half-empty bottle of whiskey and a shot glass in front of him.

"How about them apples?" said Birdie.

"My old man locked me in tonight," said Briney, sitting down with Birdie and Jabbo and Roy Strumpf for a moment. He told them about the fight at Devon. "I think they'll be all right," he said.

"Who will be all right, the Andovers?"

"No, the Carews and the Callaways and the West-hamptons. The Andovers are outnumbered anyway, and the Irish will win this one."

"And you bugged out," said Harry Jablonski, whose eyes were glazing from too many beers.

"Does it look as though he bugged out?" said Birdie, pointing to the side of Briney's face.

Briney looked at Jabbo for quite a long time, saying nothing, and when Jabbo said, "Who is this sweet little broad you brung in here tonight, Briney? You gonna take her upstairs like you take Paula?" Briney got up, excusing himself, and went to join the others, but Jabbo persisted, following him, and when he sat down Jabbo leaned over and said, "Or maybe you're gonna take her upstairs, and all three of you could —"

Briney's fist shot out from where it was resting on the table, and Harry Jablonski went back against Birdie

Hawkins who had come up behind to try to prevent trouble. Some of them in the front room heard the commotion, and they began to get up from their tables and move toward the little barroom, for most of them were Southampton natives who knew Briney Mitchel; they also knew that he was a rich summer kid and they wanted to be in on it if a rich summer kid was going to get his lumps. If the rich kid was coming out on top, they would see to it that the balance would swing the other way. Yes, and you could blame it on Roosevelt if you wanted to: even though these people owed their economic survival to the rich people for the precious three months of the summer, buying in their stores and using their services, the rich people were their sworn enemies, and it was going to give them special pleasure to watch the nephew of the sainted Aidan Carew, three generations removed from a piss-poor potato-starved family in Ireland, get his lumps.

While the rest of the world mostly starved, the Carews, Callaways, Mitchels and the rest of summer Southampton hid itself behind hedges, away from the prying eyes of the natives and the rest of the great unwashed, the rubberneckers from Queens who piled their families into the old jalopy for a Sunday excursion to get a glimpse of the rich on eastern Long Island. The hedges, in fact, were as much a part of the community as the great houses on the dunes and those houses along the maple-shaded streets that led to the public beaches. Working furiously all summer, hordes of natives kept the hedges trim, the lawns manicured, the bluestone drives raked, the houses clean, the meals cooked, the parties catered.

Tomorrow they would take their beer hangovers to
Our Lady Queen of the Sea and smile at the Aidan
Carews and the Willard Callaways, and even Lucian
Mitchel nursing his own head at the back of the church,
knowing that the rich kid whose uncle paid $100 for a
front pew had got his lumps.

"You crazy bastard," said Denny Washington,
grabbing Briney's arm when he half rose out of his
chair to await the return assault of Harry Jablonski.

"I couldn't help it," Briney said. "No, this time I
couldn't help it." He glanced at Midge. She was truly
frightened. She had seen the faces begin to gather in
the door of the barroom. Margaret Marinello pushed
through them.

"I told you not to come, you idiot, and told you to go
right upstairs and get rid of that kid. I told you, didn't
I?"

"You told me."

"But you didn't do it, did you?"

"You didn't hear what Jabbo said."

"You didn't have to sit down at his table, did you?"

"I sat down to talk to Birdie."

"Goddam you," Margaret Marinello said, and
Briney looked at her, and Margaret Marinello had the
look of a woman about to be in very big trouble. "I'll go
up. Yes, I'll go up before it really hits the fan. You.
You stay here and take your licking like a man. And
you," she said to the others, "you'd better get out of
here, especially the girls." She glanced at Denny Washington's missing forearm. "Maybe you ought to go,
too."

"You shut your mouth," said Denny Washington,

taking the girls through the back door. "I'll be right back."

So Briney stood waiting for Jabbo, who was struggling with Birdie, who was trying to hold him off. "Let him go," said Briney, and now there was a snarl on his lip. Birdie let Jabbo go, and Jabbo grabbed an empty beer bottle and smashed off the end of it on the edge of a table. Then he headed for the rich kid in the tuxedo with the scratches down his face who was waiting for him.

Upstairs in the room where they always met, Paula Kalinski was cocking an ear, listening to the commotion below. She wore only her bra and was sitting in an easy chair reading an issue of *Photoplay*. When Margaret Marinello burst into the room, she dropped the magazine and covered her loins with it.

"Get out, baby, there's trouble," said Margaret, snatching at her clothes and throwing them at her. "That rich boy friend of yours."

"Jesus, Mary and Joseph," said Paula, reaching for her step-ins.

"Get dressed and get out of here before Stanley comes, because when he comes, there won't be a fan big enough."

"A fan big enough?"

"Get dressed and get out, stupid," Margaret said.

There was a crash belowstairs, and far away they both heard the wail of a siren over the whine of the wind, and Margaret Marinello said, "Oh, Christ," and Paula Kalinski crossed herself and fell to her knees and started to pray against the bed, but Margaret grabbed her by the hair and pulled her to her feet and shook her until she thought Paula's teeth would rattle. "Get dressed! And if Stanley gets here before you leave, use the fire rope at the other side of the house. But get out of here!"

Then Margaret had to go back downstairs, and she slammed the door of the bedroom, leaving Paula in the middle of it, step-ins half off, tears coursing down her face.

27

OUTSIDE IN THE STUDEBAKER, CARLEY HARRIS was taking off her shoes. "I'm going back in," she said to Midge Crocker, who had both fists pressed against her cheeks. "I'm going back in there and get in a few myself."

"No, we have no business in there," Midge Crocker said.

"We have no business in there, but we caused the trouble, or at least indirectly caused it, and I'm not just standing around waiting for them to beat up Briney — or Denny, for that matter." Brandishing both shoes, she marched back through the rain and mud into the house just as Stanley Kalinski rolled up on his Indian.

Inside, Harry Jablonski had just lunged at Briney Mitchel with the broken beer bottle, and Briney, sidestepping at the last possible moment, let Jabbo stumble and fall across the table full of drinks, sending everything crashing. Then he jumped on top of Jabbo and wrested the beer bottle from him. Jabbo, struggling mightily, said, "You rich son of a bitch, I'll kill you, you cocksucker," and he bared his teeth, trying to get a bite of Briney's nose, but Briney pinned his shoulders to the floor.

It would have been a "fall" at Princeton, and Briney
would have won the match, but this was not Princeton,
and the people watching it all were not students. There
were no rules here in this cheap cathouse in Southampton, and the people in it were poor, sullen, half-
drunken men watching one of their own on the floor
getting it from a kid who drove his own car and screwed
girls of their own kind.

Sensing this, Denny Washington knelt on one knee
beside Briney and said, "Let him up and let's get the
hell out of here before they kill us," and Briney, recog-
nizing the wisdom of this, started to release the bull of a
man known as Jabbo, but Jabbo would not let it be
finished; he swung his freed arm and caught Briney a
glancing blow on a chin that was already bleeding, and
they went down again, taking Denny Washington with
them. Margaret Marinello, having come downstairs,
tried to break through the spectators, but one of them
had already said, "It's two on one, the sons of bitches,
let's get 'em!" and they moved in a body toward the
writhing figures on the floor, and two or three of them,
dragging Briney and Denny by their legs, and kicking
away chairs and other obstructions with their feet,
made a circle in the middle of the room, and they
kneeled on the arms and legs of the two and began a
slow, deliberate process of working them over. They
were ganging up on Briney and Denny; there was no
sense of fair play in them, and Briney could not understand this. He had been partial to the natives all his
young life; he was conversant with them. Now there was
only hate and venom in them, and Briney hated them

back, these lowest of the low, these drunken men whom he thought were his friends.

He told himself to relax his whole body, that the body could absorb the fists and shoes if it were limp like a rag. So he went as loose as he could, fending off the blows to his face with one hand, and covering his groin with the other. But somebody got a knee or a fist or the toe of a shoe under the hand that was protecting his groin, and the instant agony from it shot up through his entire body, and he let out a yell, almost like a war whoop, to diminish the pain, and he felt suddenly out of breath as he had at Portsmouth Priory a few years before when he had fallen with no tin jock on an elbow of a kid from the football team they were playing — St. George's — and they had to call time out to pump his legs and get the wind back into him.

He began to pump his legs furiously, flailing them at his tormentors, but this only stimulated more lethal blows, so he dropped his legs and rolled over on his stomach, and for the first time in years, said a prayer.

It was all done in studied silence, except for the grunts and groans of the combatants, and even the jukebox was silent. Only Margaret Marinello made noises, but they held her back, these poor, tough day laborers, and when Birdie Hawkins tried to break it up, Harry Jablonski, much bigger than Birdie, punched Birdie in the solar plexus, doubling him over, and said, "You stay out of this, you're as bad as the two on the floor."

Roy Strumpf, not knowing what was really happening, stumbled back and forth behind the ring of people, bumping into tables and cracking his knuckles. "Oh,

Jesus," said the blind man, "there will be hell to pay for this yet."

Carley Harris did manage to break through, and she got in a few swings at the assailants with her high heels. A couple of the men tried to pull her back, but they tore her dress, and she turned on them in exquisitely dignified fury, and said, "God damn you, you barbarians, look what you're letting them do, pick on a man with one arm. Oh, my God, you dirty bastards!" and they listened to her, watching her clutch her bodice, or at least they heard her, and they let Denny off the floor, and one of them took Denny by the back of the tuxedo shawl and the seat of the pants and ran him out the back door, throwing him into the night so that he splashed and slithered in the mud and rain, which probably kept him from being further injured, and he came to rest at the feet of Stanley Kalinski, who only glanced at him to make sure it wasn't Briney Mitchel. No, his flashlight told him, his quarry was still inside.

And Carley continued swinging her shoes on Jabbo and the others until finally they wrenched them from her and grabbed her by the dress and ripped it some more until the bodice came full down, and Carley, who did not have to wear a bra, stood there before them and said, "There, now are you satisfied?" Seeing that it was hopeless to continue to try to save Briney Mitchel by herself, she marched toward the back door for help, making no attempt at all to cover her small breasts, and they made a path for her, and some of them even averted their eyes, while Stanley Kalinski brushed past her without so much as a glance and barged into the melee on the floor.

Out in the driving storm, the two girls knelt beside Denny Washington, who showed no marks, but felt terribly bruised, and made sure that his only good arm was intact. "I'd better go back in there," he said.

"No, they'll kill you," said Carley. "Let's get you into the car." And they helped him to the car and Carley got a raincoat — not to put over her front, but to place under Denny's head so that he would be more comfortable. Meanwhile Midge Crocker had hurried to the front of the house and gotten a towel from the ladies' john, and was coming back to put it on Denny's face.

"Cover yourself up," said Denny, when Carley had placed the raincoat under his head.

"You would think of something like that at a time like this, wouldn't you?" Carley said.

"I could kill the demented bastards who tore your dress," Denny said.

"Yes, well, you can't kill the bastards who did it, so forget about that," said Carley.

When Midge came back with the towel, she got a safety pin from her purse and helped Carley pin up her front. And then the three waited anxiously, squashed in the front seat, for they did not know what Stanley Kalinski would do to Briney Mitchel.

The prayer must have helped Briney; the breathlessness and the agony in his groin were easing, and he was only worried about a blow to his kidneys, but they gave him none, and for this he was grateful, a mass of bruises as he was, his face buried in his arms. He heard Stanley's voice and his body tensed again; he was not prepared to be beaten to death. Something must intervene, no matter what Stanley Kalinski chose to do.

The motorcycle policeman had waited a long time for this night. He removed his gloves and slicker with some ceremony, handing them to the bystanders as though they were his seconds. Then he took his revolver out of its holster and grabbed it by the barrel end. He was going to give this rich kid something to remember him by. Then maybe he would lay off his wife and have more respect for the law. As Stanley prepared to revolver-whip him, he knew that there would be no witnesses in this place against him — not even Margaret Marinello. He leaned over Briney, preparing the first blow, and then Aunt Margaret intervened. She alone had realized that there could be terrible consequences for everybody in this. She had been freed by the circle of men, and she came through them, and before Stanley could turn Briney on his back and administer the first crack, she reminded Stanley that his wife Paula might just be in one of the upstairs bedrooms. So Stanley cursed and straightened up and returned his revolver to its holster, and, leaving the others to continue the pummeling, went upstairs and found his wife still crying with her bra on and her step-ins down around her ankles in the middle of the room. So enraged was he that he grabbed her by the arm and marched her out of the room and downstairs with no clothes on at all except her bra and the step-ins dragging from one ankle.

She stumbled and fought, trying to bite his hand, and thumped his chest with her tiny red fist, but it was to no avail; he would not let her go and cover herself up. He would teach her, this slut who was his wife. He would teach her to hang out in Aunt Margaret's waiting for a fuck from the rich kid, the phantom. He would teach her to screw around with Briney Mitchel.

Through the barroom in back they went, brushing through the sea of bodies on the floor, who turned and watched in amazement. He dragged her out the door, past Denny, Carley and Midge in the Studebaker, who watched them in the light of the windows, watched in wonder as Stanley literally flung his naked prize into the Model A. "Now go home," was all he said to her, and she started the car and drove hurriedly away, her fanny wet and cold, her step-ins somewhere in the mud between the whorehouse and the car.

28

THE MARCH THROUGH THE BARROOM WITH THE
naked Paula had, fortunately for Briney Mitchel,
stopped a lot of the action. And now somehow, with
Stanley temporarily gone, the men were reluctant to
take it up again, collectively realizing that they had
made their point. If the sight of Carley Harris's bare
breasts did not shake them, certainly the sight of the
motorcycle cop dragging his loin-naked wife out of the
cathouse did. So they stood up and began to move away
from the Mitchel boy on the floor. Even Harry Jablonski turned his back and went to the bar. And some of
the others went back into the big room out front.

But when Stanley Kalinski came back into Aunt
Margaret's, he walked right over to where Briney was
sitting up, pushed him roughly back down on the floor,
held him, took out his revolver, and was about to strike
the first, long-delayed blow, when all the lights went out
in Southampton.

"Get some candles, get some candles!" Stanley
yelled, but before they could, Briney had gathered
enough strength to squirm out from under the motorcycle cop, and crawling and feeling his way, found the
back door. Stanley had lost him and Stanley knew it, so

he stood up, and finally taking on official capacity as a law officer, tried to restore order.

Everybody was suddenly blind, like Roy Strumpf, and there were shouts and curses, and when one candle was lit it was immediately knocked over in the confusion of the men trying to grab a free bottle of beer from behind the bar, or get out without paying the bill, or maybe even trying to get in another lick at the rich kid on the floor without anyone noticing.

Roy Strumpf was banging into tables with the rest of them, flailing his arms and shouting wildly: "I tell you I seen it, I seen it! I seen it with my own two eyes, the top and the bottom of it! I tell you I seen it, the boobs of one, the snatch of the other!" He kept bumping into the other men and grabbing them and shouting into their faces, but they ignored him, too busy with their own confusion, and thinking Roy Strumpf was a fool anyway. "I can just feel her," Roy said when he could find no one to grab onto. He cracked his knuckles and pounded on the nearest table. "Yes, I can just feel her!" But nobody cared enough to ask him which girl he meant: Paula Kalinski or Carley Harris, or possibly a combination of both.

Birdie Hawkins's old man was now fully awake and not altogether aware that the lights had gone out. He knocked over his bottle of whiskey, not fully realizing it, and began to hum a sea chantey.

Briney Mitchel was outside now, bruised, bleeding, soaked through to the skin, his clothes torn. He could not find the Studebaker, and he fell once in the mud, the wind tearing at him. Birdie Hawkins came out too, and managed to find his old friend in the furious night. He leaned over and grabbed him under the armpits and pulled him to his feet, and led him over to a great maple and they leaned against it in the lee of the storm. "Maggie wants to know do you want a slug of brandy before you go. It's on the house. Stanley ain't going to lay a hand on you. He's too busy inside."

Briney swallowed — he could barely swallow — and shook his head. "Let's get to the car." Stumbling and searching in the black, they found the Studebaker from the glow of a cigarette inside. Denny lowered a window, and Briney poked his head inside and said, "Christ, do you look awful."

"You don't look so good yourself," said Denny.

A figure came up beside them. It was Aunt Margaret with a raincoat covering her head. "You all right?" she said to Briney.

"I don't exactly know."

"Well, now, get on home, all of you. Get on home and get cleaned up before your poor parents see you." Aunt Margaret turned to Briney. "And take these girls to their homes and never bring them here again, please. What a terrible thing you done here tonight." Then Margaret Marinello, madame of a two-bit whorehouse in Southampton, Long Island, disappeared in the dark.

Birdie Hawkins helped Briney climb into the rumble, the floor of it soaked an inch at least with water. Midge came back to be with him. "For Chrissakes stay in front," he said to her. "At least where it's reasonably dry." She went back to the front seat with the other two.

Denny was having trouble starting the Studebaker; the wires were wet. Birdie, standing by the rumble, shared the raincoat with Briney. "I'd come with you to the hospital," he said, "but I have to see to my old man." Birdie laughed. "And he came over here to keep an eye on *me*."

"I'm not going to any hospital," said Briney.

"Well, you ought to go over there to emergency. At least they'll clean you up and see if you have anything broken."

"My balls are broken, that's all, Bird," he said to his old friend. He wanted a cigar, sitting there in the drench of the rumble, but all his cigars were wet. "No, I'm not going to any hospital and let them put my name in the book. To hell with that noise. I'm not even supposed to be out tonight." Briney stuck out his hand and Birdie took it. "And thanks, buddy."

"For what?" said Birdie Hawkins. "They wouldn't let me close to you in there."

"Never mind. Thanks. Just thanks."

"Forget it. Hey, it was much easier in the old days, wasn't it? Playing ball and serving mass and all that?"

"It's always easier in the old days."

"Hey, and Brine?"

"What?"

"I think Jabbo's sorry, I really think he is."

"Maybe."

"He drinks too much on Saturday night."

"We all drink too much on Saturday night." Briney wished like hell Denny would get the car started.

"You wasn't drunk," said Birdie.

"A little. But it doesn't matter."

"I'm sorry about the girls, honest. And I think the other guys are, too."

Briney smiled. "The girls loved it, every bleeding minute of it."

"Are you kidding?"

"No. They'll be talking about it to their friends at the Beach Club for years. They'll be telling their grandchildren about it. About the night that Carley got her front torn down and Paula Kalinski was marched bareass out the back door by Stanley her husband, the motorcycle jockey. The night of Aunt Margaret's. My God, Birdie, these kids are virgins in more ways than one."

"Maybe you're right. But it won't be much fun for you, will it?"

"No. And it wasn't much fun for me in there, either. But someday I'll get Jabbo alone and teach him a lesson. He fights mean and dirty. But I'll get him." The Studebaker engine finally took hold, and Briney sighed with relief and said to Birdie: "So long, buddy, see you in church."

Birdie laughed. "That's a good one."

And yet, except for Birdie, there was hate and revenge for all of them in Briney as they made their way back to Carley's house on Meeting House Lane through the blow. When Denny stopped the car he said to Carley: "Can I come in for a few minutes? I mean to clean up. I can't go home like this."

But Carley said, leaning across Midge, "No, you'd better get on home. You've told me your mother goes to bed early. And if Daddy Harris woke up and found us in this state he'd think I'd been raped or something, and he'd have a stroke. No, darling, go on home and sneak in just like I'm going to sneak in, and let's hope they don't hear us."

"All right."

She gave him a kiss, across Midge, a soft one on the cheek, and then she got out and whispered good night to Midge and Briney, who were getting into the Plymouth. When they were all gone, Carley went in and up to her room without being detected. Someone, probably her mother, had left a candle burning on the landing, and Carley took it into her room and placed it on the windowsill. She sat down on her bed, a drowned rat, and undid the safety pin that held her torn bodice, and she let the remnant fall and she looked down at herself, at the remains of the Bendel dress her mother had scrimped to buy. And then she began to cry, very softly, and she cried for a full ten minutes, the tears in the flickering light of the candle running down and crisscrossing her nipples, but never quite touching them. Then she took off the dress and wrung it out and hid it in the back of the closet. She tiptoed, naked, to the bathroom across the hall and got a towel to dry herself off. Then she went back and crawled under the sheets without a nightgown on. She let the candle burn, and stared at the eerie shadows it made against the peeling paint of the ceiling. She thought about the wild night and wondered why Briney hadn't thanked her for swinging her shoes at the people in Aunt Margaret's, until she realized that Briney had probably been too busy getting beaten up to notice.

She thought about exposing her breasts to all those men, and the thought of it, of all those earthy wild-eyed local men lusting after her quite pleased her, small as her bust was. Then she placed her hands, which had been resting on the sheets, to the insides of her thighs, and she moved them up and down for a few moments very slowly, and then she joined them together and let them rest, almost as though she were in prayer. She closed her eyes and tried to sleep, but a man kept getting in the way, a young man called Briney Mitchel, and she thought about what it would be like to have Briney on top of her, and the image of it in her mind pleased her. She tried hard to sleep, to get Briney out of the way like an unwanted cobweb, and it was a long time before she actually slept.

29

MIDGE DROVE. SHE WOULDN'T LET BRINEY DRIVE
because he looked too terribly hurt. And he was hurt;
he hurt like hell. The fingernail scratches down the side
of his face burned him. He had a black eye that was
swelling, as well as a swollen lip. He could barely swallow from someone punching him in the Adam's apple.
He had a piercing pain in his right shoulder where
someone had kicked or slugged him. His wrists were
partially numb from being pinned to the floor, and so
were his ankles. He had all manner of welts and bruises
around his chest and diaphragm where he had been
pummeled, and a sharp, stabbing pain on the lower left
side of his ribs. And a bruised groin. And a twisted knee
that was throbbing with pain. Yes, he hurt too much to
drive, and they had to get from the Harris house up to
the ocean end of South Main Street. It wasn't a long
trip, but tonight it seemed interminable. The wiper
couldn't keep up with the torrents of rain. In places
water ran up to the running board. Branches had fallen
from the trees; Midge had to skirt them carefully. And
fallen wires, broken wires that crackled in the wet. She
had her nose to the windshield, but she was able to say:
"Poor Mitch. You must be hurt all over."

"I am one big bruise. But mostly I hurt *here*. Whoever the son of a bitch was who threw a knee or a foot into me here I would like to see strung up by the thumbs. And somehow, I don't think it was Jabbo."

"Carley said Jabbo spat at you. How awful."

"No, Jabbo didn't spit at me, Billy Wrenn spat at me. And I tried to give it right back to him but my mouth was too dry. In all that rain and wet from the bay, my mouth was too dry, how do you like that? It's funny, when Billy did it, it struck me right away that he was a fairy, or at least had fairy tendencies. Somehow I think only a fairy would spit at another guy."

"Well, if there's one thing at all certain in this world, it's the fact that you're not a fairy, Briney Mitchel."

"Even though I wrestle?"

She looked at him. "Even though you wrestle."

"Thank you, Midget."

As bad as the driving was, she put a hand on his leg and said, "I wish I could make you feel better."

"You can."

"Well, I'm going to fix up what I can of you when we get home."

"Meaning what?" Briney said, dropping his hand over hers.

"Meaning I'm going to wash and tend your wounds, so to speak, and then send you packing."

"That's what I was afraid of."

"You've got to get back home without them knowing, you know that. If you ever get home in this storm. But I don't know what they'll say about your face in the morning."

"I'll tell the old man the new maid scratched me when I tried to violate her."

"The new maid?"

"We've got a new maid, an Irisher, and an absolute beauty."

"Oh?" Midge was immediately jealous.

"Yes, for once Mother got a looker."

"You leave her alone."

"But I'm sure she's just as dumb as the others." He finally told Midge how he had brought himself to be locked in for the night.

"But we never should have gone out," she said.

"It's too late to worry about that now. But it would have been something if I'd brought the maid to Aunt Margaret's instead of you, wouldn't it?"

"Mitch?"

"What?"

"Don't do anything to that girl, that new maid."

"I won't." But he thought of Peggy at that very moment in her nightgown, and the image of it was hard to erase.

"And I'm glad we went to Aunt Margaret's. In spite of everything. Yes, I'm glad. I feel awful about what they did to you. And Carley's dress. But I'm glad we went."

"I know you're glad."

"How do you know?"

"Because it was exciting for you. Also, if you hadn't come with me I might have ended up in bed with Paula and a bullet through my thick head from Stanley."

It was a sobering thought, and he gave it some time in silence. They could see almost nothing in front of them but they finally found Ferry Slip. They left the Plymouth in the street and stumbled and sloshed their way up the drive, holding hands tightly so they wouldn't lose each other in the dark. They had no flashlight. They groped for the servants' entrance in back, praying God it was unlocked. It was. They went in, closed it with all the strength left in them against the wind, found two candles in a drawer, lit them and carried them up to Midge's suite of rooms.

Midge placed one candle on the night table and had Briney take off his jacket and shirt and lie down on the bed. She went into the bathroom with the other candle, took off her wet dress and got into a bathrobe, fastening it about her waist. She got some things from the medicine cabinet, took them into the bedroom, and sat down on the bed next to Briney. She held the candle over him. Midge thought he looked very sexy in the candlelight, almost like a wounded warrior home from Troy. His upper body was a mass of bruises; there was one particularly angry one at his ribs. She dried his face, patting it with a towel, and then applied Mercurochrome where Billy Wrenn's nails had torn his face. When she was finished she said, "Well, that's all I can do for your ugly mug."

He smiled up at her. "What else can you do for me?"

"Nothing, darling, really. I can't do anything about those awful bruises — except kiss them." She leaned over and kissed him ever so gently on the chest, holding the candle with one hand.

"Candles," Briney said. "Do girls really use candles in prep school?"

Midge straightened up quickly. "I don't know. I

honestly don't know." She leaned over to kiss his upper body again but her bathrobe fell open and she straightened up again, retying its sash.

"There is something else you can do." He put his arms around her shoulders and drew her face down to his chest.

"I love your hair," she said. "You have just the right amount of hair on your chest."

"You ought to see the amount of hair I have down *here*." He found the knot in her bathrobe cord.

"No, Mitch, we musn't."

He began to undo her and she made a determined effort to stop him when he loosened the knot, but he pushed her hand away and she did not move it back; he slipped his hand under her breast and began to massage it lightly, gently.

"Oh, Mitch, we'll have to be awfully quiet, darling, and be very careful . . ."

"The storm is our friend. The noise it makes."

"Oh, Mitch."

"For us the storm is almost over." He murmured something more into her hair and brought her gently down beside him on the bed. She took her bathrobe off to her waist and felt lovely and wanton, and he took one of her little erect nipples in his teeth and worked it with his tongue and his lips. He felt no pain in his body at all.

"Men should have been born with two heads," he said.

"Some of them are, aren't they?" and they both laughed, and then they clutched at each other desperately and with a quiet fury, speaking saved-up words directly into each other's mouths. And then he parted her bathrobe entirely and had his finger on her clitoris, and he was more than ready for her and she for him, when something in the nether depths of her mind told her to withhold herself from him, and she was not capable of taking his penis which he held out for her. It was something about being a "nice" girl and waiting for marriage, and though wanting him terribly she resisted him, pushing him away from her, and he fought her with what strength was left in him, for he, too, wanted her badly, but she resisted as only a determined young woman guarding her virginity can resist, and finally he fell exhausted on the bed beside her, with mixed feelings of anger and respect pushing lust somewhere into the background. He felt rejected, too, and he wanted to come against her leg or atop her stomach, but he resisted the temptation to teach her a lesson, this woman he wanted very badly and could not have. So he lay there beside her, watching the rise and fall of her breasts in the shadows of the candlelight and listening to the storm outside, watching, watching her, wraithlike and spent, as though she had consummated what she had refused him.

In a few minutes he got off the bed, wobbly, and put his soaking dirty shirt back on, and his tuxedo jacket, torn and muddy, and his pumps without socks; he let the socks lie where they were. When he was ready to leave, he leaned over and kissed her on the lips, not saying anything, not even a good night, and she was motionless. Then he snuffed out the candle so she could sleep, and went out the door, closing it behind him. The storm was his friend; he made no noise above the creaking of the old house in the wind. He left by the way he had come, the back way, and girding himself against the weather, beat his way back to the Plymouth on South Main Street.

30

BRINEY AND THE PLYMOUTH HAD A HARD TIME
along Gin Lane, even though it was protected from the
ocean by great houses and lawns and high hedges. He
couldn't see six feet ahead of him, and the car kept
swerving, wanting to go off the road to the left. There
were crackling wires and debris in his path, ripped-off
roofing shingle and other bits of houses. He turned left
on Wyandanch and had his back to the wind, which
sped the car along, but when he turned east again near
the hospital into Agapogue the car almost turned over
in the gusts that swept across the flat potato lands that
went all the way to the Carew-Callaway houses on the
beach.

But they made it; they made it to Water Mill and
Flying Point and Mecox boiling on his left, and it was
there at the Channel Pond Bridge that he began to
realize the enormity of the trouble he was in. The sever-
ity of the storm slipped into the back of his mind as he
contemplated the horrors of the night: he had already
been accused of starting the riot at Devon; he had
started the business at Aunt Margaret's, causing
Carley Harris's dress to be practically ripped off her.

And there would be other things they would think of, too, unless the storm was still his friend and took their minds off him. Well, to hell with it for now. He would worry about it in the morning.

It was blowing and raining so hard when he finally turned into the Wreck that he didn't dare douse the lights of the Plymouth. He rolled it into the garage, turned off the motor, sat back and stretched his aching body, resting for a minute against the fury of the night outside. Then he got out and started to make his weary way across the soaking grass to the trellis which he had left only hours before, for what now seemed an eternity.

He climbed it slowly, feeling his way. The ocean, it seemed, was pounding at his heels; he could feel the spray, from the booming waves that crashed below, on his soaked body. He reached the roof, pulled himself up on the edge, and began to crawl on all fours the way he had come. The wind flattened him against the slippery Vermont slate shingles, pressing him past the windows, all closed against the weather. All except Peggy Something's window. Hers was slightly open, banging in the wind above the wild night, and he suddenly heard a cry of fright from within the room. "Shut up, it's only me!" he called inside, but the girl began to moan aloud, so he slipped open the screen and dropped through the casement, closing it behind him. He found her standing in a pool of water in the middle of the room, her white nightgown barely visible in the light of the false dawn showing through the storm from the east, her hands drawn up to her face. "Shut up, for the sake of Christ!"

"Oh, it's you." She took a step toward him. "And

look at you. You look as though you have just come from the sea."

"I have. I'm King Neptune."

"You're wet," she said, as though discovering the element of water for the first time.

"And you're beautiful. You'd better go back to bed." But she stood where she was, so he put his hands on her shoulders, felt her body shake uncontrollably, and brought her slowly back down onto the bed. He rubbed her back gently, the wetness from his tuxedo getting on her, but she did not seem to mind, and she began to weep quiet tears. "Easy," he kept saying, glad for the chance to comfort someone else for a change.

She turned and took his arm and held it tightly with both hands. When she finally stopped crying, she said, "I was so frightened, Mister Brian. Not of you. You woke me, to be sure, it was the hand of the Lord, or the window did it, I don't know, but it stopped this terrible dream . . ."

"Go back to sleep now."

"I can't. It's God's wrath out there. Worse than the Connemara coast in dead of winter." He tried to push her head back onto the pillow, but she resisted. She was beautiful under his hands, and he took her around the shoulders again and squeezed her tightly, rocking her, his wetness still running down on her and onto the bed, and he pressed his lips to her ear, smelling the sleep-sweetness of her, and said, "Stop, stop, Peggy Something," and she suddenly turned her face to him and said, "Oh, Mister Brian," and brought him, with surprising strength, down on the bed alongside of her.

"I'm too tired," he said. "For once in my life I'm too tired."

"No," she said. "A man like you is never . . . A man like you . . ."

"If we get caught. But, oh, my God." His hand ran across her hips and her fast rising and falling tummy.

"I'll be quiet," she said. "I promise."

"You won't tell?"

"Never. Never. There was a man on the boat who wanted to . . . oh, my sweet goodness . . . but I wouldn't let him."

"Is that better?" Briney said, his hand caressing the sweet, warm, delicious wetness of her between her legs. "Oh, that's better," she whispered. "The man on the boat wanted me to . . . oh, you're fine, Mister Brian . . . just fine."

She began, with her soft wet tongue, to lick the wounds on his face.

Pounding, pounding, pounding like the ocean ripping at the dunes and the Wreck and a thousand other homes along the beaches of eastern Long Island, the blood, his blood, his black Irish blood ran into him, that part of him that a lot of "nice" girls in Southampton and everyplace else in the world weren't supposed to like even after they got married, and it filled his spongy tissue and made that part of him hard, as the girl under him now, almost as soaked as he, stroked that part of him through his pants and then helped him open his fly, and then that part of him was out there and standing straight up in her room, clean as a whistle from all the rain, and a little salty too, from the ocean, so that it

tasted tart and good to her when she lowered her mouth
to him.

She pleased him; she knew how to please a man. She
sucked him hard. She wanted to suck him off badly, and
she told him to lie back and relax, pushing him, and he
fell back, grateful, and let her do her will on him with
her tongue and her lips and her teeth. He reached an
arm and played with one of her fine breasts while she
sucked hard and brought him closer to what she
thought was his right, for here he was the master and
she was his servant, and she knew that there was nothing quite like this for a man, what she was doing to
Briney Mitchel. When he was close to coming, she
moaned aloud and he moved his hips, and he was almost
ready, and when he came in a great, pent-up, seemingly
endless flood, the essence of him spurted into her mouth
and swam and slipped down her throat and into her
stomach, and she found again, as she had found in the
semen of Kerry, the salt and the oil of the earth. When
she had all of him, every last drop, all that was ready
for her at that time, she lay back down against him and
kissed him with her tongue and he tasted his essence, his
own semen in her mouth.

The storm came back to them gradually, reminding
them of its reality, howling and beating as they rested,
secure that the storm was their friend. He lay spent,
with no pain in him, and presently the Irish girl toyed
with him, and sucked him again, and when he was ready
for her once more, he rose up and over her and slipped
himself inside of her. His entrance brought a spectacu-
lar cry of delight from her, not to be heard above the

storm, and anyway, Briney Mitchel did not care if anyone heard, it was that good to hear in this woman, this lovely Irish piece with her nightgown up around her neck, who must have lost it to a farm boy in Kerry, and loved it well enough to pass it around to a few other farm boys in Kerry, maybe a lot of Kerrymen except the priests.

They were lovely together; they did not miss a beat. Peggy Something's bed became a lovely, sloshy trampoline, and they truly humped and banged and clung, and Peggy Something kept coming and coming and had great joy in her heart, and when he came, they came together, and they jolted and jarred each other and she put a few more marks on him which he barely noticed, and then she lay back, heaving, catching her breath, and she had become the master and he the servant, and thus they lay, their fire smoldering, and neither of them heard Janey Mitchel leave Peggy Something's bedroom.

Briney's younger sister had stolen into the guest room, having heard Peggy Something's cries when she was wakened by the dream. She had stood in a black corner of the room, partly hidden by the door, and watched this grand fulfillment. Now at last Janey Mitchel knew what a woman was for; she saw it all — every bit of it. And in those few, fleeting minutes, Janey Mitchel was eyewitness and learned what many women never learn in a lifetime with a man. She realized for the first time in her life the power a woman holds over a man. She thought hard about what she had just seen, of the great joy and oneness her brother and Peggy Something had given each other. She thought about the role she would someday be playing in the life of a man — her man, whoever he might be. She must never forget what she had just seen, she must never forget the power and the beauty of it and, yes, the majesty of this most private of all acts she had just witnessed. It was almost as though she had been privy to an act of God, like the storm outside. For, she supposed, it was just as inevitable as the storm. She slipped away, back into her own room and watched the storm from her window, and thought more about Peggy Something and Briney Mitchel.

Briney was not able to move away from on top of Peggy for a few moments, and in that time he thought about Midge, and felt only a glimmer of guilt; Midge had had her chance and turned it down. It took a back-country girl like this Irisher to give him what he wanted, or a local girl like Paula Kalinski. At that moment in his life he felt that the summer girls could be damned. Finally, when he slipped off Peggy Something, he said, "Welcome to the U. S. of A.," and she said, "I'm glad I came," and giggled into the pillow, her nose against the rosary beads.

He had trouble getting out of the window of her room; she did not want to let him go. She kept pulling and tugging at his sorry tuxedo until he thought it might come off in her hands. He would not have been able to make love to her anymore if he had wanted to, and he told her this, and finally he was able to make her understand and she let go of his clothes. He gave her a deep, meaningful soul kiss, and then climbed out, back into the wild night, and he crawled, the storm flattening him against the sloping gambrel roof, and a good thing, too, for it was slippery and he could have fallen the other way down onto the terrace. He was almost past Janey's dormer when Janey inadvertently pushed open her casement window and knocked Briney Mitchel, her brother, the brother she worshiped, the brother she had just witnessed in extraordinary communion with the new Irish maid, off the roof. He caught the gutter, the strongly welded, squarish copper gutter of the rich in one hand — he was still quick enough — in a desperate lunge, and Janey shrieked in horror down at him, the rainwater streaming down her face. "I didn't see you! I didn't know you were there! I only wanted to tell you Daddy's waiting for you in your room."

"Get him . . . to call an ambulance," Briney said. "Or the coast guard or the navy. It's a long fall but I'll try to land on my feet." He hung there quite calmly, feeling the strength, what he had left, drain out of his arms.

"There's water on the terrace," Janey called. "It will break your fall, pray God."

Briney Mitchel began to smile. When he finally let go, he found himself surprisingly ready to do so, and just before he did, he saw by candlelight in his window his father's look of sheer surprise. Janey was beside Lucian now, her face wet but oddly chalky in the flickering candlelight.

And then he was free and weightless in the wind and the rain.

31

THE HURRICANE WAS A TEASE; SHE DROVE THE forecasters at Jacksonville, Washington and Boston crazy.

True, hurricanes had no names in those days, but this one, this tease, should have a name. She was spawned off the French West African coast weeks before, from where she blew west. There was no present day plotting of her at this point as there is nowadays; she simply meandered, undetected except by a handful of ships unfortunate enough to be in her path. She might have carried over into Central America and been gone and forgotten by the North American mainland, had she not encountered the great "alley" or trough of low pressure Denny Washington had talked about. The trough, playing her game, intercepted her. It led like a great gutter straight up the seacoast to the heart of Long Island and the southern coast of New England. She fell into the trough, her gutter, and began the trip north, teasing all the way. She flirted with Florida, but did not move in to Florida. All Florida and the rest of the southern coastal states got were high winds and tides. No, she had a more important appointment up north.

In those days, forecasts and warnings for the south-
ern states were issued by the U.S. Weather Bureau at
Jacksonville. The weathermen were befuddled by her.
The forecasters did not know what to say about her.
What was she up to?

She stayed in her gutter and traveled north. When
she had moved out of the jurisdiction of Jacksonville,
she came under that of Washington, where she was reported as being big and dangerous in spite of her teasing tactics. She flirted with Hatteras but she did not go
in there. She picked up speed. The constant warnings
about her had driven all ships away from her save two.
And, oddly and perversely, each ship reported to Washington that, from its position, the tease was diminishing
in intensity. But the reports were proved false; she did
not diminish. She picked up her skirts, as it were, and
gathered even more speed and strength, and she headed
straight for the heart of Long Island. And yet on the
morning of the evening before she struck, whole gale
warnings were issued for New Jersey, Maryland and
Delaware, but neither Long Island nor the Connecticut
shore was mentioned. Boston forecasted that she would
strike New York and move up the Hudson River Valley,
but such, of course, was not the case. Her great
chimneylike vortex moved inexorably in on Long Island
and struck that night, carrying its screaming winds
and enormous tides in its path. Yes, she slammed into
Long Island and cut a devastating swath through New
England, too, and the Mount Washington Observatory
in New Hampshire recorded a wind velocity of 186
miles per hour. Long Beach, Long Island, reported a
barometric low at the peak of the storm of 27.90 inches.

The Fordham University seismograph recorded her as having the impact of an earthquake, her waves pounded the beaches so hard. Westhampton Beach and Watch Hill, Rhode Island, were virtually wiped out; a fishing boat out of Amagansett sank with the loss of six lives. Half of Providence lay under nine to twelve feet of water. A New-York-to-Boston New Haven express train was derailed at Stonington, with the loss of two lives. Six hundred people were reported missing on Long Island and in southern New England. Power and telephone lines were out, sewers burst, and countless trees were destroyed, not to mention thousands upon thousands of homes. The storm did her job well. Her huge vortex resembled nothing so much as a round chimney up through which hot air rose from sea level. She turned counterclockwise, hurling the air upward and raising a hurricane wave of fourteen to eighteen feet higher than the normal level of the waves. She had, of course, a calm "eye." The eye of the storm went through Long Island somewhere around Bellport, west of the Hamptons. The southeast quadrant of the storm blew the hardest; it was this section of the storm that caught Westhampton Beach, Southampton, Bridge-hampton and East Hampton.

Her monstrous hurricane, or "tidal," wave, as they were often erroneously called then, threatened the homes and buildings along the beach; homes such as that of Lucian Mitchel's Wreck, one of the foolish people, as it said in the Bible, who had built his house on sand — no more than a spit of land at Flying Point in Water Mill. They took outrageous chances, these people, building their homes on the dunes, for all the delights of oceanfront living. Insurance against such a storm was virtually not to be had, and material losses were enormous.

Yes, the storm did her job, and was about to do an especially good job on the old bathing pavilion of the Beach Club, where the watchman knew he was in terrible danger but would not abandon the Beach Club because he felt obligated to guard the "chits" locked up in a safe in the old section or the Bathing Corporation of Southampton would not be able to send out bills on the first of the month.

He was making his way from the new section to the old, his body bent against the inky, howling night. Under the peristyle that circled the pool, he sloshed in his boots, staggered from wind and drink, and stumbled, but found his way with the aid of the flashlight finally to the old bathing pavilion. Fumbling for the right key, he found it and opened the door of the big office that kept the safe full of the chits. He closed the door, locking it from the inside, and went to rest for a moment against the counter.

This storm, this hurricane, with its sheets of hammering, driving water, was horrifying to the watchman, but still he would not abandon the place. He moved over to where the big Mosler stood against the wall, the black old Mosler with the fancy gold filigree, and huddled down beside it on the floor, almost caressing it, wishing he had some more gin. There was no light, of course, and no candles to be found in the big office, and his flashlight began to lose its power, and his ears started to pop from the pressure differential, and water began to come through under the door he had locked. The watchman, not wanting to get his seat any more wet than it already was, stood up and banged his flashlight in a fury, to brighten it, on the counter, which of course broke the bulb, and then the watchman had no light at all, and became fully terrified of that which he could not see, but only hear, and he wanted to go back to the new section where it would be safer, but he dared not leave the safe with the chits.

Besides, it was too late. He heard its roar first, and then he saw it in the vaguest of false dawns: the ocean coming toward him. He began to pour sweat and his heart pounded, and he thought he was going deaf from the roar, knowing it was from the peculiar pressure in his ears, and the poor wretch began to cry. He fell to his knees in the water spurting through the door and prayed to God for mercy.

When the ocean poured through the windows and split the door asunder, the watchman sprang to his feet and rushed back to embrace the Mosler containing the chits, the precious bar chits, as if even he, the watchman, would be safer for it. "Mother!" the watchman said to the old Mosler through his tears, not realizing at all what he had said. But in spite of the pressure released within the building when the windows and door were broken into by the ocean, the building exploded anyway, by sheer force of the hurricane wave, and the roof flew off into the wild dawn, and the walls fell outward and were washed away with the rush of the driving ocean, and the watchman and the Mosler with all the chits, the wooden bathhouses, the bathing suits, the coconut oil, the candy bars, the cash register (the natives who came to the public section paid cash), the cigarettes, the towels, and all that bathing required on the eastern end of Long Island that summer, were carried away, too, toward the waters of Lake Agawam and Ferry Slip.

Eckshaw, who was starchily Church of England, made the sign of the cross when she saw it coming from her second-story window. She had been awake at dawn, watching the wild Sunday break through. She had dressed up in her best clothes — not so much because it was Sunday, but because she did not want to die and face God in anything but her best. She could not see much through the rain slanting horizontally in sheets past her window, and her ears felt bloody odd; they kept popping under the eerie pressure changes. But she could make out the Beach Club through the rain: the old section beginning to fly apart before her eyes, pieces of it — shingle and splintered clapboard, and here and there a bit of a bathing suit or a clothing remnant of some kind — striking the house and falling in the water below. And then she saw *it*.

She heard herself whimper like a puppy; she thought of Midge, but she could not move even to protect herself. The ocean, the wave, the hurricane wave, seemed to rise as one huge body and slip over the dunes with ridiculous seeming ease, carrying the old section before it, and making a beeline for Ferry Slip. Eckshaw was not capable of moving, nor of shouting a warning, nor of doing anything but staring at the monster, wide-eyed and terror-stricken. The thing, the wave brought by the storm, took along everything in its path, the old section flying to smithereens as though struck by a bomb, the roof of it disengaging from the body like a great open book flying through the air heading straight for Ferry Slip. Eckshaw closed her eyes and tried to pray; she wanted to hide under the bed but she still could not move a muscle. Eckshaw had been in London during the war and remembered the long forgotten terror of the Zeppelins coming to bomb the city by night; the seed of the terror lay buried somewhere within her, and now came back in full flower. She began to tremble, watching the swift advance of the wave. She thought she heard the madame calling in the hall, and the scurrying of feet, and her thought was again for Midge, but she could not move to warn Midge, or help Midge; she was truly paralyzed with fear, and was not able to activate herself until the wave struck Ferry Slip, across the edge of Lake Agawam, with all its primitive obscene force. By then it was too late to help Midge. When the roof of the old section, the great open book, finding its landing place, smashed into the porte cochere that supported Midge's suite of rooms, Eckshaw could hear the crackling of timbers as the second story began to give and, taking Midge along with it, plunge into the swirling, debris-filled ocean water below.

32

BRINEY MITCHEL LANDED IN THE OCEAN.

The hurricane wave that had swept away the old pavilion, along with the watchman and the safe and the chits — the one that had terrified Eckshaw and collapsed Midge's suite of rooms — saved Briney's life. Had the great wave not risen from the ocean and thundered across the Mitchel terrace at the moment of Briney's descent through the early dawn, Briney might have been mortally injured. As it was, he fell into the hip of the wave, swallowed some water as it crashed into and engorged the lower floors of the house, and fought his way to the surface. He found himself being thrashed about in his own living room, as though he were a bit of flotsam in a swift-running mountain river. The furniture being smashed about were so many hazardous rapids. He had to fight to keep his head above water and fight for his breath, and he lunged at one of the Louis Quinze dining room chairs, missed it, grabbed a love seat from Altman's instead. He clung to it desperately, keeping his head clear of the water, and the torrential river of the ocean carried him with enormous power and thrust out the front door of the house, and then a hundred feet or so down the driveway before it

stopped and began to retreat, taking Briney along with
it. He found himself being dragged back into the living
room, where he floundered around among end tables,
footstools, a Dunhill humidor, empty bottles of liquor,
an antique lowboy, two tennis balls, some bathtowels, the
Saturday editions of the *New York Journal-American*
and the *New York Sun*, a volume of the *Catholic
Encyclopedia*, a wooden crucifix, a bar of Ivory soap
from the kitchen (it floats, Briney remembered when he
saw it), a pair of fishing boots and other oddments. As
the wave retreated further, he found that he was able to
control his movements more. It was all too ridiculous,
clinging to the love seat while his father, in bathrobe
and pajamas, stood and surveyed the incredible scene
from atop the landing of the staircase. His father was
calling to him drunkenly, gesticulating with the keys to
Briney's room with one hand, his other hand clutching
a glass of whiskey as the whole house shuddered from
the great wave. The ground floor began to resemble
nothing so much as a great ship foundering at sea, one
of her salons awash with water from the angry Atlantic.

Briney Mitchel, feeling safer, could not help but
laugh at his old man there at the top of the stairs.
"Come on in, the water's fine!" he called to Lucian, but
Lucian simply kept shaking the keys at Briney; Briney
could not hear what was being said. He only knew that
the old man was giving him hell, and he began to laugh
even harder, which only made Lucian more angry and
he banged on the banister with the keys. As the water
retreated further, Briney got some footing on the floor,
enough to stand partway up in, and now he began to
soberly wonder what the great wave had done to the rest

of Southampton who lived near the dunes. How had Carley, Denny and Midge fared? Yes, now there were other people to worry about in Southampton besides Lucian Mitchel and his ludicrous key slamming on the banister. Thus, for the first time that day, that summer — in his life — Briney Mitchel began to put something, somebody, ahead of himself, and that somebody was Midge Crocker.

He knew that Carley would be all right, in the house in the village on Meeting House Lane. So would Denny, whose house was on Ox Pasture Road, well back from the ocean. But Midge was something else again. He cared very much for this girl who had refused him her most precious gift; he cared for her in a special way, much more than he cared for Peggy Something, the fine Irish piece, who had given him what she had given away many times before in Ireland. Bless Peggy, he thought. She had made an intolerable evening delightfully bearable. She had more than balanced off the good against the bad for him. But now he had to see about Midge, he had to get back to her, tired as he was and hurting again from his bruises. The water was now down around his hips, and he let go of the love seat and stood up firmly in it and shouted to his father, loud enough so that everybody upstairs in the house could hear it: "You'd better all clear out of here. And get me the keys to the Phaeton." Lucian pretended not to hear, still ranting there at the top of the stairs. Briney wanted to go upstairs and shake him; he shouted again and was finally able to get Lucian to go for the keys to his car. When Lucian came back to the landing, he tossed them

to Briney, who caught them and, waving nonchalantly
at Lucian, sloshed out the front door under his own
steam, very much as though he were coming out of the
ocean on a fine, sunny day at the Beach Club.

He emerged from the house soaked through to the
skin, a sodden lump dripping ocean water which had
washed his wounds clean, and actually had a thera-
peutic effect on him. The sky was brighter now, and this
fact heartened him, and he did not hurt so much any
more. He made his way through the muck and debris
down the drive to the garage. His evening pumps were
long gone, and the bluestone, underwater, felt good on
the soles of his bare feet. With some difficulty, he swung
open the garage door where the Phaeton stood. He was
very glad to see his car; the sight of it comforted him
greatly. The water was up to her hubcaps, but her
engine was dry, and even in the dull light she was still
the shiniest car in the garage. This time Briney did not
vault into her, but climbed in slowly and cautiously and
eased himself, soaked and hurting, into the driver's
seat. Seawater came out of his clothing like a squeezed
sponge, soaking down the upholstery he had carefully
and regularly saddle-soaped, and he felt clammy and
crusty from the saltwater, and he felt fully spent. He
wanted nothing so much as to crawl into the back seat
of the Phaeton and lie down and sleep. But the idea of
Midge would not let him go, and it dragged at him and
prodded him to action.

The storm had prodded George Bohan to action, too.
He came down the stairs and went about starting the
motors of the other cars in the immense garage, the cars

that he hoped would carry the Mitchel entourage away from this perilous place. He did not say anything to Briney; he simply went from one car to the next, and Briney forgot his fatigue and started his own motor. The good, throaty, challenging noise from the engine drowned out the noise of the storm and the other cars, and brought him alive again and egged him on. He shifted into reverse and backed the car out of the garage in the diminishing rain. The tires took hold of the bluestone through the brackish water, and the roof canvas of the car began to rip away in the wind, but Briney did not care; he did not care as long as the Phaeton would run. He took a last look at the Wreck, which was at last indeed a wreck; its inhabitants were beginning to trickle out to the cars and safety. Peggy Something was one of the first to emerge. She had a raincoat over her nightgown and was smiling content-edly, looking for all the world as though it were rou-tine to abandon a house because of a storm. With one last grateful glance at her, Briney Mitchel drove down the drive through the water toward Southampton from where he had come only about an hour before.

The ocean was still pouring rivers where it had sluiced through across Flying Point Road into Mecox Bay from the ocean; there were still waves and the going was treacherous, but the Phaeton responded to its owner like a good horse. This was not the Plymouth, this was his very own car, and Briney knew what she could do and couldn't do. He gunned her through the water at the Channel Pond Bridge, which still stood, and he coaxed her and then bullied her the remaining

miles on Flying Point Road. He even sang to her. He
sang:

> *Going back,*
> *Going back,*
> *Going back to Nassau Hall . . .*

And when the Phaeton did not respond to him, when the
wiper did not work fast enough, he cursed her as if she
were a deceiving woman, and he jiggled the wiper with
the inside handle, and stamped his feet on the floorboards and shook the steering wheel, for what good it
would do, and down-shifted frequently, taking advantage of her synchromesh gears in second and high.
When at last he turned into Agapogue from Flying
Point Road, he found this higher land to be less flooded;
he was able to make better time on the road that ran
between broad flat stretches of potato land, the very
potato land upon which the Carews and Callaways had
settled. The rain still drove in on him, but now he was in
a wrestling match with this act of God called a hurricane. He hardly noticed the rain; he pummeled the
steering wheel much as he would have whipped a horse
to keep moving. Indeed, he was in a fight for his life, and
though he had done nothing all summer except chase
girls and swim and occasionally sail, he had no fear.

And as he approached the low-lying junction of Old
Town and Agapogue Roads, he saw that he might have
trouble getting through the crossroads up into Toylsome Lane, so he down-shifted and gunned the engine,
and the Phaeton plowed through the deep water like a

revved-up motorboat, bringing him safely to the other
side. He stopped the car at the top of the small hill near
the hospital and appraised his situation. He was on the
last leg to South Main Street and the Crock, his name
for Ferry Slip, and he intended to make it all the way,
in spite of some fallen trees at the far end of Toylsome.
The car had responded to him and he felt buoyed, but
when he finally got to South Main Street he could take
her no farther; there were too many trees down across
the road. So he did the only thing there was left to do:
he abandoned the Phaeton and set out on foot for the
Crock. When he had to abandon the Phaeton something
went out of him, left him, a bit of self-confidence, an
ounce of courage, and he was tired again. Yet he drove
himself, crawling over impossible tree trunks, making
his way around awesome roots of great fallen elms and
maples, fighting his way through this jungle of toppled
giants tangled with broken telephone wires and live
severed power cables to get there. The wind and the
rain however seemed to be hammering at him less, and
he was able to hurry more, anxious to see what awaited
him at the Crock.

What he found at the Crock was hard for him to
believe. Through the sheets of rain he could just make
out that the entire second story supported by the porte
cochere had collapsed under the blow of the great roof
of the bathing pavilion, and now was a mass of tangled
wreckage in the big combers of Lake Agawam, which
had become part of the ocean. Midge's suite of rooms
had entirely disappeared, along with Midge herself.
Briney stumbled forward through the muck to join the
tumultuous scene at the edge of the lake. Herbert was

running around through the water in his pajamas, tears streaming down his face. He kept saying, "But I loved her, I loved her."

And then there was Eckshaw in her best Sunday clothes, now spattered with mud, kneeling in the receding water and praying loudly for Midge. And there were two or three other servants shuffling around not knowing what to do with themselves.

And finally there was Harriet herself, in a soaked nightgown and peignoir, struggling through the water with all her strength to reach the roof being carried away by the wind and the waves in the lake. She kept disappearing under the waves and Briney shouted to her to come back, but she would not do it, she kept calling that she had to get to Midge. So Briney plunged in after her and swam out to her and grabbed her around the waist and brought her back protesting to the edge of the furious lake.

"But she's under the roof," Harriet kept saying. "I know she's under the roof."

"Then I'll get an axe and go out there and get her," said Briney Mitchel, quite matter-of-factly. She told him there was an axe on the porch, and he started to go off and get it when Herbert, coming to his senses, ran and got it and brought it back to him. Briney began to take off his torn and bloody tuxedo jacket and shirt, and Harriet helped him and said to him, "Why in the name of God didn't you take her to Greenwich and marry her?" and Briney looked at Midge's mother with puzzlement, and started to remove his pants, because he was going off to find Midge in deep water. He began to take deep preparatory breaths, standing there in the rain in his underwear shorts. Then he smiled at her and the others who had stopped running around like Herbert, and were now gathering to watch this rescue effort. "You're a fool to go out there," Eckshaw, of all people, said to him, and Harriet Crocker told Eckshaw to shut the hell up, but she wouldn't shut up, she kept saying he was a fool to go out there, and Herbert, the chauffeur in the wet pajamas, kept saying, "But I loved her, I loved her."

Briney ignored them. He grabbed the axe and waded out to the deep water, looking for all the world like an Indian with a tomahawk. He was going after his woman and nothing on earth was going to stop him from getting to her, dead or alive. He flourished the axe once and even let out an exuberant war whoop. Then he plunged in under the waves that were still rolling in from the ocean. The roof was a good fifty yards out in the lake and moving away from him, and the waves punished it like some subhuman force, making it sink lower and lower in the water. Briney dove and came up for air, and dove again, and dove like a porpoise, and swam, and cursed the storm and the axe that was a hindrance to his progress, and he wanted to drop the axe but he knew that he had to have it to get Midge out from under that roof, so he hung on to it and sidestroked his way closer, ever closer, to the sinking hulk.

He lost his underwear shorts, his final remnant, and now he was naked, and he wanted to grab the axe-handle in his teeth and swim with both hands. Finally, using his great physical reserves, he overtook the roof. With one last effort, he caught its edge and clung to it with one hand, and then he crawled painfully on top of it and rested for a moment, gasping for breath. He paused there only for a moment. Then he raised himself on his elbows, and pounded upon the roof with the axe, to find out if he could get a response from within. He got one: a weak rapping on the ceiling from inside the roof, and he took a moment to shout and wave this information to those on shore, and they were cautiously joyous, just as he was; Midge was alive.

He crawled up further on the roof and fixed himself like a living monument astride its peak, and immediately he began to feel sharp splinters in his tail, but he forgot them when he began to smash at the roof with the axe, his tomahawk. He got a small hole in it, afraid to smash too hard for fear of striking Midge. In order to reach her, he had to chop through shingles and pine planking. Once he did that, he knew enough about old roof construction to remember, he could easily pull Midge up through the rafters, usually set about two feet apart.

He cut through the shingles easily, and had chopped most of the pine planking away, when a wave, one of the great many but bigger than the others, forced him to release the axe and cling to the roof with both hands. The axe slid down the roof, tumbling, and was lost at the bottom of the lake.

He screamed a curse to the sky and wind and the rain, and began to do to the North Carolina one-by-sixes, the only thing left to do to them: he attacked them with his bare hands, furiously, pulling at the old wood and the remaining shingles until his hands bled, but not feeling the pain, nor the pain from the splinters in his tail, and he soon broke through the planking, creating a

hole big enough for him to look in and see Midge, half
drowned, coughing water, weakly reach up a hand to
him. She was submerged to her neck, and he tore at the
soft pine again and made the hole still bigger for her.
When he thought it was big enough, he reached in with
his bloody hands and grabbed her hungrily under the
arms, and with one gigantic effort pulled her naked
through the rafters from her entrapment, and when she
was clear of the hole he held her lovely, bruised naked-
ness up almost as an exhibit for the others, like a beautiful epiphany he had created with his own body and
blood. Then she collapsed in his arms, half crying, half
laughing, and he kissed her with great gentleness. He
finally had her with her clothes off and defenseless, and
it had taken a hurricane to do it, and he whispered to
her as he held her, "Maybe we should do it right here on
the roof in front of your mother and the others," and
she smiled up at him, and to his surprise and delight he
found himself getting hot, and it would not at all have
been unlike Briney Mitchel to make love to Midge
Crocker right on that roof in the middle of the lake in
front of those on the shoreline.

But there was no time to make love or even to rest;
the incoming waves were making the roof sink faster.
Clutching Midge to him so that she would not slide
away, he looked around at the waves and he saw a way
to use the waves to save them, to bring them back to the
higher ground of Ferry Slip. His eye had fallen on a
plank attached loosely to the roof, a broad plank, and
putting Midge gently aside he half crawled, half swam
over to it and grabbed it, ripping it away with his
bloody hands. He took it and rested an end of it on the

roof, and turned to Midge, who was beginning to show fright lest he be swept away. He crawled back to her and took her under her legs and shoulders and lifted her onto the plank, making her sit on it with her legs folded under her, and he knelt down behind her, and he started to hold her around the waist, but his hands moved to her breasts, and he held her tightly, and blood from his hands ran off her breasts and down her front, and he straddled her backside with his thighs, gripping her tightly with his knees, and he pushed his pelvis against her back and felt a great joy within him.

Then the two of them, grinning happily at the juxtaposition of their bodies and the prospect of imminent rescue, pushed off on the plank, and surfed slowly toward the shore, balancing the old plank, so as not to overturn it.

Midge began to lose her balance, once, twice, three times, and her hand reached back for more support from Briney, and it fell upon him in such a way that he let out a second war whoop and clung to her, and bit her ear and told her to cut that out or they would tumble from the plank. She released her grip, reluctantly, and though waves threatened to tumble them off Briney was able to keep the old board in balance, and he kept leaning close to Midge's ear and shouting words of encouragement and love to her. Midge was cold, yet warm, aroused, yet frightened, but happier than she had ever been. She could have stayed on the board with Briney forever.

From the shore they made a sight to behold, Ulysses and Venus on a surfboard in all their naked glory, bloody breasts and all. It did not matter. Those standing there up to their knees in the water waved and laughed and shouted encouragement, and punched one another on the arm, and pointed to the beautiful couple, who were themselves now laughing with all the wild glory of it.

Stanley Kalinski, who had just arrived on the scene, could not quite believe his eyes, and when Midge and Briney came close enough to think about abandoning the old plank, a big roller came in and swept them off the old board, but they came up out of it holding hands and began to emerge from the terrible lake.

Harriet, grinning from ear to ear, had a blanket waiting for Midge, which she wrapped her daughter in. For Briney, the onlookers had nothing but awe and admiration, and they did not seem a bit put out at the sight of the fine-looking young man standing nude among them, nor did Briney attempt to cover himself up. They slapped him on the back and squeezed the muscles of his arm, and Herbert came over and could not resist putting an arm around this good-looking boy.

He had brought it off: the impossible.

Only Briney Mitchel with his black Irish luck and aggressiveness could have done it: saved his own life and that of Midge. At this moment in time he loved life and he loved Midge and he loved Southampton, and he even had compassion for the natives who had beaten him up. Compassion did not often show up in him, but it was there, and he was grateful that he was alive as he made his way up to the muck of the lawn of the Crock.

He fell to his knees, completely spent, and he clutched the mud with his hands. The mud felt good.

Herbert followed him and applauded him furiously,

clapping his hands and doing some kind of a jig. Eckshaw shouted at him: "You were a fool to go but thank God you went." Stanley Kalinski was there, too, in his trappings and slicker. He stood a little in the background and Briney noticed that in all the gaiety of the scene, the cop's head was down and his shoulders were shaking, and Briney came over and looked up into the face of this big cop, and the brute of a man was weeping; he tried to turn his face away and Briney put a hand tenderly on his shoulder and asked him what was wrong. He thought it might be something about Paula, but Paula was all right, Stanley said, it was the baby. "My baby is dead," said the motorcycle cop. "A tree fell on the house and killed my baby."

Briney shook Stanley's shoulder gently. He said nothing. He didn't have to. It was all spoken in the gesture.

Midge was all right and would be taken care of. If need be, Briney knew that Stanley himself would see that she got to the hospital. He put on what was left of his tuxedo, and gave the lake one more look. The roof he had clung to, had broken open to save Midge, had disappeared under the waves. He had arrived at the Crock and rescued her just in time. Then he turned and left Ferry Slip the way he had come, on foot, making his way north on South Main Street around the great fallen trees. He looked in through the shorn hedges at some of the houses up near the beach, and people were milling about examining the wreckages of their summer lives. Some of the roofs had great holes in them, here and there a chimney had toppled, and trees lay fallen in every direction. Southampton, at least the South-

ampton of the rich, had become symbolic of life, Briney
thought, how temporary and ephemeral it all was, especially for those richest of all people who lived near the
ocean. And here, now, at this moment in time, Briney
Mitchel had something to show for it, and those other
people, there beyond the hedges, had nothing but material losses. He had saved a precious life.

He was very happy to see his Phaeton again at the
end of Toylsome Lane; happy to see his leering
brass devil's head. He got in, started her, and
headed her into South Main Street, in the direction he
had been walking. There were fewer trees blown down
here. Water was running in the gutters and he kept the
car to the middle of the road to stay out of the way of
fallen branches. The storm had been kinder to the natives. Some of the trees still threatened to fall, cracking
in the wind on each side of him. But the poor of Southampton had suffered much less. The air smelled salty
and clean and rain ran in on him, and he felt a certain
exhilaration in the early morning sweep of the storm
passing away to the northeast. When he got to the
intersection of Job's Lane, he saw that Corwith's big
front window had been smashed outward onto the sidewalk, and there were other store windows smashed, although Bonwit Teller's on the opposite corner was intact. He waited at the intersection for a moment before
turning into Meeting House Lane. No one was about
these little houses, not even Carley's. The little yards in
back were empty, except for fallen branches, and here
and there a car stood in a driveway and a basketball net
swung in the wind. These local people, these poor natives who depended for their livelihoods on the summer

people, had been spared. True, everything was shorn.
There were no leaves left on the trees whatever; it was
like an early rainy morning in the late fall when the
summer people would have closed their houses and gone
back to the city.

Briney drove slowly on, and tracking his way home
through the debris and around great pools of swirling
waters he knew that he had something — something important and dear and which transcended all of the
Carews and the Crockers and the Kalinskis and everyone else in the world of Southampton. He knew that he
had saved a precious life and he drove very slowly, this
phantom, and it seemed quite doubtful to him that he
would ever be tearing up the lawns of Southampton
with his Phaeton again.